Schaumburg's Sweet Reminisce

Sheriell Scott

Acknowledgments

To my Lord and Savior Jesus Christ...

Thank you for loving me perfectly in spite of myself, for always being more than enough for me, and for my circumstances, for the good days, and for all the days that keep me on my knees.

That which is in You, oh Lord, make it so in me.

In Jesus' name, Amen!

Ned County.

Schaumburg, Tennessee.

In my eyes, Schaumburg was the most beautiful place on earth – and I had been a few places, mostly in my mind, but none moved me quite like her. Her air was sweeter than I remembered and her gorgeous summer sun had a way of making me feel like the whole world was on fire. Her heritage embraced me like the comfort of my momma's arms and her deep, dense, fertile bottoms reminded me of my daddy's love. She never let me forget. Been dancing around in my heart for some time now and never tired once. Daddy gave his word that she wouldn't, and well, I'm sure Momma would have co-signed had she been privy to our conversation.

I's home now… and my joy is stirred.

Hard to believe I stayed away so long.

Chapter One

It was your typical scorcher of a Schaumburg summer morning. Wasn't quite sure how hot it was rumored to get that day, but the residents of Ned County were hardly a month into that old summer of '77 before they had done gone and broke more than a few of them there records that old dusty almanac told of.

Folks was sho' nuff moving in slow motion... that is, if they was moving at all. Nary a soul dared part their lips to speak on how hot it was – the heat was the last thing most anybody really cared to hear about or even lend words to, for that matter. If a person was granted the grace to live through at least one Schaumburg summer, they pretty much knew what to expect from there on out; so, most folks just sat real still and kept they mouths shut. All the same though, it'd just be hotter by the time they finished talking about how hot it was to begin with and then they'd have to have the same conversation all over again.

But now, my momma wasn't gonna let a little heat keep her from doing what she know she had to do. Never did let too much hinder her way nohow on account she knew how to pray.

Schaumburg's Sweet Reminisce

Momma agreed that it was hot and all, but having her opinion set first on things above, she was of the mind that folks needed to be more concerned with the number of souls that still needed to be snatched from damnation and eternal hellfire.

Wasn't too partial to a whole lot of complaining either – sin and foolishness didn't follow too far behind on account they came first. She always said the price that Jesus Christ paid for our souls was way too high for anybody to be striving for anything less than holiness.

Now, Momma was by no means perfect, but figured she ought not have to tell nobody that nohow. Said if folks was still walking around needing to be assured of her fallenness, they either needed to have their heads examined or start reading their Bible. Didn't spend a whole lot of energy trying to figure folks out neither; she knew all too well what the Bible said about the heart of man and made sure I knew what it said too.

> "The heart is deceitful above all things, and desperately wicked; who can know it? I, the Lord, search the heart, I test the mind, even to give every man according to his ways, according to the fruit of his doings."

Jeremiah 17: 9-10

On occasion, Momma would call you out on your sin and tell you a few of her own all in the same breath. She just simply said what she meant and meant what she said and if she didn't know what to say, well, she kept her mouth shut and people could respect that. But in spite of how she came across sometimes, most everybody knew Momma to be a true keeper of the brethren – she loved folks, and in turn, she was loved by many. Deep down, she just wanted to

2

make sure that no one she ever crossed paths with missed grace and worked at it with all her strength.

As I recall, our morning started out like any other. Me and Momma finished up our morning chores, fashioned ourselves proper, and made our weekly trip into town to take care of those things that the woman of the house was expected to take care of. Now, it wasn't all the time, but every now and again, Momma would give me a dime to buy candy or a little something or another for the occasion; but that particular morning, as favor would have it, Momma's little, leather-woven coin purse was fresh out. She must have turned that pouch of hers inside out more than a few times before she handed me one of several quarters, studying it real close like, to make certain she wasn't handing me one of her half-dollars. I was hoping she'd forget about the 15 cents, like Daddy always did, so I could add it to the rest of the change I kept in an old raggedy sock behind the loose baseboard in my room.

Growing up, I never could recall a time when we didn't have way more than we needed, but Momma always made sure we lived on way less than we had. Some might say that we had a bit more than most folks in Schaumburg, but that made Momma and Daddy no never mind. You see, my daddy never would allow himself or his family to be counted amongst those that loved money or them that robbed God. And because of obedience, the Lord rebuked the devourer just like He promised He would and blessed our family real good.

My daddy was a generous man, but now he didn't always give because people asked neither – the Spirit wouldn't allow it. He knew all about the pull of the world on a man's soul and he never wanted to help a man stay bound by strongholds and foolish vices, so he sho' nuff had to be

3

settled and sealed in his spirit *by* the Spirit before he tried to out-give God beyond a need.

If he wasn't willing to give, he'd simply tell you no and then he'd tell you why. Said the Lord gifted him with the spirit of discernment and he aimed to use it. Made some folks a little mad, but these here things were for sure: my daddy worked every able-bodied day of his life, never turned his back on a genuine need, never collected on a debt, and never counted change from your hand to his.

"Now, child of mine, you's only allowed to buy one piece of candy, ya hear me?

"Yes, ma'am." I was smiling but Momma wasn't.

"I means what I tell you, now. You know I don't take too kindly to having to repeat myself."

"Yes ma'am, I know."

Momma didn't usually have to tell me the same thing twice, but I guess she knew sooner or later she'd have to.

I could already see her and Sister Godfrey standing all prim and proper at that old dime-store counter, thumbing through the newest Woolworth's catalog. They'd stand there carrying on, telling one another how fine they'd look on Sunday morning in a particular dress with that-there hat and them-there shoes with the matching patent-leather pocketbook; all the while, Brother Godfrey minded the store and figured out what to do next from the Honey-Do list Sister Godfrey added to every other day.

While everybody else was off doing their own thing, I took my time trying to figure out what piece of candy I would buy. Brother and Sister Godfrey sold every sweet treat known to man, but when Momma said once piece of candy, that's what she meant; so whatever piece I chose, I had to make it count.

"It's getting hotter by the second, Millie. Let's you and me get on in here out the sun."

Momma pinched my cheeks, grabbed me by the hand, and led me up the front steps of the store. We stopped just short of the door, long enough for Momma to catch a quick glimpse of the thermometer that hung from the freshly painted, bright red column that looked wet, but wasn't. I know'd it wasn't wet because I touched it right quick with my finger when Momma wasn't looking.

"Whew, Lord have mercy on us all, Millie. It sho' is hot, but them eternal hellfire's gon' burn a whole lot hotter than this-here Schaumburg sun. *Lord, I pray we all be ready*," Momma whispered as she wiped the sweat from her brow and then dabbed the back of her neck and full bosom with her favorite floral-cotton handkerchief. "Millie, this here thermometer say it's 113 degrees."

I didn't know what all of that thermometer-talk was about, so I just took Momma at her word, most people did. But there was one thing I did know for myself – it was hot.

"I sho' hope your daddy carried enough ice water with him to that field this morning. God knows he don't need to be messin' 'round down there in that hollow with no less than what he need, as hot as it is. *Lord, I ask You to see after my Ben. Keep him, Lord, like only you can, and I ask it all in Jesus' name. Amen.*"

"You praying for Daddy again, Momma?"

"Your daddy need all the prayers he can stand, sweet

5

child – we all do."

Momma looked down at me and smiled and then dabbed the tiny beads of sweat from my nose and forehead with her handkerchief. I didn't think I had no sweat on my forehead, but I looked up at this woman that my daddy loved and smiled back anyhow.

I don't recall there ever being a time when I saw my momma without that pretty little cloth of hers; but I do call to mind that it always smelled real nice, just like her. Cost my daddy every last red-cent he had, but it was the only thing he could afford to buy her after they started courting. And although it had seen its fair share of sweat and tears, it was still holding up quite nicely after all those years. I guess most of that was due to my momma's proper care which amounted to a light hand washing in three-day-old well-water and a little Woolite; but I reckon more than anything, it was her love for my daddy.

She regarded that pretty little piece of cloth as something extra special, kinda like most married folks did their wedding bands. She had one of them too, and you could count on one hand the number of times she'd found cause to take it off. If it needed cleaning, she'd just take an old toothbrush to it, with a little paste, and polish it right on up with it still on her finger. I heard her one time make my daddy promise that he would see to it that she was buried in it. Daddy told her that she'd get no argument from him on the matter, but that she'd have to talk to the good Lord about it on account he had done already prayed that he not have to live one day on this earth without her.

I didn't need to know or understand everything that was behind all the sweat and tears that stained Momma's heart – or her little handkerchief over the years; but what I did know, was that this woman that my daddy loved was all the better for it because of how she loved us both back. She loved Daddy through everything and filled me up with all the love my little heart could hold.

Momma was always the proper lady, even when she wasn't at her best. Never liked being the topic of conversation and never wanted to be the cause for my daddy to have to hang his head in shame around Schaumburg, or anywhere else for that matter. And even though I was no more than just a few years out of diapers, she all but expected the same of me. She'd get one chance, one she never thought she'd come to have, and didn't want to fail me nor disappoint my daddy.

Momma had hopes of me marrying young, but only in the Lord – just like she did, and those before her. Did all she could to raise me the proper young lady and it all started and ended with the Lord.

Momma's forehead had done beaded up with sweat again, so we headed on inside the store. "Sister Earnestine. Brother Godfrey. How y'all getting along this fine morning?"

"Well now, Sister Marjorie, we just trying to maintain while the good Lord sustains us, so, I reckon we be making it just fine."

"Brother Godfrey, you just said something because it's only by the grace of God that we done made it this far. We just can't make it without Him."

"You sho' right about that, Sister Marjorie. You sho' nuff right about that." Brother Godfrey looked up yonder and gave God glory. I reckon he knew a right smart about the grace of God, too.

By now, Momma had done already gave me her

special look a second time and I knew what each one meant.

"Sister Marjorie, girl, it sho' is good to lay eyes on you. It's good to see you too, precious. It's been a while. Y'all come on in here out that blistering sun and hug my neck. Been missing y'all 'round here."

"Well, Sister Earnestine, it's good to be seen – been a good, long while, but you and Brother Claude been on our hearts and in our prayers."

"Yes, yes. Y'all keep me and my Claude in your prayers, Sister Marjorie. Keep us lifted up now, ya hear?"

"We sho' will, Sister Earnestine."

"Now, how is God's favorite child?" Sister Godfrey whispered, tickling me with both her hands – had me squirming like a little barn lizard.

I never knew how Sister Godfrey expected me to answer her if every time she asked me how I was doing she tickled me. I think she liked seeing me wiggle; but more than that, I think she just loved the laughter of children being that she wasn't blessed with laughter from any of her own.

Momma appreciated Brother and Sister Godfrey both for always loving on me the way that they did, but now as soon as we were away from mixed company, Momma would always be sure to remind me that God was no respecter of persons and that He loved all His children with the same perfect love.

Momma didn't like it when folks lied on God and if it was one thing that tightened her girdle, it was that.

"God said all that He meant and meant all that He

said and man ain't got no right to add to nor take away from what thus said the Lord." I reckon Momma had done said that more times than she could count and way more times than she felt like she should've had to.

Sister Godfrey meant well, but in Momma's eyes, lying on the Word of God while meaning well was as different as fire and water – didn't matter whose lips the lie fell from.

Momma and Sister Godfrey carried on while Brother Godfrey listened and chimed in when they offered him the chance to.

He winked at me from the back of the store through a cloud of dust that he had done stirred up from sweeping. I couldn't quite wink yet, so I just shut and opened my eyes three times fast. That made Brother Godfrey laugh until he started coughing. The dust seemed to be getting the best of him and that made me giggle and twist.

"You calm yourself down now, child. That ain't nothing to be laughing at," Momma admonished. "Brother Claude, you alright back there, ain't you?"

"Oh, I'll be alright, Sister Marjorie. Just a little dust."

"One of these days, you'll heed to what I say and sprinkle that floor before you start your sweeping, old man."

"And one of these days you'll hear me when I tell you that I can't sweep mud, Earnestine."

"Unh-hun. Well, go head on and cough up a lung then, Claude, and don't forget to dust back there when you get done, hear?"

"Yeah, alright, woman."

Schaumburg's Sweet Reminisce

And without missing a beat, Momma and Sister Godfrey locked arms and headed on over to their special spot near the end of the counter to get out the way of the dust; but not before Sister Godfrey covered my face with tiny, soft, rouge-colored kisses. I always liked it when Sister Godfrey made a fuss over me. She smelled pretty like Momma, but like white gardenias.

"Sister Marjorie, I declare. I feel like I ain't seen you in forever."

Momma hadn't been herself for months but didn't wanna trouble nobody but the Lord about it, not even my daddy. I reckon it was our little secret.

"It sho' have been a while, Sister Earnestine. Reason why I know is because I'm 'bout out everything at the house. Been real busy trying to get a few figs and the last of them peaches put up."

"Well, I ain't get a chance to put up too many of my peaches. Look like every time I turned around Claude was asking me to make a cobbler. Now, I got half a bushel of peaches left and I aim to make preserves and nothing else."

"Sister Earnestine, I ain't even now mad at Brother Claude. You know can't nobody 'round here resist that peach cobbler of yours."

"I declare, that's how I got my Claude to that altar. Yes, child, my Madea's peach cobbler and my Uncle Tunch's hot chicken sealed the deal with my Claude. Got my hands on them recipes and a few others when I was young gal – held 'em close too 'til I found me a good husband. No ma'am, I didn't waste my good cooking on every suitor looking for a hot meal. After I married my Claude, I didn't much care who got they hands on them recipes, you hear me."

"I know that's right, Sister Earnestine, but we all know Brother Claude was crazy in the head and soft in his heart for you before he even popped out his momma's womb."

Momma and Sister Godfrey got real tickled at that, like they always did when they got together; but they soon remembered that they were mature, Christian ladies needing to set an example, so they settled down just a bit. Every now and then, Brother Godfrey would look over at 'em and shake his head, but then he'd get real tickled for some reason. He looked funny back there covered in dust laughing to himself.

Momma would sometimes share with Daddy during supper what her and Sister Godfrey had laughed about that day. Daddy would laugh but he never really seemed to think what Momma and Sister Godfrey talked about was all that funny. Momma didn't seem to mind; she just said men and women was kinda different that way, but that a husband and wife ought to always have something to laugh with one another about.

Momma and Sister Godfrey headed a little further on down the counter. I made sure I stayed close but far enough distance away so not to be in earshot of grown folks talking. But it really didn't matter where I was when it came to being able to hear things. Daddy said I took after his great grandmomma Della Mae in that way. Said when they was growing up, they never did have to keep a rooster around because great grand-momma Della Mae could hear the sun rise.

"Store keeping you and Brother Claude a little winded this morning, Sister Earnestine?"

"I reckon it's been pretty steady this morning, Sister

Marjorie. But here lately, it's been so hot, folks act like they afraid to move."

Momma and Sister Godfrey laughed at that, too. I just thought it was funny the way they held on to each other when they did. Me and Momma laughed sometimes, but not like her and Sister Godfrey.

Sister Godfrey had quite a few years on Momma, but you'd never know it just by looking. They'd been best friend-girls for years. Sister Godfrey said that Momma kept her young and Momma said Sister Godfrey kept her going.

Took and told me that there'd come a day when I would have need for a woman of God like Sister Godfrey to walk alongside me. Said she was sure of it, but only after she was dead and gone. I didn't quite know what Momma meant back then. All I knew was that her and Sister Godfrey oftentimes spent the whole day from sunup to sundown shopping over in Orville without me. Said there'd be a whole lot of things I'd just have to keep living through in order to understand.

She told me, "Now Millie, you just be sho' to stay faithful to the good Lord and He'll bring whatever you need to know to your understanding in His time." Momma was right.

"Sister Marjorie, how is Brother Ben? Hadn't seen't him in a good long while neither. Working hard, I reckon?"

"You know my Ben. If it wasn't for the Lord's day, I believe he'd work hisself inside out."

"Your Ben sho' do take after his daddy, God rest his soul. Some of these rascals 'round here, young and old alike, could stand to learn a thing or two from Brother Ben

12

about hard work."

"Sister Earnestine, I pray his strength in the Lord daily, 'cause any chance of that husband of mine slowing down gon' have to be the Lord's doing."

"Make me think back on times when me and my Claude was first starting out, you know. Times was hard. I used to tell Claude all the time, 'As long as you keep trusting… and leaning into the Lord, I'll be here praying and keeping house.' Our men need our prayers, Sister Marjorie. I declare they do."

"You sho' right about that, Sister Earnestine. I was just telling Millie that I hope her Daddy took enough of them ice jugs with him to that field this morning and was of the mind to set 'em in the shade."

"Well, I hope so, too Sister Marjorie. You reckon that sun might run him on out from down there? Lord knows, it's a different kind of heat off down there in them bottoms."

"Sister Earnestine, all I can say is, Lord, make it so, 'cause I declare, Ben sometimes act like he don't know how to come down off that tractor. I tries hard not to worry after him, I do. And I loves my Ben. But now, I done had to go down there across that hollow at him more times than I care to count."

"Sho' nuff?"

"Sister Earnestine, I aim to make it plain to you."

"Lord have mercy! Go head on and tell me, child!"

Momma had done gone and got herself and Sister Godfrey all riled up. Reckon she forgot she had done already told Sister Godfrey that story more than once, but Sister Godfrey looked like she was needing to hear it just as much as Momma was needing to tell it to her again.

"Lord knows I'm grateful for my Ben. Ain't never know'd that man to do nothing unless he was bending over backwards to do it."

"Well now, that's just who Brother Ben is and we's all blessed on account of it. Always have been that a way."

"I hear your heart, Sister Earnestine, I do; but this-here last time I had to go down yonder across that main hollow after him, near 'bout done me in. Now, I ain't got nobody's lie to tell you, by the time I got down there at him, I had done got so mad and worked up, I couldn't hardly even remember why I started down there after him. Couldn't even now lay a good fussing on him on account my throat had done got so dry and parched, felt like I had swallowed a two-edged sword. Couldn't utter not one word, Sister Earnestine."

"Girl, hush your mouth!" Sister Godfrey seemed real tickled at all that Momma was saying, but I couldn't tell what Momma was thinking. She was laughing too, but she looked real serious.

"Sister Earnestine, I was coming down that path walking right hard and strong, swinging these-here hips of mine just as fast as I could, eyes stinging with sweat and wringing wet from head to toe, but I could see my Ben up on that tractor just a'smiling… just a'waving. All that smiling and waving just made me more madder."

"Child… you a mess!" Sister Godfrey cackled.

"I couldn't wait to get myself across there to my Ben

to give him a piece of my mind, and I declare no sooner did that thought enter my mind, I messed around and stumbled on a tree root and went tumbling down that path like one of them old ugly, good-for-nothing horse-apples."

Momma and Sister Godfrey hollered laughing and held on to one another, this time to keep from falling.

"God don't like ugly, Sister Earnestine. Do you hear me?"

"No, no. He sho' don't, Sister Marjorie. Lord have mercy, child. We's laughing, but you could have sho' nuff had a heat stroke messing around down there in that bottom."

"Sister Earnestine, I reckon I might have been too mad and even now too shame to done had a stroke. But now, my Ben had done come for me before I could even now get myself up off that ground, near 'bout falling down his own self getting over there to see 'bout me, ya know. Made a real big fuss over me and everything. Then he sat me down underneath one of them big old willows over near them groves and went for water."

"Well, I'll be."

"Only thing was, the water was way over yonder on the other side of the field from where he had just come. I tell you, I wanted to shout, 'Come now, Lord,' 'cause it felt like Ben was taking forever to get back there with that water."

"Of all the days, Sister Marjorie. Lord, have mercy."

"I could hear my Ben calling out to me from yonder ways across that field, checking on me, you know; all the while, I was giving him a good piece of mind."

Schaumburg's Sweet Reminisce

"I reckon that root didn't quite put you in your place, Sister Marjorie." Momma and Sister Godfrey both knew that to be the truth.

"Sister Earnestine, I reckon not, 'cause I let Satan make a plumb fool out of me that day. I was so thirsty; I didn't even now give my Ben a chance to stop the truck. I had done reached through that truck window and had my head throw'd back before I even now had the jug in my hand. Didn't even now look off in the jug for bugs. I turned that water jug all the way up, you hear me."

"Child, you's a mess!" Sister Godfrey was trying to keep herself together.

"Believe me when I tell you, that water was so hot, Sister Earnestine, I could have boiled a bushel of raw peanuts. It wasn't nobody but the Lord that stayed my tongue that day."

"My Word. You mean to tell me Brother Ben ain't have nothing but hot water down there to drank?"

"Hear me now. I had done got ahead of myself and reached for the wrong jug. The jug of cold water he had done went after was still in his hand."

"Say what now?" Sister Godfrey fell out laughing.

"When I tell you I was sho' nuff shame."

"I know you was, Sister Marjorie."

Momma and Sister Godfrey got to cackling right loud and wobbling back and forth so hard, I thought for sho' they'd end up lay'd out in the floor that time.

Mr. Godfrey was still in the back of the store stirring up dust when he looked up to see what all the fuss was about. He just smiled, shook his head, and went back to sweeping.

"Sister Earnestine, that water was hot, do you hear me? But I just had to surrender to it 'cause at that point I was too hot to be mad and too mad to be thirsty a second longer. Ben told me I ought not to had drank that hot water like that, kept trying to get me to drink some of that cool water he had, but I felt like I ain't even now deserve it. I ain't got no lie to tell you; I acted a plum fool that day."

Sister Godfrey and my momma finally settled down long enough to catch they breath. They both had tears in their eyes, the happy kind.

"Sister Marjorie? You'd go down there across them bottoms after Brother Ben again if you had too, wouldn't you?"

"Sister Earnestine, I declare I would... but I hope I'd have sense enough to remember to take my own jug of ice water."

Sister Godfrey smiled and hugged Momma. "The Bible say that laughter is like a good medicine."

"It sho' nuff is, Sister Earnestine."

"And I don't blame you one bit for worrying after Brother Ben. This-here Schaumburg heat ain't nothin' to play with."

"I bless God that all is well. My Ben is doing just fine."

"Our God is a good God, Sister Marjorie!"

Schaumburg's Sweet Reminisce

"He's a mighty good God, Sister Earnestine! Yes, He is, a mighty good God!"

Sister Godfrey and Momma locked arms and kept right on chatting as they strolled still further a ways on up the counter.

"You be sure to tell your Ben that me and Claude was asking after him."

"I sure will, Sister Earnestine... I'll be sure to tell him."

"I was telling Claude just last night that it'd been a while since we had anybody up to the house."

"Is that right?"

"Been a right smart of months now since we had any kind of fellowship. So, I'm counting on you to get your Ben up to the house with you and our Millie so we all can break bread together. You tell Ben that I said so, you hear?"

"I'll tell him just that, Sister Earnestine. We always have such a fine time with you and Brother Claude. My Ben ain't likely to let nothing get in the way of things."

"Well, that's good to hear, Sister Marjorie, 'cause I kept Claude up half the night listening at me go on and on. Now, come on over here and let me show you what I done decided on in this here catalog."

Chapter Two

Now Millie, you been sitting over there for the longest, poutin' and fightin' your sleep. If you's got a question, go head on and ask it child."

"Yes, ma'am." My tight-lip seemed to unnerve Momma just a bit.

"Well, I'm waitin. Free your mind, child."

"Momma?"

"Yes, Millie." I couldn't have been no more than five or six, but as I recall, Momma kept her nerves pretty good, at first – she wasn't as patient as Daddy.

"Do you like kissing Daddy?"

"Lord, child, yes!" Momma smiled right wide, put her hand on her hip, and clutched her pearls. Something 'bout kissing seemed to make most folks wanna show all they teeth. She gave me a once over... and then another, smiled another sweet smile, and went on back to washing that bushel of crowder peas we picked the night before. She aimed to put 'em on the table for supper.

Schaumburg's Sweet Reminisce

"You and Daddy kiss all the time, Momma."

"Yes, yes, we sho' do, Millie."

"Why come, Momma?"

"Well, sweet child of mine, that's one of the many ways husband and wife show love to one another.

"Momma?"

"Yes, Millie."

"Do Brother Godfrey love Sister Godfrey?"

"Child, can't you tell? I reckon a blind man can see that."

"Well, do Sister Godfrey like kissing Brother Godfrey?"

"Say what now, child?"

"Do Sister –"

"I heard what you said the first time, Millie."

"Well, Momma?"

"Well what, Millie?"

"Well, how come Brother Godfrey and Sister Godfrey don't have no kids? Don't they kiss, right?"

"Child of mine, whether the Godfrey's kissing one another right or not ain't hardly none of my business nor yours, ya hear? You settle yourself now."

"Yes, ma'am."

Momma went back to washing her peas and I went back to poutin' until she calmed her nerves.

"Momma?"

"Millie, what is it now, child? I declare I don't know what's done got into you with all this fast talk, but now, you go head on and ask me whatever else it is you need to ask me."

I had done wrinkled Momma's nerves and that side-eye she gave me let me know that she didn't plan on saying much else; but I hadn't yet had my young mind settled on the matter.

"I was just trying to help Sister Godfrey get a baby so I could have somebody to play with."

Momma held her tongue for a spell – she did that sometimes because she knew how words could cut. "Well, you just never no mind about all that, Millie, you hear me? You keep your mind level to the ground and stayed out of married folks' bedroom."

"Yes, ma'am."

"You get yourself on up them stairs and take a nap right now 'cause your mind on things they ought not to be on. Lord willing, there'll be time in your days to talk on such things, but that time sho' ain't now."

"Yes, ma'am." I could tell that Momma was a little put out with my fast talk so I didn't waste no time gettin' myself to my room.

Momma lifted her hands and called on the Lord like she always did when she thought she might come undone. I took the long way around her and dared not look back and have a similar fate as Lot's wife. It was times like these that I was careful not to walk too hard nor make a sound above breathing neither. I hoped she wouldn't make me stay in my room all day for punishment, but sometimes she would get busy around the house and just plain old forget. Just before I got to my room, I heard Momma laugh. I reckon she had done got all worked up over things and just had to laugh at her own-self.

After a little time went by, I could hear Momma downstairs talking to herself about how so-and-so, so-and-so, was on her last nerve. She said her peace one good time and then moved on from it. You see, even Momma had a few folks in this world that she couldn't hardly stand the sight of but loved 'em anyway.

"You can love anybody through prayer," she'd say. "You just got to be willing to pray." And after she spoke her mind on the matter, that's exactly what she did. She'd sometimes have a hard time speaking their name, but once she did, she left everything to God.

It was still mid-morning but I would force myself to take a nap anyhow. I hoped I hadn't gone and made Momma too mad. I stared all around my room, fightin' my sleep until my eyes tired and closed, knowing they'd soon open – hoping not to find Momma standing over me.

"Millie!"

"Yes, ma'am."

"You supposed to be sleep."

"Yes, ma'am." I dared not get up off that bed because Momma heard everything and I knew if she had to stop doing what she doing to come up them stairs, I was gon' get it good. I finally decided to take myself on to sleep. Daddy would be home soon for lunch and Momma would be in a better mood.

*   ****   *

"Hey Daddy!"

"Wud ya say, babygirl? You doing alright?"

"Yes, sir, I'm doing fine."

"Alright then. You help your momma out around the house today?"

"Just a little."

"Ummm, hmmm. You ain't been wrinkling your Momma's nerves none, have you?"

"Yes, sir. Just a little – but I ain't mean to."

"Alright now, I need you to fix things with your momma before I head back out to the field, ya hear?"

"Yes, sir."

"Alright then."

"Daddy?"

"What's on your mind, babygirl?"

"Why come Sister Godfrey and Brother Godfrey don't have no kids?"

"Well, God didn't see fit to bless Brother and Sister

Godfrey in that way. But you know what, babygirl?"

"What Daddy?"

"Brother and Sister Godfrey always to tell me and your Momma how good and blessed they are on account they know you."

"Daddy?"

"Wud ya say now?"

"Do you think Sister Godfrey let Brother Godfrey kiss her as much as Momma let you kiss her?"

"Well, I imagine Sister Godfrey allow Brother Godfrey to kiss her every now and then. The Lord made it alright for a husband to kiss his wife as much as he wanna."

"Daddy?"

"Yeah, babygirl."

"Is Brother Godfrey doing it right?"

"Doing what right, babygirl?" Daddy seemed a little nervous and that just wasn't much of his nature.

"Helping Sister Godfrey get a baby."

"Babygirl, what done got into you? You know me and your momma don't allow no fast talk."

"Nevermind." I reckoned I was starting to wear down my own patience. I didn't even now know what I needed to know... let alone what I was needin' to ask.

"Millie, now I ain't quite sure I know what you trying to

ask me, but it's like this here – Brother Godfrey been married to Sister Godfrey a long while so I imagine he done had a right smart of practice on how he ought to go about pleasing his wife. I wouldn't worry yourself too much with all of that there. Kissing and having babies and that type of thing is for married folks and you got a good long while before me and your momma talk with you on that there."

"Yes, sir."

"Alright then, babygirl."

"Daddy?"

"What's that you got on your mind now?" Daddy leaned forward and started to rub his head on the right side – that's how you know'd he was growing weary.

"Can you and Momma pray for Brother and Sister Godfrey to get a baby my size so I can have somebody to play with?"

"Well, babygirl, I don't believe me and your momma ought to do that there. If Brother and Sister Godfrey wants a baby, I think they need to talk to the Lord on that they own-self."

"Please, Daddy?"

"Now Millie, I believe you meddling in grown folks' private affairs just a bit. You might ought to set your mind on something else. That ain't nothin' for a child your age to be steadying her thoughts on nohow. I think it best we talk on something else now."

"Yes, sir."

Schaumburg's Sweet Reminisce

I reckoned I knew I'd always be by myself. Momma had to trust the Lord a mighty long time before I came along, and after I did, the Lord saw fit to close up her womb. She found no reason to question God any further; her and Daddy figured they'd just pray for the Lord to bless my womb.

In my coming years, Momma and Daddy would make sure I understood that the Lord had sufficient grace to fill any void that man had faith enough to hand over to Him – according to His will. They both knew it to be so, but like most folks, they had to remind they own-self of that very thing every now and again.

I didn't know how much more pitiful I could look or lonely I could be, but I knew Daddy hated to see anybody discouraged, especially a child. I figured I wouldn't say nothing else on the matter and force Daddy to take off his belt and tear my tail all to pieces, so I decided to try to make peace.

"Daddy, I'm sorry."

"Awww now – you alright, babygirl. I don't believe you meant nobody no harm."

"I wasn't trying to meddle, Daddy."

"Well, Millie, I know you probably been feelin' some kind of way for a good while now being the only child and all. I imagine it get real lonesome for you at times."

"Yes, sir."

"Me and your momma just ain't able to give you no brothers and sisters to grow up with. We had to accept the Lord's will on the matter years ago, but me and your momma bless God every day for you, babygirl. You's like our manna from heaven."

I didn't know what manna was, but my daddy made it sound like it was sho' nuff somethin' – but I was still real sad.

"Everything's gonna be alright, babygirl. Everything's gonna be just fine."

With every tear that rolled down my face, I held on to my daddy just a little bit tighter. I could trust everything Momma and Daddy told me even if I didn't understand why. The Lord told them things all the time and they took and turned around and told me.

"You know what, babygirl?"

I shook my head, wiped my nose on my Daddy's dusty work-shirt, and looked into his eyes.

"Now, I don't know this here thing for certain, but babygirl, this here's what I think. You see, old man Godfrey built like one of them great big old cypress trees down there in them Louisiana bayous. Remember that time me, you, and your momma took that trip down through there and saw all them great big ol' Cypress trees?"

"Yes, sir. I remember."

"And Sister Godfrey, well now, she a itty bitty little woman, right?

"Yes, sir." Sister Godfrey was a short, shapely woman, but petite is how she referred to herself.

"So, I reckon when Sister Godfrey want a little sugar, Brother Godfrey got to get all the way down on one knee to give Sister Godfrey what she done asked for."

Schaumburg's Sweet Reminisce

"A little sugar, Daddy?"

"That's right. But you know what else, babygirl?"

"Unh, unh."

"Well, I believe Brother Godfrey get so excited after he give Sister Godfrey a little sugar that he just have to pick her up over his head and twirl her around in the air just like this here."

Daddy jumped up from his favorite chair, scooped me up over his head, and spun me around and around until Momma came in fussing and waving her dish rag. Told us to stop carrying on before we broke something. Daddy gave me one last spin, tossed me up in the air, and let go, but I wasn't scared because I knew he'd catch me. He always did.

"Watch this here, babygirl," he whispered.

As soon as Daddy put me down Momma started screaming. But Daddy had done grabbed her and picked her up before she could even now take off running. I watched my daddy twirl my momma around that room until she was almost too dizzy to stand up straight. My daddy never let my momma fall neither.

"Come on over here, Millie. Join me and your Daddy."

Momma didn't even look my way when she called my name. She was too busy telling my daddy to stop, but it didn't seem like she really wanted him to. This time Momma scooped me up in her arms and gave me a great big hug.

I still don't know how Daddy could do all that spinning around and not get dizzy like me and Momma always did, but I loved seeing my momma and daddy love on one another, and loved it all the more when I was smack dab in the middle of it all.

Chapter Three

Why don't you come on over and hold the dust pan for an old man, Millie?"

I nodded and skipped to the back of the store to make my young strength useful.

"Little girl of mine, you not outdoors," Momma scolded.

"Yes, ma'am."

Momma rarely let me get away with anything, and if she did, it wasn't for long. Her chastening was sure to come back around again. "If you spare the rod, you spoil the child," is what she never let me forget.

"Right back here, when you done, Millie, and don't let me have to remind you neither. And don't be back there gettin' in the way, you hear me?"

"Yes, ma'am."

Right back here wasn't a specific place of sorts, but I fully understood what Momma meant by "right back here." Momma was what some folks called strict; she called it training up a child.

From the second I popped out of my momma's womb I was never more than a few feet from her at any given time, and it didn't quite matter where we were or who we were in the company of. Momma always made sure that I was within eyesight and arm's reach but out of earshot when I needed to be. I learned early on as a child to stay in my place and stay out of grown folks' mouths whilst they talking.

I made my way to the back of the store heel-to-toe so not to be tempted any more than I already was to run. I could feel my Momma's eyes watching me, but maybe she wasn't – it just always felt that way. Brother Godfrey smiled like he always did and handed me the dust pan and we got right to it. There wasn't much trash, but Brother Godfrey had managed to sweep up a good amount of the dirt that had collected between the cracks of the store's wooden floor.

Sister Earnestine always said that it didn't matter how good a job you think you did, when you sweep a wood floor like the kind most folks had back then, you could rest assured that you were leaving just as much dirt if not more behind. I never heard nobody explain how that could be, but a second sweep never proved different.

"Look like we 'bout got it all, Millie?"

I looked on either side of Brother Godfrey and then 'round about. "Umm hmm."

"Well, I'll take you at your word. Your eyes a lot sharper than mine. Alright then. This-here old tired mule on my back sho' do appreciate you, Millie. I'll see your momma about your wages here in a minute. Dump what you got there in that old bucket back yonder then go on back up front now like your momma told you."

Schaumburg's Sweet Reminisce

I hopped from my knees, emptied the battered, black metal dust pan in the trash, hung it on the nail back yonder in the short hallway leading to the stockroom, and headed on back up to the front of the store, to the place better known as "right back here."

"Stop running, Millicent," Momma called to me over her shoulder in that little-girl-don't-you-let-me-have-to-say-nothin'-else-to-you voice. Never even turned her head.

"Yes, ma'am." I stopped on a dime. The tone of Momma's voice sometimes had a way of making me do that.

"Remember what I told."

I wasn't yet running all the way fast like I always did, but I had it on my mind to run fast – and Momma knew that.

The old notion of it taking a village to raise a child applied to every child except me, especially when it came to discipline. Momma said that my raising was her responsibility and she wasn't gon' let nobody share that gift with her – nobody except my daddy. I overheard her say one time that if mommas and daddies took the time to raise they own children up proper, wouldn't be so many messed-up grown folks in the world.

Brother Godfrey hummed a tune as he shuffled from the back of the store. Daddy said he was the best tenor in all of Schaumburg, hands-down. Led the devotional hymn in church every Sunday and, by the grace of God, hadn't missed but a handful of Sunday morning services in all his years; he said singing the praises of the Lord gave him strength.

"Sister Marjorie, your little Millie sure is a hard worker. Did such a good job helping me out back there."

"Well, I thank you, Brother Godfrey. Our Millie has a mind to work hard when she wants to."

I smiled but I didn't show my teeth.

"Well, me and Sister Earnestine believe hard work should be rewarded. So, if it's all the same to you, Sister Marjorie, I'd like for our Millie to have this-here Coca-Cola. I think that might be enough to square away her wages."

I sure was hoping that my Momma wouldn't say no – but she had that look in her eyes. Coca-Cola was my favorite and she would only let me have one on Sunday evenings after supper. "Brother Godfrey, you don't have to spoil that child every time she do a little something 'round here now. Ben and me trying to teach our Millie that it's better to give than to receive."

"You and Brother Ben doing a fine job with our Millie. You don't see a lot of that these days."

"You called it right, Claude. Got a whole heap of rusty, no-count rascals runnin' 'round here."

"I'm a man of strong conviction, Sister Marjorie. The Bible says –"

"The laborer is worthy of his wages. That's First Timothy chapter five, verse 18."

Sister Godfrey fixed her hands in prayer and I was glad because I really wanted my Coca-Cola.

Momma looked over at me and smiled. She always felt proud when people made a fuss over me, but she never allowed herself or me to get puffed up. "Well, you know I'm not one to argue with the Word, Brother Godfrey."

Schaumburg's Sweet Reminisce

"Well now, there's no sense in it, Sister Marjorie, no sense in it at all." Brother Godfrey said what he said matter-of-factly and Momma let it be. I met Brother Godfrey halfway to lay claim to what was rightfully mine before any more talk on the matter got stirred up. I smiled wide and thanked Brother Godfrey for my wages.

He shuffled his feet, as to do a little dance, over to where Momma was and pulled another ice-cold Coca-Cola from behind his back. He offered it to Momma, but Momma just politely crossed her arms and leaned her head to the side like she always did when she thought Daddy might be up to something.

"Brother Godfrey, now, I thank you kindly, but I'll do fine to have a sip of Millie's."

I met Momma's smile with mine, but as soon as she looked away, I filled up both my cheeks with Coca-Cola. It burned a little bit, but I was used to it.

"Come now, Sister Marjorie, you may as well just go on and take this-here Coca-Cola; it's nearly freezing my hand right down to the bone."

"Brother Godfrey, if it wasn't for Sister Earnestine, I believe you'd give away this entire store."

"Now now, there's more than enough Coca-Cola to go around."

Sister Godfrey put her hands on her hips and looked up and over her small red rimmed glasses straight for Brother Godfrey. "Then where's mine, Claude? Look like your hands done run fresh out of Coca-Cola."

"Got an ice-cold Coca-Cola right here for you,

woman." Brother Godfrey reached in his back pocket and pulled out the last Coca-Cola. He smiled big when he handed it to Sister Godfrey and then turned around and winked at me.

Sister Godfrey laughed and swatted after Brother Godfrey. That sent Brother Godfrey a'scootin', pretending to get away. Sister and Brother Godfrey carried on much like Momma and Daddy did around the house. They always had a good time and made for good company.

If Brother and Sister Godfrey was to run plum-out of Coca-Cola, Momma was sho' to have a few bottles stashed on the top shelf of the pantry just in case we had an extra mouth or two to feed during Sunday dinner. I'm sure my daddy had something in mind when he put those shelves in, if nothing more than to please my momma.

❋ ❋❋❋❋ ❋

"Woman, you got your husband in here sweatin' and twirlin' 'round on his toes like one of Millie's spin tops. Now you's got all this wide-open space down below here. Why can't you just set these here Coca-Cola's somewhere's closer to the middle?"

"I know, Ben, but what's the sense in having all that space up there on that top shelf if I never use it? Anyhow, I wouldn't want Millie to mess around and fall into temptation. You know how she get when she see a Coca-Cola bottle, poor child nearly lose her mind at the very sight of one."

"Well now, ain't a man alive beyond temptation, but our little Mille's a good child; she minds what we tell her 'bout most everything." Daddy handed the dusty bottles to Momma and gave her a kiss on the cheek.

Schaumburg's Sweet Reminisce

"Yes, she minds on account we stay on her about always doing what's right if and when ain't a soul watching because the good Lord always is. Ain't nothin' hidden – the good Lord sees all and He knows all."

Daddy took his rag from his pocket and wiped the sweat from his face and head while Momma watched. She watched him all the time. I asked her one time why she looked at Daddy all the time the way that she did and never said anything. Momma said that she was just so in awe of God that He would give her my daddy for a husband.

"Looks like you and Momma gonna have to share this time, Millie; got a extra mouth to feed for supper." She didn't seem to be asking, but I didn't mind; Momma always shared whatever she had, so I nodded.

"Come now, child. Use your words, you hear me?" I shook my head once again out of habit, I guess, and looked up at my momma's big, smiling brown eyes. She straightened each of my ponytails and went on back to her roaring pot of collard greens and smoked jowl.

"Let's me and you share this evening, Marjorie, like old times. Our Millie been waitin' on this-here Coca-Cola all week long. How that sound to you, babygirl?"

I nodded several times as I returned the glass that I had already gotten from the cupboard. In my few short years, I had learned that the best way to share a bottle of Coca-Cola with my momma was to always measure.

"Fine by me, Ben, but if I don't soon get these in the freezer, we gon' be sittin' around sippin' hot Coca-Cola's and anybody that know anything know that there ain't nothin' worse than a hot Coca-Cola other than a cold one that you want, but can't have. Ain't that right, Millie?"

"Yes, ma'am!" I wasted no time helping Momma get those Coca-Colas in the freezer.

We always sipped our Coca-Cola after Sunday supper. Momma wanted to be sure that I went to bed with a belly full of what she cooked and not half-full of Coca-Cola. Momma could cook with the best of 'em, but she always gave me way too much and I was expected to eat it all before excusing myself from the table. Sometimes my daddy would help me out when Momma wasn't looking, but she'd almost always catch us.

"Aw baby, I was just trying to see if Millie's purple hull peas tasted better than mine."

"Well, Ben, I don't know why you would feel the need to do that. Every purple hull pea on every plate on this-here table came from the same pot."

"Oh now, woman. We just having a little harmless fun. Ain't we, babygirl?"

"Yes, sir, it's all in fun, Momma."

"Child of mine, you sit up to the table and eat your supper like a proper young child and never mind the fun for now. Millie don't need to be learning no bad habits at home, Ben; it's enough of 'em out there in the world for her to flee from."

I looked at Daddy and he looked at me. Momma was serious, but I could tell by Daddy's eyes that he'd have my momma laughing again before dinner was over.

"Little girl, don't you even think about eatin' off of nobody else's plate lest you beyond starving, ya hear?"

Schaumburg's Sweet Reminisce

Daddy helped hisself to one of Momma's fried green tomatoes while she was going on and on about how hard she and Daddy was trying to raise a Godly child with some home training.

While Momma scolded me, I could see Daddy out of the corner of my eye, smacking his lips and licking his fingers, carrying on about how good Momma's food tasted. His funny faces made me giggle which made Momma a little upset because she thought I wasn't paying no attention to what she was saying – that is, until she caught Daddy trying to get after another one of her fried green tomatoes.

Momma never stopped talking and she never took her eyes off of me, but her third eye was on Daddy and her face showed that she was growing weary. Daddy sure was funny but he was too old to get whoopings – I wasn't; so, I straightened all the way up, kept my eyes and attention on my momma, ate my dinner, and held my giggles as best I could.

I could still see Daddy out of the corner of my eye. He wasn't doing nothing, but I could see him in my mind crossing his eyes.

We laughed and talked at the table all the time, but that wasn't hardly the problem. From time to time when I laughed, I had food in my mouth and everything that didn't land in front of Momma's plate landed in the back of my throat.

"Lord Jesus!" Momma grabbed me up, pulled me across the table, and had me turned upside-down and then upright again before my daddy could even reach for me to help clear my throat. Momma was shaking like a dry leaf in the wind.

"Millie, I declare! I'm trying to raise you to be a proper and chaste young lady!" Momma looked like she wanted to cry, which made me cry.

"Now, now, Marjorie. She alright. Everything's alright."

"I know she alright, Ben. I know when my child is alright and when she ain't. Lil girl, I hope you almost choking to death done taught you a real good lesson. One that you just had to try on for yourself, I see."

"Now, Marjorie. I believe that's enough."

"You sit yourself up to this here table now. I done told you I don't know how many times."

"Woman, I said that's enough."

"I'm gone from it, Ben."

My eyes got big because my momma never talked back to my daddy and she never raised her voice towards him neither.

"I'm sorry, Momma. I didn't mean it. Don't be mad at Daddy."

"Hush up that crying now, Millie. Everything's gone be alright. Come here to me."

I felt scared for my momma. I could feel her heart beating through her chest. It felt like it was on the outside of her body. I think she may have been scared too with me almost choking to death and all – more scared than me. She unbuttoned the collar on my dress and gave me a sip of her tea while she rubbed my back with one hand and with the other she rubbed her right temple.

Schaumburg's Sweet Reminisce

I looked up at my momma and she knew why. Her tea wasn't as sweet as mine. It wasn't sweet at all. She liked to drink it like that sometimes.

Through my tears, I looked across the table at my half-empty cup and put in my mind that I would rather have what was left in my cup instead, but I knew better... knew better than to reach in that direction after the look my momma just gave me, so I just set her glass back on the table, closed my eyes, and laid my head in her bosom like I always did.

Momma's tears was still falling and so was mine.

"A man heart can't do nothing but break plum-in-two when both his favorite girls is crying."

Momma wiped both our tears with her apron and sent me back to the chair she snatched me from with a swat to my backside.

"Millie, you go on back over there now and finish your meal like you supposed to."

"Yes, sir."

"Wait a minute, Millie. Let Momma fix your bow on your dress. Momma gon' leave your dress unbuttoned for a while. Go on now, like your daddy say."

I did as I was told.

"You alright, babygirl." Daddy kissed me on my forehead, wiped the last little tear from my cheek, and then gave Momma a kiss on hers.

I walked back over to my chair, sat myself down, and

ate my supper. It was real quiet after that. You couldn't even now hear our forks scraping against the bottom of our plates. I guess that's what happens when somebody almost choke to death – nobody saying nothing.

Things like that didn't happen often, but I can remember one other time we all sat tight-lipped around the supper table. But now, if anybody ever ought to been quiet, it was my daddy. He'd come in some evenings so worn out from the field that he'd barely have enough energy to refresh himself.

I had gotten a little bit older and didn't need to be right under Momma's footsteps, but because of her third eye, she always seemed to know what was going on. That evening, Momma sat quiet mostly and picked over her supper while me and Daddy had our fun – but that wouldn't hold true for long.

"Woman, I hadn't heard you say but one word since you sat down to supper and that was "Amen" after I asked the Lord to bless the food. Everything alright, ain't it?"

Daddy didn't like sitting around for too long with nobody saying nothing. Said a home blessed by God should never look or feel like the coldness of the world whether you had a fire roaring in the stove or not. We had fun most evenings and Momma always made sure that things never got too far out-of-hand, but this evening was different.

"I'm alright, Ben. I'm alright." Momma's voice was soft. Sad.

Every now and then she would look up and dab her mouth, look at Daddy's plate, and then look over at me to make sure I was eating everything she had done set before me.

Schaumburg's Sweet Reminisce

"Husband of mine, can I put anything else on your plate? 'Course, I don't know how you can hold anything else, seeing that you done ate yours and nearly half of what I put on mine and Millie's." Momma never even looked in Daddy's direction.

Daddy smiled. "Woman, I don't think I can hold nothin' else. I'm tight as a tick."

"Umm hmm. Millie, you 'bout finished with your supper?"

I could barely get down what was in my mouth and I sho' didn't want all that was left on my plate, but I dare not talk and let Momma see a crumb of food fall from my mouth and tell her that – so, I just kept chewing what was between my jaws and nodded. When I was born, I wasn't no bigger than a gnat and Momma made it one of her earthly missions to make sure I didn't stay that way.

Daddy could sense that Momma was feeling some kind of way, and like always, his heart was set on making things better so he grabbed Momma by the hand and kissed it – kissed it again, and then again. Momma looked away every time he did. She had a peculiar look on her face, kinda like the look I would get sometimes when she had to get on to me about something that she had already scolded me about time and again. Momma looked at me and then at my daddy.

Daddy knelt down beside her. He never let go of Momma's hand. "Talk to me, woman."

He kissed Momma's hand again and Momma stood up almost beside herself. I put my fork down, but didn't stop chewing and kept watching.

"Marjorie, I'm truly sorry." I didn't know what Daddy had done did, but I believed him.

Momma looked back at me with tears in her eyes. I don't think she could have said nothing if she wanted to, though I reckon her foot tapping against that wooden floor said everything she was meaning to.

"Come now, woman. Sit on down here now."

Momma gave in but she took her time doing it. Daddy sat her down on his lap and wiped her tears like he always did – he hated seeing her cry. Momma had been crying a lot lately, but she just always said nothing was wrong.

"Woman, I'd lay down my very life for you. You got to know that."

"Ben, you don't... have to...."

"Just listen at me now. I know I tell you that all the time, but it's the honest truth. You's a good woman, Marjorie, a good mother and even better help-mate. Now, you got to believe me when I tell you that I would never purposely try to undermine you in your God-given roles. I was just trying to have a little fun. I wasn't tryin' to take Millie's mind off of what you teaching her – it brings me great joy to see you and our little Millie smile. I'm a blessed man."

Momma finally stopped crying. I had even now let a few tears of my own fall.

"Now, I can see you upset with me and I'm sorry. Talk to me, woman, so I can try and make it right."

"I'm not angry with you, Ben. I was just remembering what today once was. I woke up with it on my mind. Just a

43

little sad is all… but I'm yet grateful for all the blessings of God…"

"My Lord. Wife of mine, can you find it in your heart to forgive your husband once again?"

"Now you know I'd forgive you for anything, Ben Charles. I'm alright. Far past time I let go."

"Woman, I'm sorry. I guess I just try to put this-here day out my mind. It breaks my heart to see you hurting still with so much pain, but I aim to hurt right alongside you as long as I need to."

"Husband of mine, I'm sorry too. I don't have to be so serious all the time. I just want the very best for our Millie. I know we both do, but sometimes I feel like my best just ain't enough."

"Well, that may be how you feel, woman – ain't a ounce of truth in it, but you got a right to speak what's on your heart."

"I know your heart is for me, Ben Charles, always have been. It's so easy to love you"

"I need to tell you I'm sorry too, Millie."

"I'm sorry too, Momma." I started to cry a bit myself but held most of it in.

"Sweet girl, listen at me now. Momma loves her some Millie, you hear? I know I can be real hard on you sometimes, here lately what seem like all the time, but I don't aim to break your spirit. I just want you pleasing before the Lord, not perfect, just pleasing to Him. Lord knows I love you with all my heart; ain't never prayed for something so hard and long before in all my life. Momma's real sorry for spoiling supper this evening."

"Everything's alright, woman. Why don't I lead us in prayer?" Daddy was near 'bout in tears.

"Most holy and gracious God and Father, Master, we know that You know all things... even the deep and hidden places of the heart of man. Hem us in on every side, Lord; purge our wayward hearts and heal our brokenness. Drive out every lying, wicked, and disputing spirit from among us – even the spirit of unbelief, and help us to do what pleases You. Lord, we love You and we bless Your holy name. In the mighty name of Jesus Christ we pray. Amen."

Momma and Daddy loved on one another and on me real good after that fervent prayer, but I still had to finish all my supper before I got dessert. Our supper had done got good and cold but nobody seemed to mind; prayer always had a way of setting things right.

After supper, we took to our usual spot out on the porch. Daddy had just re-stained it and it pleased Momma well.

"What you thinking, woman?"

By the time Momma made it over to where we was, she had done walked the entire length of that porch a few times and run her hands and bare feet across every board and post she looked upon. Momma always seemed grateful no matter how big or small the gesture. The way she showed her appreciation for certain things just made people feel good about they-self. Like they had done something that really mattered. I wondered if she knew that.

"Ben, couldn't nobody nowhere done a better job on

Schaumburg's Sweet Reminisce

this porch than you. I know it ain't nothing perfect this side of living, but this-here porch you redone come real close. I'm near 'bout beside myself."

Daddy smiled real big.

"Well, Millie, what you think? You think we made your momma happy?" Daddy whispered, but not really.

"She sure do look happy," I whispered too, but not really.

"Momma is very happy. And y'all think you whispering, but you ain't – done heard every word you just now spoke."

I looked at my daddy right fast. I wondered how Momma could have heard me, but not much ever got by her.

Daddy stood to meet Momma. She grabbed him by both hands and whispered something in his ear. When Momma and Daddy started to giggle, I stopped swinging my feet and sat up straight; they just stood there holding hands, smiling and looking at each other. Wasn't nobody saying nothing, so I went back to swinging my feet.

Momma and Daddy came back over to where I was to finish drinking our Coca-Colas. Momma took a tiny sip of Coca-Cola and offered it to Daddy, then Daddy took a good swallow and handed it back to Momma.

That evening, I sat on Daddy's lap watching the both of them whisper and laugh just like I wasn't there. I didn't know why, but him and Momma was acting real strange. Daddy kept on sending me to see what time it was. I couldn't yet tell time, so I just told my daddy what number the little hand was on and what number the big hand was on. All I know is that I had to keep walking all the way to the back of the house to look at the clock on the wall. Momma didn't allow no running in the house, but I could walk fast – and I did, so not to miss nothing.

Momma sent me up to my room early that evening with a few extra teacakes and warm milk, so I didn't mind. Momma never let me have two desserts in one day. She didn't even make me get my bath before bed even though she knew I half took one the night before. Momma said a woman should always keep herself up, but if she couldn't keep herself up she was to always keep herself clean. I was sure to get a good scrubbing the next morning if the good Lord willed his Breath of Life.

From that day forward, Momma never spoke of that day again with a broken heart – only of how the Lord restored her and how beautiful her porch was.

Chapter Four

Now, can a handsome old fellow get his beautiful lady

anything else?"

"Well, since the handsome fellow is asking..."

"Oh, he's asking and he's real handsome."

"Well then, the beautiful lady will have this lovely, floral dress from Woolworth. This one right here. Put your glasses on, Claude, so's you looking at the right one. It's the prettiest one in the whole catalog."

"Ahhh haaa. That's a mighty fine dress, woman – fine indeed. Mighty pleasing to these old eyes."

"Well, I'm glad the old handsome fellow approves."

"Isn't it beautiful, Sis Marjorie?"

"I'd say so, Sister Earnestine. The fanciest one I've seen in a good long while. I believe it'd look real nice on you too. Mighty fine, indeed."

Menfolk loved to see their women all dressed up and looking good, especially on Sunday morning, and both

Sheriell Scott

Momma and Sister Godfrey knew that better than anybody.

By now, Momma and Sister Godfrey were beside themselves with laughter and soft whispers; they'd been stirring up Brother Godfrey on purpose, had him biting like a top-water in no time. By the time everything was said and done, Sister Godfrey had done talked Brother Godfrey into a hat, a purse, and matching shoes.

"Woman, come to think of it, didn't I just buy you a dress last month?"

"You most certainly did, Claude, and do you remember how good I looked in it – with the shoes and the clutch to match?"

"As a matter of a fact, I do."

"And do you remember how I thanked you for everything later that evening?"

"I certainly do, woman. I tell you what, you just write up the ticket and I'll take care of everything else." Brother Godfrey smacked and rubbed his hands together like Daddy always did just before he got ready to dig into Momma's Sunday dinner. "Well, I guess I'll leave you ladies be for a minute or two and head on down to the cellar so's I can reset them shelves back yonder."

"Claude, are you forgetting something?"

"How's that, Earnestine?"

"I wanna give you that ticket I wrote up. I got it all ready for you."

"Earnestine, you's wanting me to call this-here ticket

49

order in right now, this-here very second?"

"Yes, Claude. If I plan to pour myself into that dress for this coming Sunday, you got to call that order in right now."

"This Sunday, Earnestine?"

"Yes, this-here coming Sunday. Remember what I told you."

"Well now, in that case, I'll get right on it, woman."

"Well, Millie, I guess I'd better get back to work if my Earnestine's gon' be the prettiest little lady in all of Schaumburg this Sunday. Anything else you need, woman?" That must have been some kind of dress because Brother Godfrey seemed to be in a hurry all of a sudden. He didn't even bother to wait for Sister Earnestine to answer.

"Not right now, Claude."

"Alright now, ladies, I'll be right on back. Old man Claude Godfrey got to make another dollar to pay for all of this-here I done let my Earnestine talk me into."

"We'll be right here, Brother Godfrey," Momma said.

"I'll holler back there and let you know if I see anything else you might want to see me in, Claude," Sister Godfrey called out.

"Listen at him whistling, Sister Earnestine."

"Sister Marjorie, I aim to look so fine in this-here dress, Claude ain't gon' know what hit him."

Sister Godfrey always dressed real pretty, even when

she cleaned up around the house. Didn't matter when or where you saw her, Sister Godfrey always looked like she was on her way somewhere or expecting company.

I wasn't quite a lady, far from it, but Momma said that I still needed to know how to be treated like one. Told me to pay attention to how my daddy treated her and how Brother Godfrey treated Sister Godfrey and to expect nothing less from no man of mine.

Momma and Sister Godfrey make out like Brother Godfrey was gon' go plum-out of his mind when he saw Sister Godfrey in that dress. I didn't know why Sister Godfrey would want to do that to Brother Godfrey, making him lose his mind and all. I was just hoping that he didn't forget where he put all the Coca-Colas before he went crazy. We only had enough in the pantry for one more Sunday.

"Millie, everything alright?"

"Yes, ma'am."

After hanging up the phone, Brother Godfrey made his way on back up front. "Well woman, the lady on the phone said your dress and your matching, hat, shoes, and pocketbook will be here Friday afternoon, Lord willing."

"Well, I pray that He is. Thank you kindly, Claude. I can't wait. Just in time for Sunday morning service."

"Anything for my Earnestine. Now, before I go, can I be of further service to you ladies? If not, I's still got to get on down to that cellar and back up again to reset them shelves."

"I think we can manage on our own for a while, Claude."

Schaumburg's Sweet Reminisce

Brother Godfrey kissed Sister Godfrey on the cheek and told her something in her ear – but it wasn't hardly nobody else's business 'cause Brother Godfrey was whispering.

Sister Godfrey smiled big and clutched her pearls. "Old man, you better get."

Momma smiled and looked on. Made me wonder at the time if she didn't know what Brother Godfrey and Sister Godfrey was carrying on about.

"Sister Marjorie, it's been my pleasure." Brother Godfrey kissed Momma on the hand and then started back to the cellar.

Brother Godfrey was the only man that my daddy allowed to get that close to my momma. My daddy said if he couldn't trust a man to take care of his wife and children when he was dead and gone, he wasn't 'bout to let him get a chance to do it while he was still alive.

In our town, when a young lady was allowed to court for a husband, she always smiled and bowed her head just a little when a man kissed her hand – but if he was a man of a certain reputation, she was supposed to tell that Jack to hit the road.

Momma said if you start lettin' any and every no-good man kiss your hand, before long, he'll be wanting to kiss a whole lot of other things that don't belongst to him. Told me that it's just best for an unmarried woman to tell any man to keep his hands and his lips unto himself. Said young and old folks alike ought not awaken certain lusts before the proper time.

"No need to rush off, Brother Godfrey."

"No, no – that work ain't gone get done with me standing still. This looks and sounds like woman-talk to me anyhow, so, I need to get on out of y'all's way before this pretty little woman of mine decides she wants a brand spankin' new Cadillac. Sister Marjorie, it sure was good to see you and Millie again and tell Brother Ben that I may give him a holler sometime later this week. I believe it's far past time we go fishing."

"I'll be sure to tell him. And me and mine is grateful for the Coca-Colas."

"Anytime, Sister Marjorie. I'll be in the back if you need me, sweetheart."

"Okay, Claude, I'll put lunch on as soon as me and Sister Marjorie finish catching up."

"Alright. Take your time. You be good Millie, ya hear?"

"Yes, sir."

I didn't need to be told to stay out of grown folks' business, so with Momma and Sister Godfrey carrying on and Brother Godfrey tending to his chores elsewhere, I took another sip of my Coca-Cola and made my way to the other side of the store so I could eyeball the candy shelf a little better. I didn't reckon I'd be causing nobody no harm.

＊　＊＊＊＊　＊

Momma and Daddy always made me stand with my hands behind my back when I looked at the candy shelf so not to be quick to fall into temptation and take what didn't belongst to me. I looked at every jar twice, but I didn't see nothin' that I hadn't already had. Momma wasn't gonna let me buy no candy nohow on account I had done had a Coca-

53

Schaumburg's Sweet Reminisce

Cola, but I didn't mind, as long as I got to keep the money she gave me for next time.

My daddy told me that man should always strive in his heart to be like-minded in the things of God. I was tithing to the church long before I came to know the Lord for myself. If I didn't have money to tithe, I had to tithe from the candy I had been saving. Daddy always made me tithe my favorite piece. Sometimes if I had enough strength to deny myself, I would tithe two pieces of candy.

"Always give nothing less than your best, babygirl – and it don't matter if what you got is out of much or if what you got is out of lack, always try to out-give God even though you can't."

I kept all my candy in one of my daddy's old dress socks tucked in the front pocket of the first winter coat Momma and Daddy ever bought me. Momma said she wanted to keep that coat nice for my baby girl if the good Lord should see fit to bless me. Nobody was supposed to know about my hiding place but me. I wondered though...

Pastor Tisdale would always thank me after Sunday morning service for my tithe – but only when I tithed in candy. Momma always made sure that I had my tithe together on Saturday afternoon and always saw fit to remind me that whether anybody thanked me or not, that I was to always be a cheerful giver, as unto the Lord, of my money, my time, and my talents.

I still had half my Coca-Cola left, but it was gettin' some warm. I didn't know if Momma and Sister Earnestine was gon' ever stop talking so Momma could take us on home; but I didn't make too much never-mind about it on account I always kept my Coca-Cola top for such times.

Brother Godfrey could pop the top off of three Coca-Cola bottles at the same time with one thumb. I never saw him use nothing else. Momma said his thumb was special because it was born that way. It just looked plain old funny to me, but I never let Brother Godfrey know that I knew his thumb looked funny. It was his thumb; the way I figure, he had to know.

Daddy said when I was a wee biddy thing still in diapers, I used to be some scared of Brother Godfrey. I'd strike out running every time I saw him coming. Said one day I just reached for him to pick me up and he did. Brother Godfrey nearly cried when I laid my head on his shoulder but Daddy said I kept watch on that thumb of his like a hawk.

One time, Momma caught me staring at Brother Godfrey's thumb and told me to straighten my face and mind my manners. I wanted to touch it on account it was fat and crooked and didn't have no fingernail on it. I thought I would – just one time. I had done got up the nerve to do it, but right when I went to touch it, Momma snatched a knot in me.

Chapter Five

I could count on two hands the number of beatings I got as a child. Momma always made sure I remembered them.

After every beatin', I had to recite Proverbs 23: 13-14:

"Do not withhold correction from a child,
For if you beat him with a rod, he will not die.
You shall beat him with a rod,
And deliver his soul from hell."

Then she'd tell me how much her and Daddy loved me. Said that they loved me twice as much as anybody else and almost as much as Jesus did. Well, I already knew that my momma and daddy loved me, and it didn't matter how much, I still hated gettin' whoopings.

Most kids my age wasn't allowed to say "hell" – but I was. Momma told me that she better not ever catch me blaspheming or cussing, but I could speak the Word of God in love any time I wanted on account the Word of Truth had the power to accomplish those things that pleased the Lord. Said that if I would just say what the Word of God said, I could speak it with boldness and not ever need apologize for nothing. The Bible is man's daily portion – and man should always be ready, willing, and able to rightly divide unto others and to partake for himself.

My speech may have been delayed at birth but my hearing wasn't and Momma knew this all too well.

While I waited for Momma and Sister Earnestine to finish up, a heavy-set, gray-haired woman with a cane limped into the store. All anybody ever know'd her to go by was Mean Gurt. And Mean Gurt looked mean, sho' nuff.

I thought all old people loved children. Every last one I had ever met loved me, but I guess Mean Gurt wasn't as old as she looked.

I smiled and showed myself friendly like Momma taught me, but looked away real quick when Mean Gurt walked past and cut her eyes at me. Momma had always told me to be kind in spite of how other people treated me – and folks could be real low-down sometimes. Said that some people just couldn't help it because they hadn't yet let the Lord take over in they heart.

When people mistreated me, Momma would always whisper a special scripture in my ear over and over until we both calmed down. Momma had to whisper a lot, sometimes with tears running down her face.

"But I say to you,
love your enemies,
bless those that curse you,
do good to those that hate you,
and pray for those who spitefully use you and
persecute you."

Matthew 5:44

Mean Gurt made her way to the back of the store and

laid into Brother Godfrey about a gallon of milk that had gone bad before the date on the bottle. Her voice was gruff and her upper body swayed on account she used one hand to balance herself on her cane and the other hand to shake in Brother Godfrey's face. Brother Godfrey stood lock-jawed with his arms folded, shaking his head in agreement. I don't think he would have been able to get a word in had he had the chance to open his mouth.

That old Mean Gurt was sho' nuff carrying on something hateful. Folks had stopped shopping and was starting to whisper and stare. A good many left the store altogether. Didn't seem to me like bad milk would make a person act that ugly.

Sister Godfrey started out from behind the counter towards the back of the store, but Momma reached for her to stay put and held Sister Godfrey close to her.

"Brother Claude'll set things right, Sister Earnestine – he always do."

Sister Godfrey stayed put and held Momma's hand while Mean Gurt laid into Brother Godfrey.

"Thank you, Sister Marjorie. You know how protective I am of my Claude, but you's right, you's right."

I saw Momma's lips moving and knew that she was doing one of two things – praying or quoting scripture; although with Momma, they were one in the same. She knew that when the Word went forth, it wouldn't return void because the Word said so; but now that thing that the Word would accomplish was left to the Father.

Momma had portions of scripture she repeated over and over again when she felt herself getting ahead of the

Lord. Said it was to bring her flesh under submission to the Holy Spirit. She'd been reading the Bible from cover-to-cover every year of her life since the age of seven, the age that she was when she accepted Jesus Christ as her Lord and Savior and twice while she lay flat on her back waiting for me to arrive.

She skipped the ninth and tenth grade and was the first and only one in her family to get a high school education. Scholarships poured in all the way from California to New York City but Momma turned down every last one. Folks wasn't too happy 'round Ned County when Momma turned down all them schools.

Most folks had hoped that Momma would be the first doctor, judge, or just somebody real important in the world to get folks talking about Ned County like they did the rest of the world. But not a day went by that Momma didn't feel like she already had the most important job in the world. Even as a little child, Momma knew that her call wasn't out in the world, but at home as a wife to her husband, a momma to her children, and a servant of the Lord to wherever His will sent her. Momma may have been smart as a whip, but she was even more proud to be learned in the Word of God.

"Plenty of folks already too smart for they own good. Sooner or later they start thinking more highly of themselves than they ought and that's what keeps most folks from the Lord, thinking they know better than God; but God is the One who opens the mind."

Every now and then, Momma would run into somebody she went to school with, each and every last one of 'em wanting to know the exact same thing – why she didn't go on to college. Momma's response was always the same:

Schaumburg's Sweet Reminisce

"The Word of God teaches at all times and the Holy Spirit is the only teacher I need. I'll leave the world to learn the ways of the world, but as for me and mine, we gon' learn and do what thus says the Lord and that's more than enough for us." Wasn't much folks could say after that.

Brother Godfrey looked like a wounded animal by the time old Mean Gurt finished up her cussin', but Sister Godfrey wore the face of a fightin' woman. She didn't take too kindly to Mean Gurt mistreating Brother Godfrey, but she stayed quiet and ladylike.

Brother Godfrey finally walked behind the counter at the back of the store to pull a few coins from the register to give to Mean Gurt, but not before stopping to reach up there at that old burlap sack full of goodies he kept back all month to give to Benny Brewster who had made his monthly trip up from them Mahalia Bottoms. He'd been in the back sittin' down on a block of cedar watching that old Mean Gurt act a-plum fool. Sat there the whole time fightin' the air while she cussed Brother Godfrey up one side and down the other.

"Here you are, Benny."

"Yessur, tank-tank-tank you, sur."

"You been keeping close watch on them-there bottoms, ain't you?"

"Yessur. Alllll day. Alllll night. You aaaauullllright, ain't you, sur?"

"I'm alright, Benny. We'll see you next month. Take care yourself now."

"Yesssur. Yesssur. Neah munf. Neah munf."

Brother Godfrey made his way on back over to that old empty shell of a woman standing there with her nose in the air and placed the money in her hand. He even gave her a little something extra for her troubles and told her to come back to see him.

Mean Gurt snatched her devil's reward, which amounted to no more than a dollar and some change, from Brother Godfrey's hand and started making her way up to the front of the store to leave, all the while still huffing and cussing under her breath. Not sure how Mean Gurt had much else left to say after all that talk she gave Brother Godfrey.

If it wasn't for Mean Gurt's cane knocking against the floorboards, you never would've know'd anybody else was in the store. Nobody dared say nothing. We was all hoping for the same thing, so nobody need say it.

Sister Godfrey rolled her eyes at Mean Gurt and started toward Brother Godfrey; she had done stretched out her arms to give Brother Godfrey a hug before she even got back there at him. "Come here to me, Claude."

"Oh, I'm alright, Earnestine. I've survived worst. I do declare, that woman stir up a fuss everywhere her feet tread."

"Well, just the same, I'm glad you had your *Armor* on, Claude."

"Me too, sweetheart. Me too."

Brother Godfrey took some kind of beating that day – to his pride and to his pockets. Old nasty woman ran off everybody in the store except Benny Brewster. I imagine he wasn't intent on leaving until he had what he'd come for.

Schaumburg's Sweet Reminisce

When a man can stay humble and show love in the face of evil, that brings glory to the Lord – and Brother Godfrey did every bit of that. That's what being filled with the Holy Spirit looked like.

Mean Gurt seemed to be leaving just as fast as she came 'til she stopped dead in her tracks to wipe the cotton from the sides of her mouth, or so I was thinking, until she laughed. The next breath I drew told me that she had done broke wind and it was just as wicked as she was.

No sooner had Momma beckoned me out of the way of Mean Gurt, a young girl entered the store with her four young-in's in-tow. They ran up and down the aisles, laughing and playing like little hellions.

I took another sip of my Coca-Cola but didn't dare move from where my feet were planted to show myself friendly because I knew better. I don't reckon nobody had ever took a leather strap to them kids' backsides.

Sister Earnestine was already put out with Mean Gurt and cut her eyes long and hard at that young girl for lettin' them children tear up the store like that. She looked at Brother Godfrey with a tone that I reckon he had heard before because right after that, he shooed them children right on back out the store – young girl with 'em never said a mumbling word.

Momma ushered me further on back out of Mean Gurt's path, but before she could drag past me, all four of them children ran past her, one right behind the other knocking her cane out her hand. It scared me when she reached for me to steady herself. I stumbled backwards and nearly pulled us both down to the floor.

Right wall-eyed, I picked up that ungrateful woman's

cane and went to hand it to her.

"Stupid child, ain't you got no sense at all?" The next thing I know'd, Mean Gurt had done snatched me so hard my feet left the floor and I wet my panties. Her sweaty face was right up in mine.

"You loose my child, you old wretched woman," Momma shouted and pushed past Brother Godfrey.

"Fool child, don't you hear me talkin' at you?"

Mean Gurt's breath smelled of stale snuff. Made my eyes burn. She was some kind of mad and I thought she might kill me on account she didn't get to kill Brother Godfrey. She grew up fightin'. She'd been known to go toe to toe with men much meaner than she was, but only when she had to.

"Mean Gurt, you loose my child, I say – or you'll be resting amongst the dead this day!" Before Momma's lips stopped moving, she had done put Mean Gurt on her back. Momma looked like she could spit fire.

Mean Gurt was down, but you could tell that she was still looking for a fight. I wanted to run to my momma but Sister Godfrey pulled me back when Momma reached for Mean Gurt's cane.

"Sister Marjorie!" Brother and Sister Godfrey hollered at the same time.

Momma reared back as far as she could and came down across Mean Gurt three good times before Brother Godfrey was able to get over to her to free that cane from her hands. Scared me so bad I started shaking all over.

Schaumburg's Sweet Reminisce

"Claude, you got to do something." Sister Godfrey tried to cover my face just before Momma could lay into that old Mean Gurt one last good time. I closed my eyes and swallowed hard and hollered as loud as I could.

"Momma, no! Vengeance belongs to the Lord!"

Momma froze but still held a strong grip on that cane.

"Come, come now, Sister Marjorie. Listen to your little Millie. Let Brother Claude have this-here cane now."

Brother Godfrey grabbed hold of that cane and took it away from Momma; she didn't give him much struggle with it.

"Vengeance belongs to the Lord, Momma."

"Lord Jesus, please forgive me!" Momma hollered. She fell to her knees with tears in her eyes and reached for me.

I wiggled free from Sister Earnestine and ran and fell on my momma's neck. I hugged my momma tight and then turned to look at Mean Gurt laid out in the floor. She wasn't moving much but I wasn't sad for her.

I'd never believe that Momma could get so mad lest I'd seen it with mine own eyes. I shook my little fist at old Mean Gurt and told my momma that everything was gon' be alright whilst Momma wept.

"Sister Marjorie, why don't you and Millie go on home? Me and Earnestine, we'll see about all this here. I'll call and check on you and Millie as soon I can."

Momma carried me the entire two miles we lived from town – even though I was too big for her to be carrying. I looked over her shoulder at the truck we were leaving behind and thought it best not to ask why. Momma's breathing was husky and her eyes were welled up with tears, but she never slowed her pace. With every other step, Momma's grasp seemed to get tighter and tighter, but I just held on. The ride home in Momma's arms reminded me of the many bumpy rides I'd taken with my daddy across the hollow to his favorite fishing hole, but worse. I'd be bouncing all over the place… nearly sitting in his lap and driving my own-self before we got to where we was going.

By the time we made it home, we was a hot, dusty, sweaty mess. Momma filled us both up with cold water and then drew a cool bath for herself and then for me. We sat for a spell and then she went to put lunch on the table. She watched me while I ate to make sure that I hadn't got too hot on our way home and then sent me off to my room for a nap.

A short while later, I heard Daddy's tractor from a good ways off. I watched for him from the window in my room. Momma was still in bed, so I ran out to meet him. I jumped in my daddy's arms and started to cry.

"I'm sorry, Daddy. I tried to be strong for Momma."

"Aww now, babygirl. Everything's gonna be alright. The worst part is all over with now."

I had been waiting to hear my daddy say that ever since I laid eyes on Mean Gurt this morning.

Momma didn't fix supper that evening. Me and Daddy made do with the left-over mackerel croquettes, persimmon bread, and fried corn from breakfast without saying very much of anything to one another. Brother Godfrey called and told my daddy all that had happened. Daddy seemed sad and a bit worried. Sister Earnestine told my daddy to let her know if we needed anything at all.

Later on that evening just before the sun set, me and Daddy went in to see about Momma. She was still sleep, so Daddy sat down in his chair and hummed a few hymns.

There was something special about Daddy's voice. Some said that it could lull a crowing rooster back to sleep. All I knew was that whenever Daddy hummed a tune, after a while I could hardly keep my eyes open.

Daddy knelt at the foot of the bed with his hands raised and his head bowed in prayer until the tears came; then he saddled up Old Abraham and rode back to town to pick up his truck.

Momma was so hurt and angry when she left the store, I reckon she forgot she had done drove us into town. Before leaving, Daddy picked me up in his arms and laid me in my bed. From my bedroom window, I watched until Daddy and Old Abraham were out of site, then I went in to see about Momma. She was still sleep but her pillow was wet. I laid down beside her and patted her on the back until I fell asleep.

I don't much like to recall the hurt and anger I met in my momma's eyes that day. It wasn't at all who she was – not to me, not to most folks. But it would always hurt her soul when folks couldn't see what she saw in me; and for a good while she'd have a hard row to hoe trying to shoulder all of my pain and at the same time bear her own.

"Heaven kissed earth the day you was born, Millie." Momma said that a lot and oftentimes with tears in her eyes. "God gave me a blessing that I didn't deserve when He set you in my womb and I aim to do right by it for all my days."

Folks was glad to hear tell of my momma laying out old Mean Gurt. Said it served her right, wished they'd been there to see it with they own eyes. Didn't hear much talk about Mean Gurt bothering nobody after that day neither. But then every now and again, we'd see old Mean Gurt in Church on Sunday and not just when we was eatin'. She'd always sit in the back of the church, same pew, and leave before the benediction – didn't think she liked all the hugging and small talk afterwards; but I reckon the main thing is that she was in the house of the Lord.

Don't think Mean Gurt ever made any real friends, but then she never really showed herself friendly – not sure she knew how. Folks stopped calling her Mean Gurt and started calling her by the name her momma gave to her, Gertrude. First time she heard somebody call her by her real name, she nearly showed every tooth in her mouth.

The Sunday Gertrude got up the nerve to come before the church to give her testimony and confess Jesus Christ as her Lord and Savior, the poor woman wasn't even allowed to tell it all on account nearly every soul had done got to shoutin'. Most times, all the good Lord would have us do is show up, fall on our face, and leave the rest to Him.

Gertrude's momma and daddy had her when they was up in years and both a little sickly. They figured they wouldn't be around long after she became a young woman primed for marriage, so they made her marry young to a man that wasn't good to her... a man that didn't know the Lord. Gertrude hadn't yet leaned how to love none neither, but her momma and daddy figured they was doing right by her.

* ❊❊❊❊ *

Now some time had passed since Momma had got to fightin' but she was still feeling some kinda way, a bit shame on account of her being admonished by her own child and all; but at the same time, she was proud that I had enough Word in me to speak it in wisdom.

"Now Marjorie, I know you still feeling some kind of way about what all done happened, but how much longer you plan on wallowing in that thing?"

"Ben, you just leave me be on this now."

"Well woman, I done let you be for long enough and I aim to be honest about this here now. This here what you dealing with wears the name of pride and nothing else; it's just plain old pride."

Momma looked even more hurt. Daddy had to turn away to finish saying what he had to say.

"I can't hold my tongue on this now, Marjorie. You done made our Millie your little handiwork and every time she mess up, you take it to heart. She ain't ever gon' be perfect in that body she fitted in and neither is you."

"Benjamin Charles, my Millie ain't no idol to me. The Word of the Lord on the lips of a child is a blessed thing. But having my child rebuke me in front of folks shamed me."

"Woman, Millie ain't done nothing that you ain't done taught her to do. The good Lord done humbled you, Marjorie, and I believe you ought to count it as a blessing."

"I reckon you right, Ben. Been eating away at me like maggots. I guess I ought to be grateful our little Millie ain't afraid to speak the Truth – ain't nothing but my own pride that done turned against me."

I prayed as hard as I could every day for the rest of that summer and sometimes twice on Sunday that Momma would turn loose her pride and return to her joy in the Lord and she did.

Chapter Six

I never got to meet my momma's daddy or my daddy's daddy. Never got to meet my daddy's momma or my momma's momma neither. But my daddy said everybody born into the world got a momma and a daddy. He called it a lineage, showed it to me in the Holy Bible. Said everybody had one and everybody that had one was stuck with the one they had.

Momma kept everybody in a small, ugly green suitcase in the back of her closet beneath the floorboards with all the important papers and a few other things nobody had business knowing about. I wasn't supposed to know nothing 'bout none of all that, but I did. I only knew because that year after the weather broke from one of the worst blackberry winters in the history of Schaumburg, we had more spiders than we had names for and Momma was afraid of spiders. Everybody that knew Momma knew she was afraid of spiders, even now the spiders knew Momma was afraid of spiders. She fussed at them spiders like she fussed at me sometimes.

Momma knew all too well what was hiding underneath them floorboards in the cool of darkness. Just thinking on it nearly scared her plum-out her curlers.

One day, Daddy was over in the next town needing Momma to bring him some important papers. He had done already called the house more than a few times trying to calm her down. She even fussed at her own-self between phone calls on account she knew how bad Daddy needed them papers and she didn't want to let him down.

"I'll get them papers, Momma." I was a little rascal and there wasn't much that I was afraid of. I wasn't sure if Momma heard me or not because she was already what church folks call "prostrate before the Lord."

While Momma was busy praying, I crawled underneath her ankle-length church dresses, the nice ones she kept under plastic with a double knot and only wore on first Sunday, and reached off into the dark hole under that floorboard and pulled out that old rusty, tin box she was too afraid to get after. I figured that's what she was needing 'cause wasn't much else down there but an old pistol and the lineage she kept in that ugly, green suitcase.

I wet the bottom of my shirt with a bunch of spit like Momma sometimes did when my face was molly and wiped off all the cobwebs and dead spiders and ran back out to where she was. I reckon it was too important not to run being what she was going thru and all.

Momma was taking a good long time fussing at the Lord about not wanting go in there after them papers. I wondered if the Lord felt scared like I did sometimes when Momma fussed at me. I reckon He must have been fussing back because her whole face was wet with tears. Momma didn't even now know I had done lay'd down beside her. Whenever I thought she was about to stop praying, she started up again. I figured on covering my eyes until she finished so she wouldn't catch me staring. Every now and then I'd take a quick peak when she got quiet, but after a while, my eyes got heavier than that weight Momma was carrying and I fell asleep. I didn't think the Lord would mind 'cause I had been waiting for so long and so had Daddy.

Momma was her own kind of lady, had a way about her though, a way that was just her. Rarely did she ever go against the grain as to who she was, always the same, hardly ever not like herself. Daddy said that we all got a certain way about us, but to a whole lotta folks, Momma just didn't seem to be like a whole lotta folks.

Most folks called her Church Lady behind her back. Town gossip was that she was always quoting scripture and praying 'bout stuff that she ain't even need to pray about, but Momma would be one of the first ones they'd call when they got in a bad way. Most folks just wished she'd hush with her Bible-talk and mind her own business, but in Momma's eyes she was. She said when the Spirit of God stopped giving her business to tend to, she'd stop; but until then, she aimed to be obedient to the Spirit. The cost was too great for Momma to stand by and say nothing – a lost soul was a lost soul, didn't matter 'bout who it belonged to.

"Momma?"

"Yes, sweet child of mine?"

"You sho' do pray a lot."

"Well, Millie, you say I pray a lot, I say I don't think I pray nearly enough."

"But you pray all the time."

"And what's wrong with that, Millie?"

"I don't know. Sometimes you be crying, and fussing,

and praying all at the same time, Momma."

"Well, the Bible say we supposed to pray without ceasing and God don't mind my tears because He know what each one of 'em is for, even when I don't. The Lord thy God is my Father and I can tell Him anything I need to tell Him, knowing that He hears and that He'll answer out of His unconditional love for me. Now, I don't know 'bout nobody else, but praying is my way of lettin' the Lord know that I know that He's there, that I love Him, and that I'm forever grateful to Him for His love – whether His answer be yes or no. Prayer makes everything better when you know and trust the One you's praying too."

"But why come you be fussing at the Lord, Momma?"

"Well, I don't think I be fussing. I guess I just be expressing what's in my heart the only way I know how. Some things only the Lord knows and I'm alright with that."

When I was about the size of a sugar snap pea, I remember watching my Momma pray over a piece of a piece of gum she took from that old leather coin purse she kept in her apron pocket. Momma kept all kinds of things in that coin purse and when she moved, it moved... and so did I. I was always anxious to see what she would pull out of there.

That afternoon, I hurried over to where Momma had decided to rest herself and plopped myself down on her knee without saying a word. My eyes had done stretched to the size of half-dollars.

"You wanna share this-here lil' piece of gum with your momma, Millie?"

Schaumburg's Sweet Reminisce

"Yes, ma'am."

Now, Momma hardly ever chewed gum, but when she did, she never chewed a whole piece. Said it wasn't ladylike for a woman to chew gum to begin with, let alone a whole piece; but it was even more unladylike for a woman to have strange breath. She said a woman that chewed gum might as well ask a man for one of his cigarettes, make him light it for her, and then stand there and smoke it with him. Now that particular day, Momma was sick at the stomach and since it wasn't a sin and she was plum-out of ginger chews, Momma slid a half-piece of gum from her coin purse and broke it in half, but not before giving thanks to God.

"Calm down, child. Momma ain't got but a small piece to give you now. Rate you going, you gon' mess around and bite your tongue plum-out your mouth."

Momma made sure to remind me to chew with my mouth closed. The half of the half-piece of gum Momma shared with me sure was small, but for some reason it seemed to stay sweeter a lot longer than a whole half-piece did. I reckon I was learning the sweetness of prayer for myself through that half of a half-piece of gum.

＊　＊❋＊　＊

I woke up in the cab of my daddy's truck to my momma wiping slob from the corner of my mouth with her favorite handkerchief. I put up a good fight, swatting her hands away. Eyes still swollen from crying, she kept right on singing her favorite hymn, happy because Daddy got what he needed.

Daddy was driving with one hand and holding Momma with the other. He was happy because we were on our way to the pond, our third favorite place on earth.

74

Momma had packed a picnic lunch and at some point had talked my daddy into leaving his tractor set still for the rest of the day. We spent the afternoon and evening swimming, eating cold fried chicken and sweet potato muffins, and drinking the Coca-Colas we sunk to the bottom of the pond to keep cold. Me and Momma sat a little ways away from the bank on our buckets to where we could put our legs in the water without getting our britches wet while Daddy swam like a fish and splashed us every chance he got.

"God used you as His vessel today, Millie, at a time of great weakness for me. Your daddy was really needing them papers to get that contract up and going for that parcel of land he'd been wantin' to buy for a while now. And I was able to get 'em there to him just in time, on account of it. Always let the Lord use you in whatever way He see fit. Even when it don't make sense and no matter what other folks say or think. You hear me now, don't you, sweet child?

"Yes, ma'am." I had a mouth full of watermelon, but Momma didn't seem to mind until I started to see how far I could spit my seeds.

"Me and your daddy is sho' nuff proud of you, Millie. Yes, Lord, sho' nuff proud." Momma was trying to ring some of the water out of my hair and out of hers before it frowned up too bad. Both our heads had to be washed for church on Sunday but she didn't want me walking around too nappy-headed 'til then.

Daddy had since swam to the other side of the pond to get the boat. He'd be back over to get me and Momma to take us down and back up a few times as soon as he checked the drags he set earlier.

Momma said that Daddy would probably be a while

checking those lines, so she loosed and re-plaited the coarse, kinky, coal-black hair that hung past my shoulders and tied it down with the cotton bandana Daddy had wrapped around my neck before he went swimming. Washing and hot combing my hair took two days or better, a day and a half to wash, comb out, and air dry, and then another day to straighten and style.

"Momma?"

"What's on your mind, Millie?"

"You tied it too tight."

"Baby, I'm sorry. Come here and let Momma loosen it up some. That's better, ain't it?

"Yes, ma'am."

Momma kissed my forehead and we locked arms like her and Sister Godfrey always did when they got together. We talked about everything we could muster enough breath to speak on until Daddy came with the boat. I wondered if my momma knew she was my best friend in all my world.

The three of us sat right there on them buckets and enjoyed ourselves and one another until the sun set that evening. I didn't own a care in the world. Momma and Daddy always saw to that. It never entered my mind that I would one day find myself without them. Besides, a child shouldn't be burdened with such thoughts nohow; but the course of life just seemed to have a way of not caring sometimes. Momma and Daddy were all that I needed and I was all that they had; but if Satan could've had his way, I never would've made it into this world.

"But God!" That's what my daddy always said anytime

things was going bad. "But God!" He told me to always trust in that.

One of the things that brought Momma the most joy over the years was bringing the lineage to Thanksgiving. The lineage had its own special way of encouraging Momma like nothing else on Earth ever could.

When she talked about our family history, she said it gave her the strength of a hundred chariots of war; the only other thing that gave her greater joy was having me. Said there would never come a day when she would forget the humbled look on Daddy's face when he held me in his arms for the first time and that made her so proud.

Momma kept the lineage wrapped inside a heavy plastic bag which she kept inside a leather pouch inside the inner zipped pocket of that old green suitcase. The lineage had been passed down through the years and between Momma's family and Daddy's family, they could account for nine generations. The photos were cracked and worn out around the edges and there was yellowing on the backsides, but you could still see all the faces alright.

Folks married early back then and made big families. The babies came when they was meant to – sometimes back-to-back-to-back. Looked liked all women did back then was have babies, sometimes 12, 13, 14 children birthed to one family. During them times, folks considered everything about having a baby a blessing. Those that died at birth was counted amongst the living and they even gave place to those lost to the womb.

Daddy's lineage looked like they hadn't been too long left the cotton fields. Momma's lineage looked a bit more proper; but, be that as it may, Momma and Daddy paid that never no mind because the same sovereign hand of God that was on one family was the same sovereign hand of God that was on the other.

When Momma set the table for Thanksgiving, it was always something to behold. As far back as I can remember, she always set the table three days before the big day. Sometimes folks would drop by to pick up food that Momma had prepared or offer a dessert of some kind for the occasion. Most times when folks paid you a visit, they'd usually sit and visit a spell – so if they did bring a dessert it'd be nearly gone by the time they left. And that was alright by Momma because she didn't eat everybody's cooking nohow.

Momma took much pride in setting her Thanksgiving table, but as I grew older, I started to realize that it was more about the love she had for family. Each Thanksgiving always seemed better than the Thanksgiving before it.

Momma always let me share in the credit of how everything turned out, but she had her own particular way of doing things. The only thing she would ever let me do was dust off the chairs and the table legs, nothing else. I always took my time and did my best. I would dust until Momma told me it was enough. One time, she got so busy she forgot where she'd left me to my chores and got to running 'round that house calling for me, thinking I'd up and run off – but I was under the table the whole time, sleep.

Come suppertime, every inch of that table would be covered with Momma's special touch. Everybody and everything had its place. The family heirlooms, the pear-and-muscadine wine that went untouched year after year, all the different side dishes with the funny names, right down to the desserts that me and my daddy dreamed about all year.

Daddy always told Momma that apart from the Marriage Supper of the Lamb, there wasn't no finer

Thanksgiving Day meal nowhere. That always softened Momma's heart, but the special thing for her about Thanksgiving dinner was our guests.

Before I was even now really old enough to understand what was going on, I remember trying to count all the pictures in the frame and then carefully counting the slices of cake under Momma's cake dish two or three times. I was just starting to count to ten pretty good, but was a little scared I had done-forgot how. Momma was close by watching and quickly realized what was twirling around in my busy little head and got tickled.

"There'll be more than enough cake for you and your daddy, Millie. So, stop your counting, child."

At that age, I was happy that I had a momma that could read my mind.

"I see you been practicing your numbers."

"Yes, ma'am."

"You's a smart child, Millie. Me and your daddy tell you that all the time, but man can't know nothing apart from what the good Lord plants in his understanding."

At some point before the big day, we'd sit around and visit with every last one of them pictures whilst Momma dusted 'em off to make ready for the frame, that way it wouldn't be so much talking with our mouths full at the table during dinner – something my momma hated ever since she was a little girl. Momma realized that not many folks had the same upbringing that she did; but too many times she'd find herself across the table from folks doing a bit too much laughing and talking and sooner or later she'd end up eatin' something that somebody had done already chewed and it

Schaumburg's Sweet Reminisce

just wasn't right, just wasn't proper.

Days before, she'd place all the photos she had in that special picture frame she bought from Woolworth. She'd spend a few minutes at a time looking closely at each one before finding the perfect place for it in the frame which was always the same place she found for it the year before.

After the frame was mounted and made steady on the brass plant stand that momma worked at nearly half the day polishing, she prepared a grand place setting for our guests – a lot nicer than the others at the table, even my daddy's. The lineage sat at one end of the table across from Daddy; Momma always sat to Daddy's right and I sat to his left, even when folks came to visit after church on Sunday.

Momma and Daddy sure had some stories to tell about the lineage. Momma had come to learn quite a bit about our kinfolk in her years of living, especially when it came to how her ancestors wholly trusted in the Lord to make a way out of no way. I felt like I knew 'em just as well as Momma and Daddy did, even though I didn't know 'em-know 'em.

"What's on your mind, Millie? What's got you walking 'round here with your lips all poked out. You feeling alright, ain't you?"

"Yes, ma'am."

"Come on over here and let me check you for fever. Well, you ain't warm, child, but you ain't cold neither. Sit up here on my lap so Momma can love on her sweet girl."

"Momma?"

"Yes, baby? Tell momma what you got on your mind."

80

"Will I ever get to meet the lineage?" I didn't really understand death, even though we talked about it in Sunday school all the time. All I knew was that a person didn't want to close they eyes in death still lost in they sins. And to be honest, I didn't understand all that much about life yet neither; but all I heard my momma and daddy say, I saw them do.

"Well, Millie, I pray it so. The Bible say that all of God's elect will see and know one another in eternity."

"Well, what day is eternity, momma? I'm ready for everybody to meet me."

Momma smiled and held my face in her hands and said, "No one knows the day nor the hour of Christ's return except the Father, Millie. But you know what?"

"No, ma'am."

"If you really think about it, in a roundabout way, you done already met the lineage."

"When momma? I don't remember."

"It ain't in the way you thinkin', but let Momma think this-here thing through for a minute."

"You want me to ask Daddy, Momma?"

"Naw, now… I don't need you to ask your daddy. I'm just trying to find a way to make what I need to say plain so's you can understand it. Let Momma think here a minute."

"Momma?"

"Wait a minute now, Millie. Give me a chance to settle this-here thing in my mind."

Schaumburg's Sweet Reminisce

"But Momma..."

"Don't you go and 'But Momma' me. What's done got into you?"

"But Momma, them supper pots is boiling over."

"Sho' nuff, child? Set still your thoughts a minute, Millie. Momma'll be right back."

Momma didn't take long, but I reckon not. She didn't like to waste time doing nothing on account it was always something else needin' to be done.

"Whew, child. Thank you. We was 'bout to have more food wasted on the stove than we was gonna be putting in our bellies." Momma looked back toward the kitchen and smiled.

"Momma?"

"Yes, sweet child of mine?"

"Do you know what you gonna say yet, Momma?"

"I do now. Come on back over here and sit on Momma's lap and let me try to sort it out in your mind. Then I want you to go take a nap, you hear?"

"Yes, ma'am."

"Now you's a smart girl, so I want you to just listen at me real close, ya hear?"

I nodded. But this time, instead of saying anything, she just gave me her special eye and rested my head on her bosom. I held her neck tight and closed my eyes. I was getting a little too big for her lap, but she seemed not to mind; I surely didn't. Every time she held me like that and rocked from side-to-side, I felt like everything would always be alright – no matter what. Said her Momma used to do her the same way.

When I was born, one doctor after the other told my momma and daddy that I would never utter a word, at least not one that anybody could make out. Made Momma real good and mad. Said she took and got all them high-and-mighty doctors in a room at the same time and told every last one of 'em that they needed to fall to they knees and repent because every word that had done parted they lips on the matter was a lie straight from the pit of hell.

"Millie, you's the sweetest child I know and I ain't saying that just because you's mine. I say it because I know it to be true. The day I birthed you into this world was the happiest day of my life. When that doula laid you across my bosom, my heart was filled with the warmth of what felt like a million suns all shining at the same time. Everybody that had something to say but not worth hearing told me I would never have children, but God saw different. That's why it's so important to put everything before the Lord. You's the only child I got. Anything that God does always turns out to be more than enough and me and your daddy is eternally grateful.

"You see, Mille, sometimes, for a time, the Lord has a way of keeping his children when we don't even wanna be kept, and blessing us when we know we don't deserve it. God loves his children with an unsearchable love, a special love fit just for that child. A perfect love. His own Son knew it to be so. That's why He laid down His life on the cross. And it ain't no doubt in my mind that while He hung there on that cross, that before He died, He knew that it would one day all be worth it."

Schaumburg's Sweet Reminisce

I listened as hard as I could to what my momma was saying without so much as a nod. She could talk about the goodness of the Lord all day long if she needed to whether she had anybody there to listen to what she had to say or not. She always had a praise of thanksgiving on her lips. Even thanked the Lord for stuff that she didn't yet have – did it all the time before I showed up.

"You's Momma's heart, sweet girl, and you's cut from a real special cloth."

"Why come it's so special, Momma?"

"Well, I believe the reason why that cloth is so special, Millie, is on account of love."

"Love, Momma?"

"No question about it. You come from a long line of slaves, share-croppers, and prayer-warriors, Millie. And back then, if kinfolk didn't have nothing else, they had love, and in a lot of ways, it was the only thing they had that they could give freely of. Our people wouldn't be living like we living today had it not been for somebody with enough love in they heart and faith in God to pray for generations to come. From the heart reaches the heart and I reckon I believe that's how the lineage is able to love on you now, Millie, after all them many years they been gone."

Whenever Momma had her special say about the lineage, she always took and told us first about my daddy's daddy Sydney Bartholomew Fouraukis. Everybody called him PopPop. Blessed me on his own death bed while I was still in my momma's belly. Momma was barely showing at the time and only a handful of people even now know'd she was with child. But, being that this was the farthest along she had ever come in her struggle to carry a child full-term, PopPop saw fit because he was a man of great hope. Said he had done blessed all his other grandchildren and that it was to be no different with me. PopPop didn't know when the good Lord would send for him; but what he did know was that it wouldn't be before his time – either way, he was ready.

PopPop talked with Momma from time to time of how he hoped and prayed that the Lord would be gracious, if only to allow him to lay eyes on me and maybe hear me cry one good time. He told Daddy that my momma was gonna have some kind of time getting me here, but that he had faith that we'd both make it on the strength of the good Lord just fine. Told my daddy not to waiver none and not to doubt, but to only trust the Lord.

"Son, the Lord's will was purposed for that child in Marjorie's belly before you ever even come to know her – just like it was purposed for all them other children that didn't make it. Now, you and Marjorie both might think you got cause to fret and even now complain, but ain't no sense in it. Ain't no since in man worrying 'bout nothin' if he done prayed in faith. Marjorie is strong. Have to be to been done lost all them many children and still be in her right mind; but she gon' need to see you standing firm in your faith before the birth pangs come, son."

PopPop's last words before his soul left his earthly shell were, "Lord, I's ready." Momma said he never even shut his eyes. Daddy walked over to his bedside and honored him and as soon as he did, after all those years, PopPop's eyes released one lone tear. For some reason, that made my Daddy smile.

Schaumburg's Sweet Reminisce

PopPop died at home in his own bed wearing his favorite suit. Woke up that morning asking my daddy to help him into it. Didn't want to leave this life any other way.

"Reach up in there, boy, at that favorite brown suit of mine and help your old man into it."

"Wantin' to go to church this morning, old man?"

"I reckon I got one more first Sunday left in me, Son."

Momma took the pocket square from PopPop's favorite suit jacket and soaked that tear right up off his face. She held on to that pocket square for my daddy along with PopPop's Bible and saved the suit for herself – she often liked to see PopPop in it. Momma really had no idea what she would do with that suit and even after all that time, Daddy never did get as big as PopPop. Momma said people just stopped growing after a certain age, but Daddy said he knew a whole lot of people that kept growing on account they wouldn't back up from the supper table.

I don't reckon nobody really know what to expect after death; but it's enough talk of it in the Bible to sho' nuff make a person wanna find out before they leave this here world. God appoints death to every man from the beginning and no man can live a second beyond that time. PopPop was alright with that, and lived his latter days by faith; believing that when he was finally absent from his body that he would be present with the Lord.

Momma said that PopPop would sometimes stare out into nothing, like he might have had something heavy resting on his mind and then just like that, he'd start humming his favorite hymn in such a way to where you didn't even need to know the words it would be so powerful and sound so good.

I guess we all know that as sure as we living, we dying; it just seemed like PopPop knew something most other folks didn't.

Momma and Daddy told a lot of stories about the lineage, but they talked about PopPop more than anybody else. I guess that's why PopPop was my favorite. I liked hearing Momma and Daddy laugh and talk about the lineage; but, while they carried on, I liked to lay out in the floor and take my time looking at everybody. Sometimes Momma would get to crying and carrying on so much that Daddy would make her sit on his lap until she hushed up. I wished I got to sit on PopPop's knee like I sat on my daddy's every chance I got; or even empty the ashes from his pipe and fill it up again with his favorite tobacco. But Daddy didn't smoke no pipe 'cause Momma wouldn't let him.

The lineage grew smaller over the years. Had done dwindled down to just us pretty much. Times had changed and people just wasn't making babies like they used to, had other things on they mind. Had a few kinfolks a little further south, distant relations that didn't care to be bothered with nobody, but who they cared to be bothered with. Daddy said every family got a handful just like 'em.

Chapter Seven

Seemed like it was just yesterday we made that five-hour trip to Desmond to visit Momma's side of the family. Only one other time I remember ever being that far away from home. Everybody was to meet out at the old Dreggs' Plantation for what was supposed to be a family reunion of sorts for the few family members that was left. Momma said that everybody had been living for themselves far too long and wanted to try to get everybody together more often – together, like family should be.

Daddy hitched up his trailer and his prized homemade BBQ grill to the back of the truck, packed that big old pork shoulder in ice at the bottom of a double-barreled drum he'd turned into a cooler along with everything Momma had put together for the meal, and we headed on down the road.

Momma had worked real hard to make sure everything was just right. While she rested from her kitchen labors, me and Daddy took and had a little taste of everything. We was careful to be real quiet on account Momma didn't like us sneaking in her pots. She'd prepared a bunch of Sunday-style fixings with cakes and pies and a blackberry cobbler; figured she could heat it all back up after Daddy took the shoulder off the grill. Seemed satisfied enough that most everything would be nice for everybody;

but now, that potato salad is what worried her. She had done convinced herself that it would spoil before we got a chance to eat it. Daddy thought it'd be alright; said we had more than enough food anyhow, enough for seconds or thirds if anybody so chose.

An hour into the trip, Momma was still checking her list until Daddy asked her to let him see it. When she handed it to him, he stuck it in his left front pocket and then held her hand.

"Now woman, I believe you done did your best and if it's anything we need that we ain't got, we gon' do without it. You ain't got to worry about pleasing nobody but me and the good Lord; and we both determined we was satisfied three days ago."

Momma looked at Daddy's hand resting on hers and then out the window again.

"It ain't like you to worry this a'way and I don't like it one bit, now. Everything's gonna work out just like the good Lord intend for it to."

"Alright Ben. Alright. I'm gon' leave it all up to the Lord."

"That's my girl."

That old plantation was mostly just land now. After the old roof fell in on the big house, everything else around it followed suit and rotted away for the most part. But now, somebody stole all them beams and folks was sure of it. Wood that old and with that much history was worth a right smart of money. Just as well. Nobody in the family cared none to pay the taxes on it or keep it up, so it just went to ruin. A lot of history was hidden and dwindled down between them beams – some good, but mostly bad.

Daddy said he would have offered to pay up the taxes owed on that old place to keep it going had he known. He know'd it would have made Momma real happy to keep that kind of history in the family. Momma said they could've took and held on to it to give to me and my husband if Daddy thought there'd ever be a man born worthy of me.

They say that old place had been given to my Great Granddaddy Kane by his master's wife Ms. Clarissa way before she died. Said that Granddaddy Kane was the closest thing she had to a child and he had well earned it. Worked every inch of soil on that plantation since he was knee-high to a gnat. But as wickedness would have it, evil settled and resettled into the hearts of both blacks and whites.

Whites didn't want 'em to have it 'cause a lot of them still felt like a black man still had no right to nothin'. A right smart of black folks felt like it was a slap in the face for a slave to lay up in his master's house no matter what bed he slept in. They'd rather see that big house burn to the ground with Granddaddy Kane in it before he made his master's house his home. And some black folks was just plain jealous and still living in fear, still believing that they wasn't worthy of nothin' but crumbs from the white man's table.

But Granddaddy Kane believed what the Bible said. And even though he couldn't read or write, he heard an old preacher man declare from Proverbs 13:22 that "the wealth of the wicked is stored up for the righteous." Granddaddy Kane believed every word of what that old preacher man told him that day and held it close. It nearly took him all his life to see it come to pass, but it did.

Right after Ms. Clarissa took to the bed, the deed to the house and a lot of other important papers come up missing. The law clerk took and said that the ledger they kept record in over-town made it look like Ms. Clarissa hadn't paid a dime toward them taxes in a right smart of years. Ms. Clarissa and Granddaddy Kane knew that wasn't right. Any blind man could see clear as day where them pages had been tore out that ledger and Ms. Clarissa wasn't settling for that lie. She was determined to set things right for Granddaddy Kane before she died – and she did.

Ms. Clarissa happened to write to some important folks she knew up north and they wrote back; went back and forth like that for a few seasons and before all was said and done, Granddaddy Kane was signing his name to the deed to his master's house with a big old X on account he never did learn to write his own name.

Granddaddy Kane knew how most people, blacks and whites alike, felt. He'd heard all the whispers and felt the stares, but he kept his head held high, a kind word on his lips, and his shotgun loaded; said his home had a new Master and that his door would be open to anybody that came in peace. He said that his God lived there now, and if not one soul ever came knocking, he'd still have all the company he needed.

That was a blessed thing that Ms. Clarissa did. She was able to set things right before she died. That big house was in pretty good shape, on account Granddaddy Kane kept it up himself. Wouldn't hardly have a thing to do to keep hisself busy and that worried him a bit – being a man of labor and all. Houses built like that could last several generations over, but if they sat empty too long, they'd start going down just like anything else, even man.

Granddaddy Kane gave away most everything in that house except what he figured he needed and that was nothing more than a place to rest his head, a place to sit, and a few pots to cook in. Had done lived there a good number of years before the floorboards on them steps gave way. Good thing he used 'em everyday – never would have found that pile of money his master had hid beneath 'em. He wasn't sure if Ms. Clarissa knew about the money or not, thought twice if she hadn't hid it there herself and forgot it over the years.

Granddaddy Kane lived in that old house on that plantation all by himself for a good many years – 20 or better if they countin' right. Widowed long before all that at a fairly young age, he reasoned that the pain was too much for his heart to bear and he never did take another wife.

Every now and again, Granddaddy Kane would take on boarders as long as they wasn't female to keep a little money in his pocket and pay the taxes on the land. He'd run 'cross a fella that was down on his luck, give 'em work, and a place to stay for a while 'til he could get back on his feet, but Granddaddy Kane had rules.

The man had to work six days a week, worship the Lord on Sunday; be in by a decent hour or else don't come knocking, and keep his hands off of Granddaddy Kane's pistols unless they was knee deep in it. Them was the rules. And if for some reason they couldn't remember all the rules, they was to do all that the Bible say to do.

For as long as Granddaddy Kane lived in that house, folks whispered, but he didn't pay that no bother and kept right on living. Some even tried to argue that Ms. Clarissa had done gone plum-out her mind towards the end. Said that by the time Ms. Clarissa was ready to depart this earth, she was thinking that Granddaddy Kane was her master when she gave him that house; but that was a lie if ever one was told.

Sheriell Scott

Granddaddy Kane saw a lot of change in his lifetime, some to his good, some not; but by the time he shut his eyes in death, there was hardly a soul around that wasn't negro and doing alright for himself. And the few white folks that remained, well, they was sorta like family, but not quite. It'd be some years later, but negroes near 'bout owned everything in Desmond except each other.

Granddaddy Kane always knew that a mighty change would one day come, a change that would take a good long while to come about; but, not knowing what kind of change it would be, he was content in just being able to live long enough to get a glimpse of the beginning of it all.

Even more than that, Granddaddy Kane wanted that old plantation to remain in the family for as long as the family name remained above the earth as an inheritance to his children's children; but if nothing else, he wanted to leave a Godly inheritance. So, he lived out his days the only way he knew how – chasing after the Lord. Granddaddy Kane believed that if a man was blessed to live to be the oldest man alive and didn't leave a Godly example for those who would live on after him, that man lived his whole life in vain and it probably would have been better had he not lived at all.

Not in all his days did Granddaddy Kane expect to outlive so many of his kinfolk, young and old alike. Seemed like the longer he lived, the further away from God they ran. He wasn't surprised by it none. He sensed the division long before then. Matter a fact, he could see it outright 'cause it wasn't like they was trying to hide it. Never wanting to hear much of what nobody had to say or be around in company even, but they always had they hand out, casting lots for this here and that there to where wasn't nobody even now yet in the grave.

Schaumburg's Sweet Reminisce

That there hurt Granddaddy Kane's heart. Had he heard it from anybody else, he probably wouldn't have paid it no mind, but he couldn't deny what he'd seen with his own eyes and heard with his own ears. He wanted to be long-gone before they decided to divide any further. He'd much rather remember his family the way they were, when times were knucklebone hard.

All Granddaddy Kane could do was hope that he had lived a life that honored God because as far as he was concerned, as soon as his spirit left his body, they could have burned that old plantation to the ground and cursed the land barren.

That old plantation had been bought and sold a few times over before the family's secrets started coming out. Before Granddaddy Kane died, he left a right smart of money hidden in that old house and a little money on the clerk's ledger, but not much on account he still had his eye on 'em over there from years ago when Ms. Clarissa was still living. He didn't have much, but what he did leave would have suited any man right kindly, for a spell anyway.

Most of Momma's kinfolk was already pretty settled with they own families and land, but had to work sho' nuff hard to keep from going to ruin. A few years before Granddaddy Kane passed on, the family didn't seem to have much interest in him or that old plantation; but at the same time, everybody got in such an uproar when Granddaddy Kane asked my daddy to oversee things after he was dead and gone. He knew my daddy could handle himself and that he'd do right by the heathens he was leaving behind. Things just didn't sit well with my daddy though knowing that Momma would have to deal with all that foolishness, so he took and bowed out.

Anyhow, Momma and Daddy didn't stay around too

long after Granddaddy Kane went home to be with the Lord. Daddy didn't want no parts of that family mess that he saw brewing. Had made my momma many a'promises before he married her and was aiming to make good on each and every one.

Momma and Daddy never kept secrets because secrets at some point turn into lies. But now, Daddy knew how sensitive Momma was when it came to her kinfolk, so the only way he knew how to protect her was to only share with Momma what he found to be true and to only tell her what he thought she could handle.

He heard things. Unsavory things. Things that ought not to be.

As soon as the money ran out, so did Momma's so-called kinfolks. And as time would have it, the county took over the land and turned it into a public meetin' place. Folks had picnics, revivals, weddings, and whatever else they needed a nice open space for. County didn't hardly even now have to worry about money to keep that old place up. Whoever was in jail at the time was put to work on the plantation. Place stayed real nice all the time.

With all that hush-talking they'd been doing about Granddaddy Kane behind his back, Momma wanted to believe that pride got the best of 'em to where they was just too shame to ask for help; but Daddy knew better. Sometimes folks was just given to a slothful spirit, looking to get something for nothing, and he didn't take too kindly to that way in man and despised it even more coming from family.

The way Momma's kinfolk come across sometimes, that is, if they figured to be bothered at all, was like they was owed something. It seemed like they all just woke up one day and didn't feel like being family no more – and that there tore Momma apart inside.

Didn't know how bad things was until one of them boys took and tried to put his hands on my momma because she wouldn't agree to sign off on that deed so that they could sell that old place and split the money; but, drunk or not, Daddy wasn't having it. As far as he was concerned, no man would ever lay hands on my momma and be the same – figured he might let him live but he'd never be the same man he once was. Momma tried to tell Daddy that her Cousin Joe was drunk and that he had barely grabbed a hold of her, but that didn't stop my daddy from grabbing his shotgun and taking a ride. He stayed out all night searching for Cousin Joe and Momma stayed up all night crying and praying until he got home.

Didn't see Cousin Joe for many years after that. Some wondered if my daddy had done found him and got up with him that night. Daddy confessed later that he didn't know what he would have done had he met up with Cousin Joe, but it wouldn't have been good; said he was glad that the Lord allowed things to play out the way they did that night. Said he felt real shame to have that kind of hate enter his heart for another man, let alone family.

When Cousin Joe did finally come around again, he had done married and managed up on a whole heap of kids. Come to find out, Joe had done got drunk one Sunday morning and put his hands on the wrong woman; and for his troubles, she stabbed him within an inch of his life. Seemed like everybody everywhere had done had they fill of Cousin Joe and just assume his old lady leave him for dead – wouldn't have been no bother for folks to look the other way neither. But even after all of that, she hung right on in there with him and didn't leave his side until he was able-bodied again. And then on top of that, she gave him seven children. Had them kids one right after the other, two sets of twins.

Made Daddy feel even worse about ever allowing hisself to get that mad at Cousin Joe. He reckoned that had he found Joe that night, them children wouldn't even now be born. He wasn't proud of it but he was most sure of it. And even though all of that happened ages before, Daddy humbled hisself and apologized. He loved on Cousin Joe and Cousin Joe's kids as if they was his own – didn't matter that they was nearly grown.

Cousin Joe was a changed man and any and everybody that had ever met Cousin Joe back in his day was glad of it. Daddy had grown in the Lord, too. He'd still do what he had to do to protect me and my momma, but he'd never go looking for a man with murder in his heart ever again, no matter what. Uncle Joe apologized, too; said that he had learned his lesson and now that he had his own wife and kids, he kinda felt that he'd have set out the same way my daddy did that night, only he would have never stopped looking for the man who dared put his hands on his woman. Back then, Uncle Joe would have probably killed a man for a whole lot less and everybody knew it, so everybody stayed out of his way.

Momma hated seeing her kinfolks divided amongst one another and shortly after Granddaddy Kane passed on, Daddy decided that it was time for them to move on too. So, for a season, Momma would have to love them kinfolks of hers from a distance. Didn't hardly recognize 'em anymore nohow. When Daddy told everybody that he and Momma was leaving, he knew that it would divide the family even more, but he wasn't the one to be bothered with that kind of nonsense. Every chance they had to do right by my momma, they chose not to and my daddy was sick and tired of seeing

Schaumburg's Sweet Reminisce

Momma's heart hurt. All he knew was that if any a'soul came around asking questions, they'd better make sure they was able to answer a few of his. God had blessed him with a wife that he would give his very life for and that's who he'd be concerning hisself with keeping happy.

* ＊＊＊＊ *

We finally got to Dreggs and everything was just how the man on the phone with Daddy told him it would be. Momma was more than pleased and got right to work.

"Woman, what you think about everything?"

"Well… things sure have changed, Ben." Momma stood off to herself with her hands on her hips and looked all around for a while. Daddy went to her, hugged her from behind, and whispered something in her ear that made her laugh. After a while I went over and hugged Momma from the front.

"Child of mine, there's work to do and it ain't gonna get done with us just standin' 'round here talkin' 'bout it."

"Yes, ma'am."

Momma pulled out the burlap table cloths and told me where to put this and that while Daddy fired up his grill. The new barn the county built east of where the big house once sat made real nice for the kitchen, even had two small washrooms out back – one for the men-folk and one for the women-folk, not black and white like the days of old.

It didn't take long for me and Momma to set up, so once everything was ready, we waited around and sipped on some of Momma's special muscadine-mint tea. Waited for what seemed like forever.

Daddy had been done pulled that pork shoulder off the grill so not to dry it out and the fixings had been warm for a good while. Momma tried to keep herself busy doing nothing, but after a while she just couldn't take it no more and broke down crying. Daddy walked over to her and just held her in his arms. Momma was hugging him so tight I thought she might break my daddy half in two, but she didn't. Daddy didn't say nothing. He just let her cry.

"What's wrong, Momma? Momma, what's wrong? Daddy what's wrong with Momma?

"Well babygirl, I believe your momma got a broken heart. She'll be alright here after while."

By the way Momma was crying, it must have been broke for a good long while.

My plate was almost the size of my daddy's – he the one who fixed it. Momma looked right at it and stared for a bit, but didn't say nothing; she just tucked a cotton napkin inside my dress so I wouldn't soil it and told me to eat my supper. Daddy talked about how good the food was just to keep a sweet spirit in the air. Momma barely ate at all. She probably swallowed more tears than anything else. My daddy's favorite girl was a strong woman but some things just seemed to cut her deep, right down to the white meat.

I cleared the table and then chased me some butterflies while Daddy rubbed momma's feet and shoulders. They talked a while and then Daddy laid hands on Momma and prayed. She seemed all the better afterwards. Daddy always seemed to get Momma to a better place.

"Millie. Millie, you come on now."

"Yes, ma'am." I ran over to Momma and gave her a

great big hug. I loved hugging my momma 'cause she was so soft and always smelled real pretty. I reckoned that's why my daddy hugged on her all the time too. "It's gon' be alright, Momma."

"Thank you, my sweet Millie. It makes Momma happy to hear you say that."

"You welcome, Momma."

"You wanna give your momma a hand with this-here ice cream?"

"Yes, ma'am." I wanted to keep chasing butterflies; but I didn't really know what would happen if I told momma no.

"I promised your daddy I'd make his favorite." She looked me over and then straightened my hair and clothes, just like she always did.

I looked at Daddy and smiled. He loved my momma's homemade chocolate, blackstrap molasses, and walnut ice cream. I loved Momma's homemade orange, maple-cream ice cream; but, I was fine with having Daddy's favorite. Me and Daddy didn't know how Momma came up with all those many different flavors, but we did know that they always tasted real good. You couldn't buy ice cream like Momma's nowhere, not even in those fancy parlors up north. Folks would probably look at you kinda sideways if you was to ask 'em for persimmon, ginger, and lemon-grass ice cream.

"I'm as tight as a tick, but I sure could use a lick of my favorite ice cream, woman."

"Well, you heard your daddy, Millie. Let's get to it. I brought you some play clothes to put on; just help Momma get started here and then you can play all you want."

"Yes, ma'am."

"Grab that box of rock salt from the blue crate for me please and then you come on behind me."

"What you need me to do, woman?"

"You just sit there and rest your hands, Ben Charles, 'cause you wasn't quite finished rubbing my feet."

"I reckon I can do that."

Me and Momma got the ice cream started and then I put on my play clothes. Daddy chased me around until he got tired and then he pushed me and Momma on the swings. Momma did most of the talking while we ate our ice cream. Me and Daddy never said much of anything, we just nodded.

In spite of everything, we still had some kind of day. Daddy told Momma that he thought we might ought to try it again; Momma agreed, but not really. He said sometimes it takes people a little time to come around, but we as Christians should never grow weary in doing good – it's what the Lord would have us do.

We wasn't in no rush to get on back, so later that evening we drove a little ways out to where Momma's people was living last. Like most families in the South, kinfolk all lived in the same little cluster like the generations before 'em, so it should have been fairly easy to spread the word if you was trying to get everybody together.

I reckon that family mess that sprung up a good while back still hadn't worked itself out, but that didn't stop Momma from reaching out over the years. Not so much as a whisper from none of 'em in all that time – until Momma's first cousin Rudy Mae picked up the phone. That's all Momma needed to put everything in motion.

Daddy thought it just seemed strange that not a soul showed up after all that back and forth planning Momma and Cousin Rudy Mae had been doing over the past couple of months. Had done talked with Cousin Rudy Mae for over an hour before we even left the house that morning.

"Cousin Marjorie, I done got in touch with everybody from the least to the greatest and everybody's coming. Everybody. Yes Lord, everybody's aiming to be there. Sho' nuff gon' be good to see you, Cousin Marjorie," is what Mamma said Cousin Rudy Mae told her.

Daddy didn't wanna just leave after coming all that way without knowing the reason why he found nothing but sadness in my momma's eyes for the better part of the day; didn't want to drive all the way back with a spirit of judgment stirring in his heart neither.

My daddy was a reasonable man and he didn't allow much to get underneath his skin – half the time, you never would know that he was even now upset until he opened his mouth and made it known. But the fact that my momma's heart was nearly in a million and one pieces broke his heart and the whole thing had done unnerved him to no end. Anybody who knew my daddy knew that he only got to the bottom of things that concerned family face-to-face. So, we got on down the road and made the hour's drive out of the way not knowing what to expect.

Them dirt roads could be tricky, so Daddy made sure to drive real slow, so not to miss our turn. If that turn caught you sleepin', you'd have to drive way on out yonder almost to the next county before you could get turned around.

We drove a good little piece before we found that cluster of houses.

Momma grabbed for Daddy's hand before he could reach for hers.

*　　*✳❈✳*　　*

Much time had passed since they moved away and struck out on they own together. Things seemed hardly at all like they once did, but Momma and Daddy was sure to be yet holding on to what they had together.

The sun had done gone down, but we could still see pretty good. Daddy pointed out the tree he and Momma used to meet at when they was kids. That was the only place they was allowed to meet until he could be trusted with my momma. Daddy smiled and laughed as we drove past, but Momma's mind must have been elsewhere because she was looking straight ahead.

"Woman, you still remember our little spot, don't you?"

"I remember. Spent every chance we got together under that old, great oak."

"What was that ya daddy used to tell me?"

"Ben Charles, you still remember that?"

"Every word, woman."

"Ben Charles?"

"Wasn't no way I could forget. That old man reminded me I wasn't welcome every time I came 'round there to see you."

"Just 'til he knew he could trust you with his babygirl."

"'There ain't ever gon' be a man born from a woman to come between me and my wife or me and my only'st babygirl. So, you may as well go on way from around here, son. Just quit comin' 'round here knockin', now.' I declare that's what Bo Hatcher told me."

"Sound just like 'em," Momma chuckled. I laughed too on account my daddy sounded real funny talking like my granddaddy, William "Bo Hatcher" Yarby.

"But you know what I did, babygirl?"

"Uunh Unh."

"I kept right on knocking every chance I got. Yes sir, I was determined to make this pretty, young thing my wife. Determined, sho' nuff."

"Ooooh wee, Daddy."

Momma laughed into her handkerchief and then waved at the evening air. I laughed and waved my hand because I hadn't yet had no man give to me no hanky of my own. "And each time you knocked, you tried my daddy's patience ever so and again. I'm just glad he didn't shoot you that one time, Benjamin Charles."

"You and me both, woman, because that old man never missed."

"Millie, your daddy was the only suitor man enough to come 'round to face your granddaddy, so I paid all those other suitors no never mind. Your daddy was something special. Still is."

Daddy stuck out his chest and smiled real big. "I remember your old man stopped me dead in my tracks the first time I came 'round there asking for you. You remember that, woman?"

"Remember it like it was yesterday. Cried myself to sleep that night. Didn't even now eat supper."

"Wouldn't even now let me set foot on that old porch and dared me to lay eyes on you, yet alone speak your name in his presence. He'd much rather see that old mean, mangey hound lay up there with all them ticks and fleas than for me to walk up them steps and knock on that screen door to see his babygirl."

"Daddy hated that old dog, too, Ben Charles. Said he always smelled right strange."

"Some days I couldn't tell who had it worse, me or that mangey hound; but everybody had done already told me that old Bo Hatcher was a hard man, and even harder when it came to his Marjorie Rose. But I'd made up in my mind that I was gon' come to him like a man. I had my speech knitted together, you know, about how I was gon' ask your daddy if he would allow me to court you."

"Ben Charles, I declare, I was scared for you that day; Lord knows I was. I was up there in my room looking out the window, just a'pacing and praying, praying and pacing. I saw you when you come 'round that bend in the road up yonder. I had done got so beside myself, Momma had to even now make me hush."

"Woman, I reckon I sho' needed 'em, that day. Now I may have been seeing things, on account I was way on back yonder on that road, but I declare I thought I saw your daddy smile from underneath that wide-brimmed, straw hat of his.

Schaumburg's Sweet Reminisce

Never did lift his head, but the only thing running through mine was the thing he told me last time I came 'round there at you.

"'Son, now I done told you, you ain't welcome 'round here. After today, you need not ever let your feet touch the dust on this-here road, not naan 'nother time' – and it wasn't no doubt in my mind that he meant every word he said.

"I know'd he saw me coming, so before I lost my nerve, I picked up my steps. Soon as I did that, your old man raised up from his seat, real slow-like. Looked like he was heading back into the house and no sooner than he could reach up, I was staring down the barrel of his shotgun."

"'I thought I told you to keep way from 'round here, boy.'"

"I tell you I ain't never been so shook before in my life, but, babygirl, all's I could think about was my sweet Marjorie. Woman, I could see you waving at me out the corner of my eye from your window upstairs. I swallowed hard and started toward the porch and that's when your daddy knew I meant business. I was sweating so hard, looked like I could've took a bath where I stood, but as soon as I heard your daddy rack that shotgun, my whole body went cold. I closed my eyes long enough to whisper a quick prayer and while I still had my eyes shut, I said what I'd come to say. As soon as that last word fell from my lips I turned and started high-stepping real quick-like before your old man had a chance to shoot me between the eyes. I declare I didn't know if I was gon' make it off your daddy's land alive or not; but I couldn't go back home to my old man and tell him that Bo Hatcher had run me off. I didn't wait 'round for your daddy to say not one more word, no sir; but, I had done already made up in my mind that if I made it home alive that day, I was coming back to try and win your heart no matter how many times it took.

"Lord knows, I was grateful that your old man didn't shoot me dead where I stood. Made it all the way back down somewhere 'round up in here, just below the edge of this-here bend in the road and tossed my hat straight up in the air. Boy, your daddy didn't like that. He got one off on me – bullet was just a breath shy of grazing my right ear. Nearly scared the life outta me. I ran all the way home and fell into my daddy's arms. Had him pretty shook too on account I wouldn't half say nothing because I couldn't half make out a thing he was saying, couldn't hear out naan' one of my ears, but I had managed a big grin on my face. My momma was beside herself, fussing over me like I was a newborn baby.

"Next day after supper, I sat down with my old man and told him everything that had happened. Made me tell him twice, out of earshot of my momma 'cause he knew she'd be feeling some kind of way. Daddy reared all the way back in that old rocking chair of his and didn't speak a word for a good long time.

"After a while, he said, 'You know, son, I ain't ever know'd old man Bo Hatcher to miss nothing he was aiming at. If he wanted you dead, you'd sho' nuff be dead, son – that's the truth on the matter. Ain't no doubt in my mind 'bout that.'

"'Bout that time, the blood ran cold in my veins on account I didn't wanna die, but I was going back there that same day to win my Marjorie's love."

"'I raised you a man, Ben Charles – always remember that.'"

"Yes, sir."

"'You watch yourself with Bo Hatcher's daughter, now. If she ain't the one you willing to die for, leave her be.

Schaumburg's Sweet Reminisce

Hear me on this thing now.'"

"Yes, sir." 'Bout that time, he popped me upside that right ear of mine and smiled wide, lit his pipe, and went on in the house.

Daddy always said that a man ain't worth marrying if he ain't willing to die for his woman whilst they courting, 'cause if he ain't willing to die beforehand, nine times out of ten he won't be willing after they's married. Momma agreed.

Momma's heart seemed like it had started to stir a bit. I watched as she patted the nape of her neck with her pretty little cloth and primped her hair on both sides. "Lord knows I would be so shame at the way Daddy would carry on, but I would be so happy to see your handsome self waiting for me out there on that porch. I could hardly get ready for peeping through them curtains every five seconds."

"I remember that day your momma walked out on that porch whilst your old man was giving me a hard time, stood in between us, put her hand right in the middle of his chest, and invited me to Sunday dinner. Woman, your daddy got so quiet I thought he had done gone and swallowed his own tongue."

"Now that day, I sho' nuff remember, Ben Charles, and I was just as wall-eyed as you was at the time; but a little later, Momma would help me understand how important a wife's touch is to husband."

"That-there what your Momma did, had me scared for the both of us, but boy, that was one of the happiest days of my life. I ran all the way home and paid my sister to whip up a couple of her sweet potato, walnut-pecan custards to bring with me the next day. I came early. Yesssir, I didn't wanna be late and your old man not let me in. Had all your cousins out in the yard messin' 'round with me about all them shotguns your old man kept in the house. And sho' nuff, just like they told me, it was a shotgun in every corner."

"Momma hated having all them guns in the house, but that was Daddy's rule. She couldn't turn him on that. He aimed to protect his home and everybody in it at all cost. Never was able to teach her how to shoot though; that's where Momma drew her line."

"I sho' was glad your momma met me at the door that Sunday evening and not your daddy. The whole way over I was just a'hoping and praying that your old man hadn't changed his mind."

"Ben Charles, I thought Daddy would die where he stood when you handed Momma them flowers."

Momma and Daddy both got real tickled at that.

"'Son, don't you know many a'men lay in they grave on account of steppin' to another man's woman?' And I reckon I might've know'd one or two of 'em he was talkin' 'bout."

"Your momma walked over to your daddy and kissed him on the mouth."

"'You hush now, Bo Hatcher, that's enough. Let it be now; give the young man a chance. He's a good boy – everybody seems to know that but you.'"

"Daddy's heart changed towards you after that day."

"You know, that was the first time your daddy treated me like a man. All them times he turned me away, I'd walk down that road sometimes and see him sitting up there on that porch and as soon as he seen that I seen him sitting there, he'd get up and go on in the house and shut the door. But I'd come a'knocking anyhow. I knew I ain't stand a chance going toe-to-toe wit 'em, so I figured I'd wear him down."

"Momma hated how hard a time Daddy used to give you. 'Course, now she had her eye on you too, but she liked you – was like a son to her. Used to tell me that all the time. Said that as a man, my daddy needed to know that you'd always do right by me no matter what."

"Woman, my heart filled up with you the first time I laid eyes on your pretty little, bow-legged self. I promised myself that I was gon' make you my wife and I did."

Momma looked at me and smiled.

"I wasn't too long saved, but the Lord had a'hold of me. Yesssirr, He had my attention and so did you, Marjorie. That day I told the Lord that I didn't know what he had planned for my life, but as long as you was in it, I was on board."

"Oh Ben."

"I know everything ain't been perfect, woman, but you done gave me a good life."

Momma lifted her chin high and looked out the window away from Daddy. Him and me both knew what that meant; Momma never did take to well to kind words said about her.

"Now, woman, I need you to hear this here."

Momma looked straight ahead as to let my daddy

know that he had her attention.

"We've had our struggles, more than a few, but the good Lord seen us through every one. Grateful that you been by my side all these years; couldn't have made it this far with nobody else. Wouldn't now even have wanted to. I've held you in my heart, Marjorie, since the first day I laid eyes on you and much like a fool, I'd probably curse the day I open these-here eyes of mine and not find you here. This-here heart of mine is gon' always be open towards you. That's my promise to you and to the good Lord."

"Husband of mine, the good has always far outweighed the bad. Things ain't always been perfect, but you've been the man that I've needed you to be. Whole lotta women can't say that, but I can. You helped me keep what was precious in the sight of God and stuck by me when I thought I'd lose my mind. You've done your best to honor the Lord and in doing so, you've honored me and I love you for it, Ben Charles."

"That was always the plan, woman... That was always the plan."

"My daddy was mighty proud when I told him that you hadn't spoiled me – near 'bout brought tears to his eyes."

"I miss that old man. Your momma too."

"I miss 'em too, Ben. Lord knows I do."

*   *****   *

The road that led up to the house was long and full of deep trenches. Good thing Daddy left that trailer behind.

"Boy, I know they have a time getting in and out of

111

Schaumburg's Sweet Reminisce

here when it come a good rain. Y'all hang on now; it's pretty rough up through here."

"Be careful, Ben. Ain't much light up through there."

From the road, all's we could see was a weak flicker from what we imagined was an oil lamp running low on oil. A heap of old cars filled the front yard and no telling how many mangey mutts, but it very well could have been more mutts than it was cars. Seemed like we could hear music playing from inside the house, but Momma said it was probably them old, bottle wind chimes hiding in the trees.

The house soon went dark and Daddy stopped the truck. Momma grabbed me close to her bosom and covered my face. I could feel her heart beatin'. It sounded scared like me.

"Everything's alright, Millie. You just stay close to your momma, now." I reckon daddy knew I'd be scared.

Momma kept saying that she didn't feel welcome and told Daddy that we may ought to just leave well enough alone. Momma and Daddy had a way of hearing one another and not hearing one another, but sooner or later they'd end up agreeing with each other... They always did.

Daddy eased back on the gas and started towards the house. We could see the house a lot better now; it looked run down. It was good and old, true enough, but it sho' didn't look like nobody ought to been living there. The only sign of life that old house had now was that big boney hound-dog barking on the porch. We finally made it all the way up to the house.

Momma looked all around. I think she might have still been a little scared on account she hadn't stopped

112

squeezing me.

Daddy looked all around too and then told me and Momma to stay put; but Momma didn't look like she was about to move anyway. I raised up when Daddy got out of the truck.

"It's alright, babygirl." He could see the fear in my eyes. I looked at Momma and she nodded in agreement.

Daddy dimmed the lights on the truck to where he could make it to the porch without running into nothing. He took and grabbed all them boxes out the back of the truck and carried 'em up to the house one stacked on top of the other and set 'em down on the porch. He only had to make two trips.

Me and Momma watched Daddy's every move. I didn't know what I would do if something was to happen, but I already knew Momma was praying in the Spirit. I could tell because I could feel her breath on the back of my neck and the harder she prayed the tighter she held on to me.

Daddy straightened his pants and wiped the sweat from his brow before he knocked the first time. He knocked a few times more, but nobody came to the door. Before he knocked each time, he'd turn around to check on me and Momma. Momma waved for my daddy to come on back to the truck, but Daddy wasn't ready to give up just yet – even if the windows was covered up with mismatched sheets to keep peeping eyes out.

He walked from one end of the porch to the other and then back again, peeping through whatever crack he could find, but not before stumbling over something he got caught up with underfoot. He managed to stay upright.

Schaumburg's Sweet Reminisce

"Lord Jesus! Be careful now, Ben!" Momma lifted my head and sat up to the edge of the seat trying to see what Daddy had tripped over. Said it looked like he had done managed to get his foot hung up in that old dog's chain runnin' 'round on that raggedy porch.

"Something don't feel right 'bout this here, Millie." Momma had done got a little put out, so she started up the truck.

"Come on back now, Ben! Come on now! We ain't welcome!"

That big hound got stirred up and started sniffing around them-there boxes, but Daddy got after him and chased him back off the porch into the yard. I guess he had more bark than bite.

Daddy started off the porch and was about halfway to the truck when the door to the house opened just a little ways. But wasn't nobody standing there.

"Lord Jesus! Ben Charles! Ben Charles, you get yourself on to this truck now!"

Daddy turned around to go back, but the door shut again.

"Ben, baby, just come on now. You done all you can."

Daddy turned for the house, but I guess he figured Momma was right and headed on back to the truck instead. He probably had done worn out his welcome.

"Well, woman, I don't quite know what to think about this here. Kinda puzzled. I guess me stumbling 'round on that-there porch this late ain't the smartest thing I could be doing, but seem like to me somebody would've come to the door."

"I was hoping and praying you didn't get your head blown off running back and forth up there in the dark peeping in folks' windows."

"I was praying too, woman. Would've been well within they right if they'd wanted to pop one off in me, too."

"You wanna try any of these other houses round here, woman? It's up to you."

"Ben, I'm ready to go. I think it best we just get on back down the road to Schaumburg. We's a long ways away from home and it's already dark."

"I guess you right. We can try to straighten everything out tomorrow."

"Ready to get on home, babygirl?"

I nodded because I was near 'bout half-asleep.

"I sho' do appreciate you trying so hard, Ben. I sho' nuff do."

"I reckon you was right, Marjorie. By the looks of things, I'd say your peoples may done fell on hard times. Everything's gon' be alright, though. We'll figure it out."

Momma stayed quiet.

"I know how important family is to you, Marjorie, but we gon' deal with this the way we do everything else – with the help of the good Lord. He'll show us what we need to do next."

Schaumburg's Sweet Reminisce

Before we could get turned around good and back out to the main road, the porch door opened again, wide this time. Daddy stopped the truck and looked back to try to see who it was. Somebody had done run out on the porch and started after them boxes of fixins' we left.

"What is it, Ben?"

"Woman, I believe them's white folks living up in there."

Momma looked back out her window. I was too tired to look, but I was listening at 'em both real close.

"A whole heap of little children. Four, seven, nine. Nine children I count, Ben."

I reckon I thought I was too tired to look until Momma mentioned children. I raised up quick to see if there'd be any girls my age for playmates.

"Woman, is we at the right house? Got to be, ain't we?"

"We's at the right house, Ben. I know this old house like I know the back of my hand. I was conceived in that-there house, born in that-there house, and grew up in that-there house."

"Reckon we ought to turn 'round? We can go on back now, if you wanna."

"Ben, now I appreciate all you done. Made this-here day special for me, but I'm nearing my peace on all of this here. I reckon I'm just too heartbroken at this point to talk to anybody about anything. Reckon you ought to be getting pretty tired too, ain't you?"

"Well, I guess we might ought to leave well enough alone for tonight. I don't know who that is up in there, but I imagine all them kids need a place to stay for the night. I can call Cousin Rudy Mae tomorrow and try to get her side on all of this here. Just try and set your mind easy, woman."

"I'll be alright, Ben."

That next day, Daddy spent all morning and half the afternoon on the phone with everybody, but Cousin Rudy Mae. I know because I spent half the time on his lap listening when Momma wasn't calling me to do this-here and that-there. Daddy just kept talking and nodding and writing, talking and nodding and writing.

"Mille… Millie, come in here to me."

I ran to see what Momma wanted. "Yes, ma'am?"

"Your daddy still on the phone?"

"Yes, ma'am."

"Well, take this-here glass of sweet iced tea in there to him for me, please."

"Yes, ma'am."

Daddy saw me coming and stood up to meet me. I only spilled a little, but I didn't waste none on the floor. He gave me a big sip like he always did and then drank the whole thing down just like that.

Daddy covered the phone so that lady he was talking to wouldn't think he was gettin' fresh with her. "Daddy, sho' do appreciate you, babygirl."

"You welcome, Daddy."

Schaumburg's Sweet Reminisce

I was just about to hop back up into daddy's lap.

"Do this here for me, would you, babygirl? Go get ya momma and tell her I need her to come in here to me for just a minute."

"Yes, sir."

"And ask her to bring me another glass of that sweet iced tea, please ma'am."

"Yes, sir."

I didn't know if Momma heard Daddy tell me what he told me, but she already had a glass of tea in one hand but waited until I made it over to where she was to pop me on my butt with the other hand for running through the house again.

"Child of mine, ain't gon' be too many more times you gon' hear me tell you 'bout runnin' in this-here house, you hear me? I'm gonna get you real good now."

"Yes, ma'am."

Daddy alwayst' to say that I run so much on account I was plum-full of joy, but Momma said if I was that full of joy that I should run outdoors plum-cross the world 'cause it's folks everywhere in this world that could use some of the joy that I had.

"You ain't no wild horse waitin' to be broken, Millie. Temptation rests on every hand and you got to learn to take the way of escape when it's set before you – we all do."

"Yes, ma'am.

"Next time I'm gon' tighten them bloomers, hear me?"

I nodded and hung my head. Momma rarely whooped me, but when she did, it always seemed like it hurt more than it should. Momma didn't like to half-do nothing. I didn't mean to be disobedient, but I just couldn't always remember everything that I wasn't supposed to do.

"Use your words, child. You's gettin' to be too old for that."

"Yes, ma'am." I hung my head even lower. "Daddy, want you to come in there where he at, Momma."

"Alright, I'mma go see what your daddy want. You hungry?"

"No ma'am, I don't think so."

"Well now, Millie, is your belly near 'bout empty or near 'bout full?"

"Momma, can you look for me 'cause I can't see inside my belly?"

I always did think that was a funny thing for Momma to ask – had never heard nobody say that before about somebody's belly outside of her.

"Millie, pull your dress down, child. Nobody need be looking at your bloomers and I mean *nobody*, do you hear me? Don't you do that no more. What's under there ain't for nobody to see."

"I won't do it no more, Momma."

"Well, see to it that you don't. Now, I was planning for us to eat the rest of these fig biscuits for supper this evening, but I reckon I can make some more."

Schaumburg's Sweet Reminisce

"Momma, I think my belly is all the way empty." I covered my face with my hands to hide my smile and then ran over to hug my momma. I only got to eat one fig biscuit that morning and I was hoping to eat another one before they was all gone.

"Child of mine, Momma's belly 'bout empty too. What you think we ought to have with these-here biscuits, Millie?"

"I'll just eat biscuits, Momma. That's all I want."

"You gon' have to eat more than a biscuit, Millie, 'cause you gon' be hungry again before supper. I reckon I can cut up some cheese, a few of these-here apples, and the rest of that ham we had left over from last Sunday. I imagine your Daddy 'bout ready to eat a little something, too."

Momma laid our lunch spread out on her favorite wooden cutting board and covered it with a piece of white cheesecloth, just until she went to find out what Daddy needed. Wasn't nary a fly in the house, I guess she just wanted to be proper. Daddy hated flies, especially when he was cleaning fish or trying to eat watermelon – and even sometimes when Momma cooked cabbage.

Momma grabbed me by the hand and we headed toward the back of the house where Daddy was; but not before stopping in front of the mirror near the parlor for Momma to primp her hair and smooth out her blouse and skirt. I smoothed my hands over my dress too; Momma smiled. She loved it when I made like a little lady, but she never let me forget that I was still a child.

Daddy stood up when me and Momma walked into the room. He did that all the time for Momma, me too – most times.

"Woman, you gon' always be a sight for these old sore eyes of mine."

"Well, thank you, Ben Charles." Momma gave my daddy a kiss on the lips and handed him that glass of sweet iced tea. "Now, I declare you been on that phone all morning, so I knows you got a heap of things to tell me." Momma sat down in the chair next to the one Daddy was sitting in, so I started for his lap.

"Yes Lord, woman. Look like our peoples done had a lot going on. I'm almost beside myself about all this-here that been told to me."

"Well, go on and tell me, Ben. You got me a little nervous. Now, I don't want you to feel like you have to spare my feelings; just tell me everything that was told to you."

"Alright, woman. Gimme just a minute here and I'll tell you; but, as your husband, I'm gon' always protect your heart."

I had already hopped back on Daddy's knee and had even took another sip of his sweet iced tea while he was talking to Momma.

"Millie, how 'bout you let your momma have your favorite seat for a just a minute here so I can talk to her."

I didn't want to sit nowhere's else; I always sat on my daddy's lap. As soon as Daddy picked me up, I got butterflies in my stomach, but they wasn't much like the giggling kind.

"Just for right now, okay, babygirl? You can have any which one of these old knees back as soon as me and your momma done talking 'bout Cousin Rudy Mae."

Schaumburg's Sweet Reminisce

My little heart was hurt, but Momma and Daddy didn't believe in me always gettin' my way. I stood there for a minute with my chin on my chest and lips poked out fightin' back the tears. Daddy rarely said no to me, so it made me wonder if I had done something wrong.

Momma had caught me playing with matches a few days ago and tore my bottom up one side and down the other. I wondered if Daddy knew. He probably did. Momma and Daddy told each other everything. Sometimes they'd be up talking long after I was made to go to bed. They'd get up the next morning and still be talking. Seemed like the only time they didn't talk was when they wasn't together.

It didn't look like Daddy was gonna change his mind, so I slow-walked myself over to the chair where Momma should have been sitting and wrung the hem of my dress around my fingers until I couldn't. Back talk of any kind wasn't wise, so I sat there poutin' careful not to let a sound depart my lips.

"Thank you, Mille. Momma appreciate your generous spirit."

"Well, woman, I just hung up with the nursing home. The nurse over there say Cousin Rudy Mae had a pretty bad night last night; doing a lot better this morning. Kept 'em on they toes over there near 'bout all day yesterday. Said Cousin Rudy Mae told everybody that would listen that she had a party to go to and she didn't wanna be late. Doctor over there say she struck with Alzheimer's, done had it for some time now. By the time they got her over there to the nursing home, she had done got herself in a real bad way. Doctor say she nearin' the end, but she strong, doing a lot better than they thought she would."

"Lord have mercy, Jesus, Ben." Momma looked like

122

she wanted to cry but she didn't. She just held herself.

"Cousin Rudy Mae done been over there at that nursing home going on three years now. State had to put her in there on account they couldn't get in touch with nobody. Couldn't get a word out of her for months, had 'em wondering if she could even talk at all."

"Sound like my Cousin Rudy Mae had done been left to waste away all on her own and what not. It ain't right."

Daddy could hear the hurt in Momma's voice. "Don't go blaming yourself, woman. Sometimes folks just don't take too well to places they can't call home. They can go down in they body and they spirit real quick-like if they ain't careful."

"Ben, I just should've kept trying."

"Marjorie, I ain't gon' let you get started, now."

"Well, tell me this here then. How was I able to talk to Cousin Rudy Mae if she over there at the nursing home? I been dialing the same number I been dialing since I started dialing it."

"Well, it wasn't until a few months ago that they was finally able to forward that phone line over there to the nursing home. Reckon that's why you was able to get your Cousin Rudy Mae on the line when you called. Still had the phone listed in Cousin Emmitt's name. His account over at the bank had done dried up on account Cousin Rudy Mae would forget to take the checks by there to have 'em cashed. Had a right smart of 'em stuffed in a drawer. Was even now using some of 'em to light that old stove. I don't reckon she burned too many, but the bank was able to make good on them she had left."

"Well, I sure am glad I was able to put my hurt and my pride aside and call my Cousin Rudy Mae when I did. Been trying off and on for years to bring my family together."

"God healed your heart right on time, Marjorie. Ain't no telling how long it would have been before we found out about this here."

"Was they able to run down anybody else?"

"Naw, not that I know of. Said somebody would call every now and then and hang up – all that started round 'bout the time they put a hold on the account over there at the bank."

"Hold?"

"Took and said somebody was getting after Cousin Rudy Mae's money somehow or another. Said a few times somebody had done brought a note over there to the bank tryin' to make it look like Cousin Rudy Mae was wanting to cash a check and give them the money. Had done put a big X where her name was supposed to be. After that last time, they called the house but couldn't get in touch with nobody. Kept calling. Kept calling. So, to be on the safe side, they put a hold on the account until they was able to either lay eyes on Cousin Rudy Mae or talk to her."

"Ben Charles, you reckon they'll be able to find who done that?"

"Well, baby, I sho' hope so; but that could have been any old low-down rascal trying to get after Cousin Rudy Mae's money."

"Well, the only thing I ever know'd Cousin Rudy Mae to be able to write was her name and Cousin Emmitt's name.

And the reason why come I know is because when she finally did learn how to write it, she asked me if I'd help her find a frame for it, and I did. I bet it's still hanging in that old house somewhere."

"I remember that. Cousin Emmitt was some proud of his Rudy Mae that day. That was a good, long while ago."

"Well, I hope they find the rascal that's been stealing my Cousin Rudy Mae's money and after they find 'em, they need to be made to pay back every dime no matter how long it take."

"I'm with you on that, woman. And it shouldn't make no never mind whether she living or dead, to tell you the truth about it. Your Cousin Emmitt lost his mind fighting in that war and Cousin Rudy Mae is entitled to that money, do you hear me – every last, red cent."

"Well, I'm just so glad to hear she doing better. You know we got to go see her as soon as you can get a break from that field now. Lord, I feel happy and sad all at the same time."

"Well, Lord willing, I figured we take a drive up there this Sunday after church. Folks at the nursing home gon' set everything up for when we get there. Ain't no sense in putting matters off no longer. We going this coming Sunday to see 'bout your Cousin Rudy Mae, woman."

"I'm so grateful, Ben. It warms my heart to know that I just might get another chance to get everybody together after all these years."

"Woman, I like the sound of that. It's been a long time coming."

Schaumburg's Sweet Reminisce

Momma pressed her curls in place, picked up Daddy's mason jar still full of iced tea, took a sip, and then handed it to Daddy. "I wonder what Cousin Rudy Mae might be needin'. I know she could use a few things – a woman always can. I'll pull together a real nice care box for her. And I should be able to find a picture or two that I can part with. I already got two in mind. And I know I can find two little frames to put 'em in. Can you think of anything she might be needin', Ben? Anything at all? Did they say anything over there at the nursing home 'bout what she might have need of?"

"Woman, I think them pictures might do Cousin Rudy Mae some good. Babygirl, what you think?"

"I don't know, Daddy." I knew, I was just still poutin' a lil' bit, but I was glad to see Momma's heart not resting so heavy no more.

Daddy finally took another swig of his tea. He tried not to drink while Momma was talking, but Momma wasn't letting up. She wanted to make that care box real nice for Cousin Rudy Mae – and I did too.

"Millie, you wanna make your Cousin Rudy Mae a nice card?"

"Yes, ma'am."

I was 'bout done poutin' and had started to listen in on Momma and Daddy talking back and forth again. I hoped Cousin Rudy Mae would like my colors, most everybody else did. Momma said it was because I took my time and did it from my heart.

"You think we ought to tell her we's coming, Ben?"

"We can call back over yonder there and talk to the doctor to be on the safe side, but I don't think it'd make a difference one way or another. If she did remember, by the time we got there, she'd probably been done forgot."

"I can't wait to see my Cousin Rudy Mae's precious face."

"I'm sure she gon' be some surprised. Sho' nuff so if she able to make out who we be."

"Them folks over yonder said Cousin Rudy Mae sit right there by that phone almost every day now since you been calling. She took and wrote your name down on a piece of paper and set it right there by her phone. Said she threw a fit until somebody taught her how write it."

"Did she now?" Momma smiled.

"Said Cousin Rudy Mae be 'round that nursing home asking everybody she see if they'd done heard her phone ring."

"Always have been the one never wantin' to miss out on nothin'." Momma laughed.

"Doctor told me to tell you to keep calling on account it do Cousin Rudy Mae a world of good. They all thought she'd be gone by now from a broken heart long before that Alzheimer's claimed her."

"All that time me and Cousin Rudy Mae carried on, I never would have thought that she was losing her mind, but I reckon that doctor know what he talkin' 'bout. Maybe I was doing more talking than listening."

"You know, woman, I was hoping that this whole thing

would turn out to be something silly. Never would've thought it'd turn out to be something like this-here."

"Me neither, Ben, but we gon' count our blessings."

"Each and every last one. Babygirl, you excited to meet your Cousin Rudy Mae?"

"Yes, sir."

I hadn't yet met none of Momma or Daddy's peoples, none that I could remember.

"Well, Marjorie, on the one hand, I reckon it gotta be kinda bad not to know sometimes whether you coming or going; but on the other hand, the way the world is today, I reckon it might just be a blessing not to have no parts in it all."

"My, my, my. Husband of mine, you just said something."

"Anybody you talk to this morning have anything to say about them folks that's living in that house?"

"I talked to the sheriff. Said the family that's been living there was from up north. Man seeing after 12 children between him and his late wife. Fell on hard times and then even harder times a few years back when his wife up and died. Him and them kids been traveling here and yonder trying to catch a break. Reckon he just took up living there 'til he could figure out what to do next."

I was hoping to get by there on Sunday to see them children Momma and Daddy was talking about. I know I saw some little girls on the porch about my size I could play with. I didn't much care if they skin was like mines or not, hair neither.

"Sheriff said everybody just up and left one day. Had no idea what had happened to Cousin Rudy Mae, figured she took up with the rest of the family."

"They just up and run off and left Cousin Rudy Mae over there all by herself?"

"Looks that a'way, woman."

"Lord have mercy. Sometimes it be your own family, but we gon' leave it all to the good Lord."

"That's right, baby. We know what we know and now we can do something about what we know and leave the rest to the good Lord."

"Ben, reckon how that man seeing after all them children?"

"Well, I reckon he might be doing alright. Sheriff said every last one of them children is in church on Sunday and in school during the week. Don't get to see much of the daddy on account he always working. Work way out there in Chester on that old hog farm on Sunday, do a little farming with another man during the week and then for another man all day Saturday.

"Sheriff said he seemed like a God-fearing man and he just didn't have the heart to make him leave on account he had all them children. Didn't seem to be causing no problems and wasn't nobody making a fuss about nothing, so he just assume let 'em stay on. Had done fixed a few things around there to try to keep the place halfway livable. House didn't have no power electricity, so they used the wood stove to cook and heat water – even now got that old well up and running out back. Wanted to know if we'd be alright with him and his children staying on there for a while longer."

"Well, I'll be. Man working seven days a week to feed his family; I reckon the man probably too tired to feed his own self."

"Sho' sound like he could use a helping hand. You know of any reason why he can't stay on there at least until we can get back by there to meet him and find out for sure?"

"I'm of the same mind as you, Ben Charles. Cousin Rudy Mae ain't going back there if I got anything to say about it. I'll pull together some of the ladies from the church to see if they have anything they need rid of and we can take it on by there for 'em when we go see 'bout Cousin Rudy Mae."

"As unto to the Lord, woman." Daddy loved it when Momma operated in her gift. One of the many reasons he loved her so much.

"Every chance I get. You's a good man, Ben Charles."

"You think so, woman?"

"Can't a soul tell me any different."

Momma smiled and rested her face against Daddy's head and then held his chin gently in her hands and gave him a peck on the lips. That made him nearly show all his teeth. Seeing Momma and Daddy make nice with one another always made me smile. They didn't seem to care who was around. It was like nobody else mattered and wasn't nobody's business if they did.

From that next Sunday forward – once a month during the winter months and every other Sunday during the spring, summer, and fall – we packed up the truck to go see Cousin Rudy Mae faithfully until she died. Momma always took Cousin Rudy Mae something nice and never once did she ever think about not going, even when she wasn't feeling quite right.

Before Cousin Rudy Mae passed, Momma got with the folks over at the nursing home and planned a special day up at the plantation for all their sick and shut-in to spend with they families. Momma's heart was dead-set on having a family reunion even if she had to have somebody else's family do it. 'Course, now some of them folks over at that nursing home didn't have no family, but we all tried to make sure that those that didn't felt like they did.

We got to the nursing home early that Spring morning so Momma could fix Cousin Rudy Mae's hair and put her face on. Cousin Rudy Mae looked nothing like the Cousin Rudy Mae I was used to seeing and by the way she kept touching her face and all, I reckon she was thinking the same as me. She sat and stared at herself in the mirror for the longest time and Momma sat and stared at Cousin Rudy Mae staring at herself while me and Daddy waited for them to finish.

Daddy told Cousin Rudy Mae that she was gon' have every man in town making a fuss over her. Cousin Rudy Mae smiled, took Daddy by the hand, and told him to hurry up and put her in the truck – she didn't want to keep 'em all waitin'.

Everybody told Cousin Rudy Mae how pretty she looked in the yellow dress Momma handed down to her. Momma had only worn it maybe once or twice so it may as well have been brand new; fit Cousin Rudy Mae just perfect even though she had picked up a little weight since the last time we saw her. Momma said that little bit of weight Cousin Rudy Mae had done put on wasn't nothing, said it looked good on her, had done got too po' anyhow.

We wasn't the only ones partial to Cousin Rudy Mae's looks. A shady, white-haired, fair-skinned fella who lived at the nursing home seemed to think Cousin Rudy Mae looked right nice too, but more than most folks. A few of the nurses had done already told Momma to watch herself and Cousin Rudy Mae around that man and to make sure that I didn't wander off by myself.

Momma let that old rascal admire Cousin Rudy Mae from a distance for just a short while. She even let that old goat tell Cousin Rudy Mae how nice she looked. I heard her tell Cousin Rudy Mae to make sure she kept that rascal at arms-length. Cousin Rudy Mae smiled when Momma said what she said, but I couldn't tell if she was smiling at what Momma had said, or if she was smiling at the man grinning at her. But knowing Cousin Rudy Mae, she may have just been smiling to be smiling – she did that sometimes.

We stayed the whole day with Cousin Rudy Mae; had a mighty fine time, too. Momma's heart had been a little heavy because she didn't know how much longer it would be before the good Lord called Cousin Rudy Mae on home. Once Momma got wind of the man with the fancy camera, she told him that my daddy'd be willing to pay top-dollar if he could spare a photo; she wanted a part of Cousin Rudy Mae that she could hold in her hand after she was gone.

Daddy stood close by just to make sure she didn't offer him up the farm to the man as payment. I don't know what Momma told that man with the fancy camera, but by the time she finished talking to him, he had done got so excited, he took a picture of everybody wanting one and didn't charge 'em a dime. Most them folks had never even had they picture taken before. Momma was well pleased and mighty proud to be able to get that picture of Cousin Rudy Mae to add to the rest of the lineage.

We'd never forget the time we had that day; and in just a couple of years Cousin Rudy Mae was gone. Momma had settled it in her mind that Cousin Rudy Mae was probably the last of her family and wasted no time adding her picture to the lineage. We all was real sad for a while, Momma mostly, but we soon returned to our joy. We was grateful for what little time the Lord allowed us with our Cousin Rudy Mae.

Chapter Eight

Momma and Daddy knew a whole heap of people.

Wasn't a place they set foot to where they didn't meet somebody that knew somebody they knew but didn't know them – just friendly folks that a'way, a lot like Sister Frieda and her late husband Brother Albert. But now, as friendly as Momma was, she would never invite a male stranger into our home if Daddy wasn't there and wouldn't allow one to stand on the porch too long asking all kinds of questions neither; said it wasn't proper.

Quite often they would invite folks over to the house for a little food and a whole lotta conversation – didn't matter who, didn't matter when. Momma would invite 'em over and then call up Sister Freida Mae Johnson to fill up the rest of the house and yard. Daddy always seemed to be the last to know, but he never seemed to mind; he loved to fellowship almost as much as Momma did.

Now, Sister Freida was way on up there in age, but you never would tell just by looking at her. She and her late Albert used to entertain like Momma and Daddy did, but always on a much grander scale. Not sure how they come by all the money they had, but Momma always used to say that people should mind their own blessings and with the same mind be a blessing.

After Brother Albert died, Sister Freida passed the torch on to Momma – those big get-togethers reminded her too much of her late Albert. One would think that after being in the company of so many folks, a person would be filled up with love, but that wasn't always so with Sister Freida. She always made sure that everybody had a good time, but it wouldn't be long before she started to feel lonesome for her Albert, and Momma understood that.

While Brother Albert was alive, him and Sister Freida kept record of every family in every town they had ever lived. Well, them records and everything else was lost to a fire while Sister Freida was away up north helping her youngest babygirl with her first child. Other than her nine children and a wedding photo she kept with her all the time, Sister Freida felt like that was all she had left of Brother Albert.

Sister Freida went and got herself in a real bad way after that fire. Spent a whole lot of time to herself. It'd be weeks sometimes before anybody would hear from her. Hadn't been to church or taken The Lord's Supper in months and the elders had done had enough. A right smart of 'em got together with they wives to go check on her; took with 'em a few fixins' and most importantly a Word from the Lord. Sister Frieda wouldn't even now answer the door. So, they called on Sister Ida and no sooner than they could get the need off they lips, Sister Ida had everything ready.

When the day came, over half the church showed up to help out. Sister Ida never took no for an answer; she'd been known to worry the mess out of a mosquito. They all marched right on over to Sister Freida's farm to love on her for a while in the name of our Lord and Savior Jesus Christ. The womenfolk gave that house a working over from the ceiling to the crawl space while the menfolk cleared off, fixed

135

up, and mended that three and a half acres the house was on. They left the rest of the farm to do what farms do.

With Sister Freida being up in age and all, Momma prayed and asked the Lord to prepare her heart and her spirit before they all got there.

It wasn't that Sister Ida didn't mean well; it was just that she liked to take over most things, most times. But everybody that knew Sister Ida knew that everything she did, she did out of love.

Sister Ida went on and on in her prayer that morning 'bout how they was gon' storm the gates of hell and snatch back their beloved Sister Freida from her grave of loneliness and despair and told the Lord that they wasn't going knocking. And sure enough, Sister Ida strolled right on up Sister Freida's front steps and opened the door like she lived there.

Sister Ida was clothed in the Full Armor of God that day and with one hand on her hip and the other clutching her Bible, she walked every inch of that house, quoting Scriptures and assigning chores and whatnot until every able-bodied soul she'd done laid eyes on had something to do. And if Sister Ida asked you to do something, well, you just went head on and got to it.

Sister Ida was a retired school teacher from West Virginia, you see; never married and no children birthed from sin – so, she was a lot better at giving orders than she was at taking 'em. She had done gone and got herself so wound up that she started outside to where the menfolks was with they chainsaws, slang blades, and tillers and such.

But now, Deacon Yancey could sense Sister Ida's zeal from a mile away. He knew she was on her way on account the wind had done picked up a scent of perfume that only Sister Ida would dare wear. He stopped Sister Ida dead in her tracks before she could get a word in edgewise and quickly ushered her back on up to the house. Sister Ida smiled and clutched her pearls like she oftentimes did in the presence of Deacon Yancey.

Whole lotta womenfolk didn't think Deacon Yancey was all that much to look at on account he was old and round with sad eyes, but he was a good man and Sister Ida knew that.

"Well, Deacon Yancey, look like y'all menfolk coming right along. It's a right smart of ya out here. You think y'all'll be able to manage by yourselves? You know, us ladies ain't girdled too tight in our britches to help out, now."

"I think us menfolk know best when it come to menfolk matters, Sister Ida. No need to trouble yourself nor the rest of the ladies."

"Well, you might be right, Deacon Yancey, but the Lord can use any of us for anything. If you find yourself in need, don't be too shame to ask for help."

"Well, I thank you, Sister Ida, but from the looks of things, you ladies have more than you can say grace over. They could probably use your help in there – I believe it so. I think we can handle this manly labor on our own out here. I thank you kindly, Sister Ida. Good day, now."

"Well, just let what I said sit with your mind, Deacon Yancey. I don't mind rolling up my sleeves for the cause of Jesus Christ."

"Sister Ida, now I done already told you that your place ought to be in that-there house with the rest of the womenfolk. Now, if it's all the same to you, I can't stand 'round here talking to you all morning. I's got work to do and I aim to get it done before sundown."

"I reckon you right, Deacon Yancey, the morning is getting along into the day." Sister Ida had one more thing on her heart to say to Deacon Yancey. "Deacon Yancey?"

"What is it now, Sister Ida?"

Sister Ida could tell that Deacon Yancey was growing weary, but she'd say her peace. "Only that which is done for Jesus Christ shall last."

"That's a good word, Sister Ida. Reckon it's time we both get to it if we aim to get anything done at all. Good day, Sister Ida."

"Good day, Deacon Yancey."

Sister Ida smiled and turned to walk back up toward the house; Deacon Yancey couldn't do nothing but shake his head. He wiped the sweat from his brow, but then turned around and looked back at Sister Ida and smiled. I reckon he was glad to see her go.

Some of the ladies standing earshot of Deacon Yancey and Sister Ida laughed to themselves, and it wasn't no secret as to why. Everybody knew that Sister Ida thought Deacon Yancey had a sweet spot for her, but truth be told, she really got on his nerves. Sister Ida was a proper woman and wasn't no man-chaser, but she loved her some Deacon Yancey. She figured sooner or later she'd wear him down before he got too old.

Sister Ida was loved by many and her gift of service was a God-send to the church. If you needed to get things done in a hurry but in an orderly fashion, Sister Ida was who you called on. She had a way about her that most folks didn't quite understand, but she had a sweet spirit about her that folks couldn't help but love.

Deacon Yancey and Sister Ida got married not too long after that. Made a nice little life together taking in young wayward orphans to train 'em up in the Lord. Deacon Yancey drug his feet hither and yonder on it, but in due time Sister Ida was able to make him see different. Raised a right smart of orphans in their old age – children from all over. Lived long enough to see some of those children get married and have children of their own.

Near 'bout every time Sister Freida and her late Albert put together one of them shindigs, somebody or another was bound to find out that they was kin to somebody or another. Most times it was way, *way* on down the bloodline, but blood was still blood. And by the end of the night, Brother Albert made sure that everybody and all the problems that they thought they may have had was put before the good Lord. Some folks that wouldn't even now step foot in a church on Sunday morning would show up, sit and talk, and break bread with 'em, and was made to feel welcome. Didn't bother Brother Albert not one bit. He figured saving souls was the Lord's work anyhow.

Most everybody told stories about their lineage whether they felt proud or shame. Some had more stories than others, but then, some just made up stories as they went along on account of not having no kinfolks left or much history to draw from. Those who had a lot to say, gleaned as far back as the oldest living patriarch or matriarch was able to remember, mostly God-fearing slaves and sharecroppers. But every now and then, Momma and Daddy would stumble across somebody's family who made history in some way or another. Back then, it wasn't uncommon for people to strike out on a prayer and a plan. And because most folks didn't have much of nothing, they had to trust God for everything.

Older folks believed that it was just good for folks to get together often and share with one another whatever good or whatever bad they had going on at the time.

People's hearts are oftentimes heavy with many a'troubles. You never know, sometimes a person might be grinning like an old chess-cat, but be hollow on the inside.

"Most young folks coming along nowadays don't take much care to get to know they own peoples, and that's a mighty sad thing. A person could end up marrying they own blood," Momma would sometimes say.

Daddy would always laugh when Momma said what she said, but he always told her that she was right. They both knew it to be so, but never spoke on the matter directly. Momma could get real serious when it came to her faith and her family.

Daddy said some people never do give thought to the call of God on they life; most folks just live until it's they time to die. Said that type of thinking can cause a person a whole heap of grief in life. But once you give a man wise counsel, it's left on him to choose which side he gon' stand on.

"You got to allow a man to make his own mistakes and suffer his own consequences – that's how a man becomes a man. Either way, one thing's for sure: any man leaving home need to leave in such a way that if he needed to come on back, he'd be welcomed." PopPop told my daddy that when he was just a little runt. Daddy never forgot it.

There was a whole big world outside of Schaumburg,

not all good but not all bad neither. Whole lotta folks was running toward it for one reason or another. Many would leave and forget all about family 'til they fell on hard times or 'til somebody died.

Chapter Nine

Millie, you know our people was learned in the Word of God early. And they lived by the Word of God – and what was expected was understood without it having to be said because it was lived out before 'em. There was to be no talk of any other way, except the way of the Lord. You see, way back then, whatever God said was what it was gon' be – no ifs, ands, or buts about it. And that way of doing was passed down from generation to generation. My momma and daddy took what was taught to them and taught it to me. And your daddy's daddy and momma took and taught your daddy what was learned to them. And so now, me and your daddy take and try to teach you everything that was taught to us. Yes Lord, our families been training up generations the same way as far back as we's been able to trace our family's roots. When you really think about it and take it all to heart, our lineage been loving on you since before you was even born."

Momma talked on. "One thing PopPop used to always say, 'If a man can't be but one good thing in life… let him be a vessel of love, and if he so happens to find grace for one more good thing, let him be a vessel of light.' As children of God, we got to make sure that nobody misses grace."

I didn't really know what Momma was trying to say but she had tears in her eyes, so I just patted her on the back and told her that I did.

"Momma's alright, my sweet girl. I sure do miss PopPop. I miss all our kinfolk that done left here."

"Momma?"

"What is it child?"

"How is the lineage gonna know me? Ain't none of them ever seen me and I ain't never seen none of them neither."

"Millie, you just trust the good Lord for heaven and they'll all know who you be when you get there."

During Thanksgiving, Momma would let the lineage visit until late Sunday evening then she'd gather 'em all together and kiss each one before she put 'em back in that little, old ugly green suitcase. It was kinda like she was saying goodbye for now, but not forever – just for a few seasons.

When I was born, I looked just like my great-great-great-grandma Maylene on my momma's side when she was a child, except for the funny-shaped birthmark under her left eye. I didn't have no birthmark, but I had a head full of hair just like her. Momma said that I wasn't gonna ever have to worry my mind about being as big-boned as she was.

Couldn't half-tell how old nobody was in them old pictures, so we just guessed. Folks way back then barely knew they own age; had more pressing matters to be worried with. Momma said PopPop used to always say that he was as old as dirt on account he come from it.

Schaumburg's Sweet Reminisce

Daddy always told me that I had my PopPop's eyes – eyes the color of over-ripe muscadines so big to where you almost couldn't hardly see the white parts. PopPop was born half-blind and his sight would come and go for a right smart of years until God's will proved different. When God saw fit to give PopPop his full sight, PopPop didn't sleep for days. Spent the better part of his young life trying to see everything that he figured he had done missed out on. Left home early and didn't give too much thought to settling down. The way he figured, a family would only slow him down and he wasn't wanting to miss nothing else, just in case God decided to change His mind again – PopPop didn't truly yet know the hand of the Lord.

PopPop was always real serious, too, even about small things. Always made a fuss when it came to idleness. Wanted everything done right the first time or not at all; didn't really matter how long it took so long as it didn't take forever. He didn't feel the need to have to explain or repeat hisself too often neither. And he never was the type of man to make problems for hisself; he respected folks and folks respected him. A man of few words, but you always remembered what he said.

Nobody ever know'd PopPop to cry none neither. But now, Daddy remembered the first time he thought PopPop might come close. It was early one evening and PopPop had come in from the bottoms from all day planting for fall harvest. He turned down the tractor just like he did every evening, but this time he took the keys out the ignition. Any other time he'd leave the keys in the tractor so he wouldn't have to hunt for 'em the next morning. But that day, PopPop just sat there. Couldn't have moved if he wanted to. It had come time for PopPop to go on to the house – something folks said when they'd gotten too old and too tired to work.

Just so happened, Daddy was on his way in from the field and decided to check on him. He could see from a'ways off that PopPop was yet still out in the yard. It was something about PopPop sittin' there the way that he was that stirred him a little bit that day. PopPop rarely tarried after a hard day's work. PopPop was just sitting there looking straight ahead, as still as a thousand-year-old oak.

Daddy sat in his own truck waiting for PopPop to make some kind of movement, but he never did. He even revved the engine a couple times. Nothin'. That was enough for Daddy to hop on out that old truck and head towards the old man.

"Hey there now, old man!" Daddy yelled out to PopPop from across the yard.

PopPop never moved. Never uttered a word.

Daddy said as fast as he was walking to get to PopPop, he still wasn't walking fast enough to out-walk the beat of his own heart. He thought it kinda strange for PopPop not to so much as even look his way and it shook him a good bit.

PopPop had gotten on up in age and didn't want nobody telling him what to do, how to do it, or what they thought he might ought to be doing neither. When folks stepped too far out of line with him, he often joked that he hadn't been on his momma's breast for quite some time. Sounded funny to most people when he said it, but he was really trying to tell folks in a roundabout way to mind they own business. There was only two people PopPop took orders from – the good Lord and his sweet Mae Ellen Rose; and now that his Mae Ellen was dead and gone, PopPop was primed to do exactly what PopPop wanted to do when he wanted to do it.

Schaumburg's Sweet Reminisce

PopPop's stubbornness stood to give Daddy the blues from time to time. Every now and then you'd hear talk about a farmer somebody had done found down and around them bottoms slumped over with his tractor still running; or like the time they found that young fella down there across the creek in a field sliced up something awful. Boy had done got too hot and dry out there working in all that heat; got caught down there between them big old tires and when they turned him loose, them blades caught him. Tractor plowed here and yonder all across that field and come back over there on him.

Only thing PopPop had to say to that was that when it was his time to go, it'd be his time to go; but until then, he had every intention on getting his seed in the ground on time and his crop out the ground when the time came. PopPop wasn't the type to worry about today's trouble or give too much thought to the troubles that lay in wait for tomorrow neither.

"Hey there, old man. Everything alright?"

PopPop's eyes was open, but he sat tight-lipped. Daddy said he just needed to touch him – so he did.

"Hey there, boy…"

"You alright, old man? Had me a little worried there."

"Yeah? Well now, boy, what you worrying about?"

"I reckon, you was just sitting a little too still for me is all. Called out to you. Even now revved my engine."

"Welp, I reckon you be right."

"How's that?'

"I'm old. I guess my time done run on down and near 'bout out."

Daddy said he remembered that PopPop spoke real low, but slow and a matter-of-factly.

"Yes, sir. I reckon that be so." Truth be told, PopPop had been an old man.

"Trying to make a 100 though, ain't you, old man? Lord willing?"

And He was. "Lord willing, son. Lord willing. But, I don't reckon I can take a breath beyond the time the Lord done set for me. Don't even now want to nohow. If He say tonight, tomorrow, or 99, I'm ready."

"I reckon you right, old man."

"God's been mighty good to me, son. I know it for myself."

"Yes, sir. Seen it with my own eyes."

"I believe it's long past time for me to take it on in. Been on my mind a while. All day today. Couldn't now hardly settle my thoughts."

"Is that right?" PopPop was always sho' nuff' with what he said, but Daddy would have to see it come to pass. He already knew PopPop wasn't 'bout to put his tractor out to pasture until he was good and ready.

"Who you think you fooling? I'm your Daddy, boy."

My daddy said PopPop couldn't help but chuckle about it. They had done had their share of strong words on the matter over the years, but in love.

"Welp, if that's your plan old man, I stand by you on it." To hear PopPop say that it was time to rest made my daddy happy.

"Yep, that's my plan. That's my plan, son. Been working that soil down there in them bottoms long before you was even now born. Never wanted to do nothing else in life except farm; it's all I know. My daddy, my daddy's daddy, and his daddy before him worked every day God allowed. Each one died in his sleep."

"Is that right?"

"That's right, son."

PopPop's heart was heavy. Daddy could tell, so he rested his hand on PopPop's shoulder and turned to leave him be. Said by the time he walked away, PopPop's whole body was trembling; may have been on account of him trying to hold back the tears. Daddy never did know if PopPop broke down or not; he just couldn't bring himself to hang around to see him humbled in that way.

The way PopPop's momma died might have done broke PopPop early and dried up all his tears. Shut up his emotion.

Momma said that that was just PopPop's way and he didn't waste his time comparing himself to no other man on nothing – white, black, or other for any reason; said if the Lord saw fit to give him tears to cry, he'd cry 'em and if He didn't, he wouldn't. Didn't believe in sittin' around wasting tears on hisself – but if he ever did, God knew the reason behind each tear and that somewhere in His Word he promised to bottle 'em all up. PopPop said it'd suit him just fine to cry out to the Lord and Him alone, 'cause once he did, he could be done with the matter; wouldn't be no need for tears.

PopPop may not have been quick to the draw when it came to crying, but if you was to spend any amount of time with him, he'd be sure to show you his heart. Momma said he just couldn't help it.

But now, Momma's daddy, Bo Hatcher, wasn't so selfish with his tears. He always cried when he communed with the Lord in that way and cried non-stop for days when my momma's momma, Grandma Audrey, died. He'd always hoped to leave this world before she did, but at the same time he didn't want to leave this world without her. Most folks already knew what Granddaddy Bo Hatcher made pretend that he didn't – he didn't want his Audrey Elizabeth taking up with no other man once he was dead and gone, and that was all there was to it.

Growing up, Daddy wanted to be strong just like his daddy – but there would only ever be one PopPop.

As a young man, PopPop worked picking cotton and cutting tobacco to feed hisself after he struck out on his own. Saw a man stripped naked, strung up, and set on fire and was made to stay and watch him burn to death. White men nearly beat PopPop half to death on account he kept fightin' to get away to help set the man free.

PopPop would hold on to what happened that night in his heart and mind for years until he just couldn't hold it in no more. Told it to an old preacher he boarded with while he worked his crops. What he'd heard and seen that night stayed fresh on his mind and had done nearly eat him up on the inside. Had him thinking back on the days when he was half-blind. Said that old preacher had done took bits and pieces of what he'd told him and preached the whole tent happy one night during revival.

PopPop took to himself two brides but died a widower. PopPop lost his first wife Queenie and their only child during child birth. People say Queenie was a good woman, a beautiful woman, and a stretch older than PopPop; but her mind was left fragile from her first marriage. Momma said that that wasn't no kind of marriage though. Poor child was made to play wife to her own daddy after her momma died. Like me, she was the only child and not much family around. Wasn't no more than nine or ten years old and looked like every bit of her momma. Bore no children with her daddy which was a blessing if you looking at that thing the right way.

"Man ain't got no right to lay with his own flesh. Such things just ought not be; it's a sin against God, like all sin." I don't recall Momma ever mentioning what happened to Grandma Queenie no more than once or twice; but when she did, she always got a strange look about the eyes.

God released Grandma Queenie from that abomination on account her daddy died a young man or so they say, but the damage had been done. Whole thing messed her up real good. Ate her plumb-up on the inside. Her and PopPop was happy, but they struggled a spell.

Then there was my grandma Mae Ellen Rose Fouraukis, PopPop's second wife, my daddy's momma who made him a widower at a good and ripe old age, but sooner than PopPop would have liked. PopPop never remarried. The Lord had blessed him with two beautiful wives and two equally beautiful marriages that he honored from beginning to end. Said that he could be content on his own so long as the Lord extended the grace. So, after the death of Grandma Mae Ellen Rose, PopPop stayed committed to the Lord and worked the soil in every acre of every bottom he knew of like an old work-mule six days a week from sun-up 'til nearly his own sun-down.

Chapter Ten

Whatcha's on your mind, son? And don't say nothin' –
'cause I knows better. Talk to your old man."

"Been thinking' 'bout asking Marjorie to marry me. Start a family. Done had these feelings for a good long while now, since the first time I laid eyes on her."

"Mmmm hmm. You ain't done went and got Marjorie in a bad way, have you son?"

"Nooo. No, sir."

"Mmmm hmmm."

Daddy remembered the look in PopPop's eyes. Similar to the one that let him know that he had better think twice about lying and a third time if he was even thinking about changing his answer before he and his Marjorie married.

"You met long and hard on it with the Master, son?"

"Yes, sir."

"Well, I reckon you heard from Him?"

"Yes, sir. I believe I have."

"Mmmm hmm. Well, I know your heart is for her."

"Yes, sir. I love her."

"I reckon you got a right smart of money saved up?"

"I'm just 'bout able to afford the house she done had her eye on. Need a little work, but ain't nothing I can't handle. Even now done been by there a few times. Man that owns it say he'd make me a fair offer on it and hold it for me if I could keep his hay fields cut for a few seasons. I believe I can take him at his word."

"Mmmm hmm."

"I'm thinking about asking her after Sunday evening service."

"Well, I know you not asking... but I'll tell you what I think – Marjorie is a mighty fine woman, son; and I mean no disrespect, but I think you know that. What I'm getting at is that I believe Marjorie'll make you a mighty fine bride... a mighty fine helpmate, and a real good mother to your children – if the good Lord see fit. I done watched her over the years with my own eyes; how she done served in the church. Her first love is unto the Lord. Don't you go bothering with that in no kinda way, son. Ya hear me? You'll be all the better for it."

"Yes, sir."

"Is you a man, son?"

"Sir?"

"Nothing hard about the question, son. Is you a man

or ain't you?"

"Yes, sir. I am."

"According to whose standard?"

"You and Momma raised me right."

"Son, me and your momma raised you to honor and obey the Lord. You wear the Fouraukis name, but you's created in the image of God and His standard is the only one that matters."

"Yes, sir."

"Now, I know how Marjorie feel about you. I heard it from her own mouth. She talk with me from time to time. Talking to Marjorie been able to help me gauge if you doing right by her or if you ain't and I aim to believe what she tells me. Keep doing right by her and the good Lord will honor your marriage, son."

"Yes, sir. I aim to do that."

"You been courting Marjorie as long as I can remember. Glad to see this-here day. You done had to learn a few things – patience is one of 'em. You can thank Marjorie for that-there. A woman supposed to make a man wait. A patient man ain't quick to cheat nobody, not even his ownself; but every man need a good woman to help make him better. Lot of funny things about a woman – most things you won't ever understand, so don't go run off trying. It'd take you your whole life to try and figure out your Marjorie. Same way for me with your momma all them years.

"I done showed you how to protect and provide, but only God can give a man what he need to love his wife according to His standard. You got to stay connected to the Lord no matter what. You follow me, son?"

"Yes, sir."

"Any man taking on a wife enters into a covenant with God. Marriage carries a lot of weight – nothing else like it; and God is serious about His covenant of marriage, so you and Marjorie need to be serious, too. You ready and willing to die, son?"

"Sir?"

"Don't sound like it."

"Don't know what you's askin', Daddy."

"You got to be ready to lay your life all the way down for that woman before you even now ask her old man for her hand. Only thing that can severe that covenant you's thinkin' 'bout entering into is death. And son, you got to be sho' nuff ready and willing to die for Marjorie without even having to think about it – and she gonna wanna know that you willing and so is her old man. But now, you ain't gon' be willing to die for her unless you willing to die to your ownself as unto the Lord. If you got to think about it, back up all the way and wait 'cause if you ain't willing to do that, she ain't the one that God would have for you.

"You my boy, but if Marjorie had any doubt in her mind on the matter, I'd tell her not to marry you. I'm telling you this son because I love you and I come to love that woman that you done chose to take as your wife. If I didn't, I'd keep my mouth shut up like a barren womb.

"If there be any part of you feel like you need to wait, you back up off of that-there and don't part your lips to ask

Schaumburg's Sweet Reminisce

Marjorie nothin' of the sort. Act like the thought never come into your mind. Man don't ever wanna ask a woman to marry and then change his mind. It ain't right. You need to have your mind made up before you take a knee, 'cause if her daddy come see you man-to-man on the matter on account his babygirl heart torn all to pieces… you gon' have to see 'em man-to-man – won't be no way around it. Ain't nothing no different that any real man would do for his daughter. I reckon what I'm saying to you is sinking in. You ain't stopped sweating since you came in and sat down."

"Yes, sir. I reckon that'd be why I'm sweating."

"You talk to her old man yet?"

"No sir, I wanted to get your blessing first."

"Well, if you sure 'bout this thing, and I don't doubt you know what you want, you don't need to put off no longer talking to her old man. He may need time to think and pray 'bout this-here thing. Marjorie come from good people, but a man be a certain way about his daughter, rightly so. If for some reason he don't give you his blessing, give him some time and then go back man-to-man. I'll be fasting and praying on your behalf."

"Yes, sir."

"Your momma told me that you was still her little baby boy before she died. She was proud of that. I reckon she'd still be proud, wouldn't she?"

"Sir?"

"I'll be, son. You know, it's almost always on account of sin that married folks never do get the full blessing of the marriage bed the way God intended. Reason being, one or the other, if not both, enter into the marriage covenant already defiled. That ain't how God intended. Little do they know, they only cheatin' they ownself.

"Now I hope and pray that ain't the case with you, but if it be so, you settle that thing with God – settle everything with the Lord first; and then you talk to the old man before you ask Marjorie for her hand. If her old man be anything like me, he gon' probably just ask you outright about your relations if he ain't already. You been keeping company with his babygirl for some time now. I know I'd sho' nuff ask that rascal if it were my daughter and dare him to lie to me.

"If the old man give you his blessing, you gonna need to have a long talk with Marjorie. You got to enter into marriage with nothin' hidden and nothin' unconfessed. And I mean *nothin'*. The heart and the mind need to be content. You don't want her weighed down after you's married on account of foolishness. Search yourself real good, and if you still serious about asking her to be your wife, let her know what kind of life you got planned for her. If she in agreement, you and her go over and set with the preacher for a spell.

"Got a soft spot in my heart for your Marjorie and you know how your momma felt towards her. Marjorie was like a daughter to her. Remind me a lot of the woman of God your momma was in a roundabout way. You just do right by her, son. Not too many women like Marjorie. I believe you know that."

"Yes, sir. I know."

"Just do right by her, son. Just do right by her. 'Cause if you don't, I don't think I have to tell you what her old man aim to do to you; and if the good Lord see fit to bless you with any children of your own, you won't even need to

Schaumburg's Sweet Reminisce

question this-here what I'm telling you. Now, I've said my peace."

Chapter Eleven

Most everybody that knew my daddy Benjamin Charles Fouraukis and my momma Marjorie Rose Fouraukis knew me… Millicent Rose Fouraukis – my momma's sweet child and my daddy's babygirl, Millie for short.

Momma and Daddy was childhood sweethearts but nearing the other side of life before I finally came along, their only living offspring.

Daddy farmed land that had been passed down to him from his Great Granddaddy Gideon Myles Fouraukis while Momma kept house and everyone else in line. Said the Lord would keep her in line so nobody else need not try.

Daddy always said when he died he only wanted to be remembered as a faithful servant of God – nothing more, nothing less. Momma on the other hand couldn't have cared less if she was remembered or if her name was even uttered by man, for good or for bad, so long as she heard the Lord say, "Servant, well done."

As a young child, folks often wondered if there wasn't something wrong with me upstairs. Some chose to be kind when asking, but for those who didn't, they never had to be put in their place a second time if Momma had anything to say on the matter.

Reckon it strange to never hear a baby cry none. I even now had my speech backed up a good while after I was born. Back then, the handful of doctors we had was stretched out over several counties and it could be months before you saw one; but Doctor Jesus was who we always called on first anyhow. Momma and Daddy prayed over me every chance they got and Sister Godfrey got up a group of ladies from the church to fast and intercede on my behalf; and in His own special way and in His own special time, God answered.

To hear Momma and Daddy tell it, when God finally saw fit to loose my speech, every thought that entered my mind parted my lips. Spoke better than most grown folk, too. But I was a shy child and mostly carried on only around Momma and Daddy. I reckon I knew what to say all along, but the words just wouldn't come.

Because I didn't talk, I reckon a good number thought I couldn't hear on account every now and then, I heard things a child my age shouldn't. Picked up on things quick, too. But Momma was quick to make me turn loose them things that wasn't proper for a child. I made more than a few meals out of bitter root for "gettin' fresh at the mouth," or what grown folks often called "talkin' all over myself."

I talked so much, I doubt I ever said the same thing the same way twice. I even talked in my sleep. Momma always thought I was having a bad dream, but Daddy just laughed and tried to make out what I was saying.

"Ben, I best go check on Millie. She been talking in her sleep for I don't know how long. Sound like she having a bad dream."

"She alright, woman. She just catching up on her words. Kinda funny hearing her make a fuss in there most every night."

"Well, I don't know, Ben. I can't half make out what she saying. And you know how dark it get in that room in there."

"Marjorie, she alright. How you figure she know it's dark if she sleep? Moon shine bright as day thru that window in there anyhow."

"Don't you get fresh with me, Benjamin Charles. I'm going to see 'bout my child, right now. I need to make sure she alright and my mind ain't gon' rest 'til I do."

"Well, woman. What if your husband have a bad dream?"

"Ben Charles, I reckon you might ought to wake up from it, feel your way through the dark, and come on in there and check on me and Millie."

"I ain't trying to start no fuss with you, woman."

"Well, that's fine by me 'cause I ain't much in the mood for none."

"I just miss you beside me every night, Marjorie."

"I know, Ben. I just need a little more time. Just a little more time…"

Momma would always come in and lay across the foot of my bed. She would lay hands on me and pray most times, too. Her hands were firm but soft and her prayers probably made a few angels cry. Sometimes I'd wake up and if her eyes were closed, I'd watch her until I couldn't hold mine open no more. At some point, Momma would pray herself to sleep and then make her way back to Daddy just before sunrise.

That night was the last night Momma slept at the foot of my bed; she knew her wifely duties couldn't go untended for too much longer. She told me that a wife had to be able to hear her husband's heart even when his heart was shut plum-up and ain't saying nothing, even when it seem like it ain't nothing there. Told me I would have to learn to love past all the fear, pain, pride, and anger to get to it; said most men would have at least one if not all and if he didn't, he hadn't lived long enough.

I slept in the same bed with my momma and daddy from the day I was born until I was three years and a day old. Momma didn't much want me to leave her nipple let alone her side. I was one of only a few babies heard tell of that slept sound through the night. Daddy was grateful for my sound sleep on account he rose before the roosters crowed. Momma did too, but that didn't stop her from stirring throughout the night every chance she got. She'd look me over, up one side and down the other nearly 100 times a night to make sure I was doing alright. Sometimes, she'd wake me up on purpose just to look in my eyes and visit with me.

Daddy would never agree to anybody or anything taking up space in the marriage bed, even me. But he was wise enough to know that he didn't have a dog in that fight. He didn't agree but he understood; said that it was something or another about Momma not being able to fully trust the will of the Lord. He would never say that to Momma, but he knew she knew he already knew.

Said it didn't make sense for him to build that big old

fine crib my momma said she just had to have if I was just gon' sleep in the bed with them. Momma made talk like that crib was so big it could hold three, four, five children easy. They had hoped for a full quiver, but God saw different.

I gave Momma and Daddy back their marriage bed, but I didn't go far. I slept in the fancy crib that Momma kept in arm's reach of her. It was a good while after that before Momma saw fit for me to have my own room, but, once I was in bed, I couldn't get back up unless I had to *use it*. Back then if the man of the house heard a stir, he'd grab his shotgun and ask questions later.

I was a bit awkward as a child, my own kind of precious. Momma kept me bathed, my hair combed, my teeth brushed, my clothes neat and clean, and always greased my lips, knees and elbows. I was beautiful in her eyes and no one could tell her any different.

"You hold your head up, Millicent Rose, I say. You ain't got a thing in this world to hang your head about. You's been created in the image of God and for God's good pleasure."

The callous stares always seemed to send Momma right into a tizzy, but she'd catch herself most times. Me being the only child she'd ever been able to carry to term, Momma was overly protective and rightly so, I guess.

It was a rough carry, too, but she left it all in the Lord's hands. Stayed bed-ridden for six of the nine months.

Momma took ill for a spell right after I was born, but Ms. Willa, one of the last two doulas left in Ned County, nursed Momma back to health in no time. Made sure she ate real good, so I could eat good, too – put a good bit of weight on the both of us.

Schaumburg's Sweet Reminisce

Ms. Willa had no children of her own, but knew everything there was about birthing and raising one.

Gossip was that after all those years, she went the way of the dust never having known a man in that way. Said when she was born, the doctor couldn't now tell if she was a boy or a girl; didn't know what to make of things down there.

But now, Ms. Willa, she'd watch them-there old doctors real close-like. Listened to every word they said. If it was anything she didn't agree with, she'd wait 'til they left out of respect, and then she'd tell the sickly to forget everything that old lying doctor had just told 'em.

"I tell you this-here – you keep listenin' at that old doctor and you sho' nuff gon' be in a bad way and out a whole lot of money and either way gon' suit him just fine. Now, I ain't saying he wrong about everything, but he ain't right 'bout a lot of things," Ms. Willa would say.

Ms. Willa was smart as a whip, but she never let on. Kept a prayer on her lips and everything she needed to nurse a person back to health in a little old scrap of burlap tied up with a slither of purple velvet ribbon tucked away in her bosom. Spoke on things with just a few words unless she was serious. Hadn't had no more than a lick of schooling, but she knew more about these old clay vessels of ours than any of them doctors and they big old fancy words.

Ms. Willa lived on with us for a short while after Momma got better – Momma and Daddy just didn't feel right about sending her back across that hollow to that old empty house she hollowed out of a tree.

As far as Momma and Daddy reasoned, Ms. Willa couldn't wear out her welcome if she tried; asked her to stay with us for as long as she wanted. She was glad to stay on, but just for a spell. She wanted to keep an eye on me and make sure that Momma was strong and back on her feet as a wife and new momma before she parted ways.

Ms. Willa didn't have no more kinfolk left that she know'd of, wasn't all that close nohow. Never gave too much thought to how far-gone the years had gotten. I guess Ms. Willa was too busy bringing life into the world and didn't have time to be sittin' around grieving over life that would soon be going the way of the dust – not hers nor nobody else's.

"Anybody looking for me… just tell 'em to look out yonder, cause I ain't hard to find." Ms. Willa was good people. Always seemed to make the most of what she had wherever she was and with whoever she was with until she got word that the next womb was ripe to give birth.

Anybody she spent time with wanted everybody else to know. The lessons of wisdom stored in them long silver matted locks of hers made for a blessed woman and folks near and far wanted to share in 'em with her. So no, Ms. Willa wasn't hard to find. Anybody needing to get to where she was wouldn't have to put forth much effort at all.

After some time, the call finally came. Ms. Willa blessed our home with prayer, grabbed up her little suitcase, and struck out to help soothe the birth pangs of another labor. We'd never get to spend time like that with Ms. Willa again; death notice said she lived to be 107 years old.

To hear tell of it in the Ned County obituaries, Ms. Willa enjoyed herself pretty good in life. Lived on very little and off the land, yet had everything she needed and always gave based on the reward she knew she had waiting on her in heaven. Ms. Willa knew of her fair share of joy in life.

Schaumburg's Sweet Reminisce

They say before she died, she had done delivered somewhere upwards of 3,000 babies or better. For every child she helped birth into this world, she drew a line on the wall in her tree house and even now marked the ones that didn't make it in red and gave each one a name, a name that she wanted them to have.

Ms. Willa often told of how the Lord would wake her up in the early hours of the morning from a sound sleep. Said He'd tell her to get up and get on her face to pray for the children He saw fit to let live. Most times she'd pray, but sometimes she'd just sit quiet or in song, close her eyes, and try to remember their faces.

Ms. Willa knew God had given her a special work to do and she aimed to do it all before she died; wondered sometimes about all those babies that didn't make it. But Ms. Willa, she didn't fret none. She knew she'd see every last one of 'em again – she just had to wait 'til she got to heaven; and she didn't mind waiting, because she loved the sound of screaming babies.

But now, Ms. Willa would have some dark days while serving the Lord and one day in particular haunted Ms. Willa's soul until the day she died.

One rainy Sunday morning, just before daybreak, Ms. Willa got the call. Needed her help catching babies to a 13-year-old child full of some man and another's wicked seeds. Poor child was a little touched in the mind and up until the time her womb was ready to give way, she ain't know nothing about nothing that was going on. Babies was coming early. Ms. Willa said once them labor pangs hit, she ain't ever seen that kind of fear in all her days.

Child went missing for three days. When they finally found her, she had been torn all to pieces, almost dead. Few months later, her belly started swelling.

Poor child just wasn't strong enough to deliver all them babies – was just a baby herself. Labored nearly all day and died before she could deliver the first one. When they finally opened that poor child up, looked like demons had been fighting inside of her.

That thing torched Ms. Willa's soul. Had her spirit in tears for years after that; didn't know if she could keep doing what she knew in her heart the good Lord put her on this Earth to do. The day that little child died, a part of Ms. Willa died with her.

Ms. Willa was reminded that the will of the Lord is always for the greater good. All them children dying that day took a lot outta folks – brought the whole town together though. Death sometimes got a way of doing that. Folks didn't understand why God would let such a thing happen; had a whole lotta folks doing a whole lotta soul searching. Blacks and whites from all over showed up to the funeral that day. A sight for sore eyes to see so many sharing the same church house with more than a few with the heart to sit down next to each other on the same pew.

Ms. Willa didn't always understand why 'bout some things, but she was wise enough to trust the providence of God even when she didn't.

Ms. Willa couldn't bring herself to catch babies for almost a year after that child died, that is until Mrs. Josephine took need of her and put out the call. Ms. Willa served as Mrs. Josephine's doula-wife for well over 40 years – and two husbands. She was 56 years old when she conceived that last child. Married a man almost 20 years her senior on account her first husband up and died on her. Mrs. Josephine wasn't but 13 when she took her vows before God the first time. Just didn't like being off by herself, she needed to be married, and men didn't seem to mind settling down when it came to Mrs. Josephine on account most men said she rolled and stacked like fresh bales of hay.

Ms. Willa knew of only a handful of other women that babied that late in their years – my momma being one of 'em. Got her to thinking. She hadn't caught a baby for Mrs. Josephine in many years; her own children had since done given her great grandchildren. It didn't take Ms. Willa long to encourage herself in the Lord. She figured this would be the last one on account Mrs. Josephine had done already birthed 12 children and would soon be going through the change.

I used to overhear Momma and some of the mothers from the church talk about the way of a woman that they call "the change." Never did have much good to say about it; but that thing they called the change was hush-talk, just like when it came time for a young girl to flower. Said the change messes with a woman's nerves real bad; sometimes cause a woman to plum-lose her mind five or six times a day. Said it could cause a woman to mess around and run her own husband off if she wasn't careful. All that woman-talk seemed a little strange, had me scared some, and I knew then that I didn't want no parts of none of it.

No sooner than two days after Mrs. Josephine's thirteenth child was born, the poor woman's uterus fell out right where she stood. Said Mrs. Josephine shouted "Glory!" and then fainted before she could shout "Hallelujah." Ms. Willa said that the poor woman's body was just plain-old tired of having children.

Chapter Twelve

Most folks won't own up to it, but if truth be told, there be a little something wrong with every last one of us. A little crazy and a whole lot of sin. Funny how folks don't mind lying to they ownself, but get mad as fire when somebody lie on 'em.

The way I see it, a person's life story is best told in they own words. I never been big on talkin' 'bout myself, but I don't know nobody that know me better than me. I just as well let folks think what they gon' think by what they see me do rather than by what they hear somebody else say.

Momma praised God that I was coming into my own as a young seeker. She prayed daily that I'd soon be loosed from Satan and welcomed into the Ark of Safety. I wouldn't go another Christmas without my own Bible. Got my very own grown-folks' Bible, special-ordered and bound in a heavy cognac-dyed hide with my name braided into the back cover by this old dark-skinned Creole-Indian migrant from Louisiana – called hisself Yeti.

Any time anybody had need of him, they'd send word by one of his old carrier hounds to let him know what they needed and when. He'd trained them hounds of his better than any army general could one of his own soldiers.

Schaumburg's Sweet Reminisce

Yeti could make most anything any reasonable mind could think of, and he had a way about him that most folks liked; them that was well-off called him eccentric. Met everybody in the same spot, at the same time, at the edge of the woods underneath the big red oak, the one that leaned. If you didn't like what he made for you, he'd give it to you for free and throw in a jar of wild mulberry, hot pepper, and muscadine jam. But I only heard tell of that happening one time and that was only because the woman wanted the jam.

Didn't allow folks to lay eyes on him too often; lived life free, tucked away, and off the land. Everything he owned, he used and everything he needed, he knew how to come by without so much as a dime in his pocket.

From near and far, everybody that passed 'round that way joked about how strange a fella he was, said that he looked like he just stopped aging. Nobody really knew how old he was, just certain that he was good and old. Even Yeti had to laugh and admit that he'd lost count, but he always said that he just hoped to live long enough to see tomorrow. Little did he know, he had folks wantin' to make sure his name lived on forever.

Yeti had traveled near and far over the years and somehow or another a bunch of his pictures wound up in some fancy book. Anybody that had ever met him wanted other folks to know they know'd him. Man from South Georgia tracked him down through a girl Yeti courted years ago. Said she was still mad as fire at him, but a few dollars in her hand seemed to make her forget and remember all at the same time. He'd been trying for months to find him. They say that old Georgia boy handed Yeti one of them big ole cashier's checks for a right smart amount of money but Yeti told him that he'd settle for his truck. They shook on it and old Yeti drove that truck 'til it rusted out. After that, he filled that truck bed with dirt and moss and started growing these funny-looking mushrooms that everybody just had to get they hands on. Talk over town was that a few youngin's had done tried to run off with a few of Yeti's mushrooms but the hounds got to 'em. Nearly chewed 'em up. Lotta folks thought Yeti ought to put his hounds down, but Yeti wasn't for it.

Momma hated what happened to them wayward children but felt like them mushrooms might have been the work of the devil anyhow and wanted no part in it. But she was well-pleased with Yeti's work on my Bible cover and said she didn't know nobody hungry enough for the Word of God to steal a Bible; and in the same stern breath, she assured me that I wouldn't be losing mine. She didn't much care if I read or understood anything else, but I was to study and learn that Bible daily.

Daddy said he thought I ought to start with the Book of Proverbs. I was to read it three times over before starting any other book and to put into practice what I learned every day. After Proverbs, Momma thought I ought to study the Book of John, my daddy's favorite, so that in time, I'd come to receive Jesus Christ as my Lord and Savior and be able to witness with the help of the Holy Spirit to some lost soul.

We would sometimes read together after supper, Daddy and me. Momma would sit and listen in while she put her curlers in her hair. We'd take turns reading verses of Scripture until I fell asleep. Half the time I didn't understand what I was reading, but Daddy told me to always pray for understanding before and after I studied God's word, and in due time, He would open my understanding and reveal His heart and His will to me.

"The Word of God teaches at all times, babygirl. All you got to do is be ready to obey It when It speaks."

Schaumburg's Sweet Reminisce

The Spirit of God had been wooing me to the foot of the cross for a while and one Sunday morning I surrendered my whole self to Jesus Christ and received Him as my Lord and Savior. I didn't even feel myself walk up to the front of the church. After I was baptized, everybody came around and welcomed me with the right hand of fellowship into the family of God.

On fifth Sundays, Pastor Tisdale would let me read the Scriptures from his Bible during service while he delivered the sermon; I got to read the church announcements every other Sunday when Sister Flossie Carver was away visiting her sister who had taken ill. I always felt like I wanted to preach a sermon of my own standing on top of that wobbly pine box proclaiming the Word of God, but I just ended up saying "Amen" or "Hallelujah" if Pastor Tisdale said something that I'd heard before or when Momma or Daddy did. All the mothers would love on me after service and that made Momma proud, but she always reminded me to seek God's reward and not the praise of man.

Momma took to schooling me from home. It had been her and Daddy's plan all along, even before I was born. Momma believed God for my speech just like she believed God for me and she knew in her heart that God would answer, but not until He got good and ready. Said a person can't learn nothing until the good Lord open the mind nohow.

"You get your lesson today alright, babygirl?

"Yes, sir." I looked at Momma all wall-eyed and she looked at me and then we both looked at Daddy.

"We getting there, Ben."

"Well, babygirl, by the time all is said and done, you

gon' be as smart as your momma."

I looked at Momma and smiled. She smiled back and then told me to go wash my face and hands for supper. Look like something happened on the inside of me when I heard my daddy say that. From that day on, I promised Momma I would always try my best.

Momma was a good teacher. Taught me everything from the Bible to the birds and the bees. Even taught me how to use proper English, but didn't make me use it all the time on account she hardly ever did. Only time I had to was when I was in mixed company, folks of certain importance. Any other time I could express myself in any way I wanted as long as I wasn't lying or talking all over myself. Her thoughts on the matter was that proper English didn't really make folks 'round Schaumburg no never mind as long as they could believe the words comin' out my mouth. She taught me a bunch of that fancy math she liked so much too, but told me I'd probably have to leave Schaumburg if I ever wanted to use it.

Every year they'd send Mrs. Gladys Powell out to the house to test me in my learning. Her and Momma didn't make nice at first, but Momma settled down after a while and Mrs. Gladys opened up. Momma and Mrs. Gladys were schoolmates from the first day of school to the last. Truth be told, Momma was way smarter than Mrs. Gladys and Mrs. Gladys knew it; everybody did. Year after year she'd come and her and Momma would share just a little bit more with one another. They come to be real good friends after that.

As time passed on, I'd finish school early, just like Momma, except I'd finish one year sooner than she did and that made her and Daddy proud, real proud.

I came into my womanly way for the first time over in

the night. Momma had always told me that it would be a special day for me and for her, but I didn't find a thing in the world so special about it — still haven't 'til this day.

I knew Momma would be up in a little while, so I didn't wake her. I lay there in my womanly way, scared and trembling, wondering why God would allow such a thing. I had heard talk of this-here thing that had come over me and I didn't like none of what I'd heard.

I didn't have to say not one word that morning; Momma knew. She had to give me one of her sanitary napkins to wear that morning until we could go find a size fitting for me. The front of that pad covered my navel and the back nearly rested in the small of my back. For the first time in my young life, I didn't wanna be no girl — but I didn't wanna be no little dirty, nappy-headed boy neither.

"You check your bloomers every chance you get, Millie, ya hear? I don't want you messing up your clothes."

"Yes, ma'am." I didn't know why she felt like she had to say that in front of my daddy, but she did. I stayed in my room until after he left for the field that morning.

I was so fightin'-mad, I wanted to cry, but Momma already was. I figured it didn't make sense to upset the house any more than I already had, so I held back my tears. I could tell the whole thing caught Daddy off-guard because he left the house that morning without his breakfast or coffee.

Momma called out to Daddy a few times, but he was long-gone. She was so wound up that she didn't even realize that Daddy had already kissed her goodbye and told her he'd be home early for lunch.

Momma's daily mission usually started before her feet hit the floor in the mornings, always with a spirit to serve. She hadn't stopped walking or talking since she woke up that morning, but that was every bit of her. Seemed real beside herself about me becoming a woman and all. Much more than I was.

"How you feeling, Millie? Is you cramping any? What about your head? Is your head hurting you?"

"No, ma'am."

"Well, you just wait for it."

"I don't like being in a womanly way, Momma."

"Child, not many womenfolk do. You just be grateful you didn't start your period your first day of high school over there at that school-house like your momma did. I near 'bout worried myself to death all day thinking that everybody knew what was going on in my bloomers. I couldn't wait to get myself home. Momma had been telling me that I would become a young lady soon, so she started making me carry a sanitary napkin or two in my pocketbook just in case and I was so glad she knew what she knew because it turned out to be true just as sure as I'm sittin' here."

Momma smiled and scrunched my Shirley Temple curls into place.

"Geraldine did such a good job on your hair, Millie."

Geraldine was known around town for her press and curl; had been doing her own hair since the age of 11. Had seasoned many a straightening combs in her day.

"Thank you, Momma."

Schaumburg's Sweet Reminisce

"You welcome, baby. Go on and finish up your breakfast, now. Reckon we ought to be gettin' started."

Momma made things as nice as she could for me for my first day of high school, but I still wouldn't be going no further than the kitchen table. Bought me a few fancy school clothes and a little stain for my lips. I even now got to take school pictures every year, too.

My womanly pains starting rising up halfway through the morning, so Momma figured it best we call it an afternoon and sent me to go lay down.

"Millie, you go rest yourself, now. As soon as I can get this-here water to a boil, I'll bring you a hot water pad. It'll make you feel better."

I didn't know what Momma was gonna have me do with that hot water pad; I was just glad to know that there was something that God had in His plan to make me feel better.

I slept right through lunch, and just as well, on account I felt shame that my daddy knew I was in my womanly way. After Daddy left back out for the field, Momma came up again to check on me. I fell into her arms before she could sit down good, just like I did when I was younger. Momma's arms had healing in 'em – I know'd it for myself.

"Your daddy told me to tell you he missed you at lunch today. I told him you was probably just a bit shame-faced. I reckon he felt some kinda way too. Told me to tell you that you gonna always be his babygirl."

Momma talked mostly and I listened to all she had to say about such things as carrying myself as a proper and chaste young lady; but Momma had already taught me most of what she said by the way she lived, so she really didn't have to say much, if anything at all. But I was glad she did.

"A lady should always look and smell like a lady, whether she got fine clothes to put on her back or nothing but hand-me-downs; whether she got running water and sweet oils or if she ain't got nowhere to bathe but from a creek; whether she got hair that run halfway down her back or no more than she can pinch – a lady should always look and smell like a lady. But above all of that, a lady should be pure on her marriage night."

But now, Momma thought that there was only one thing worse than a loose woman and that was a woman trying to be a man.

Momma stayed on the matter of my purity more than anything, but she made sure to tell me that it was God's will for me to save myself until marriage – not hers. Little did she know, marriage and the marriage bed were the farthest things from my mind. I didn't take too kindly to boys; they always seemed to have a strange way about 'em. I guess maybe they felt the same way about me.

Daddy would be home soon and expecting supper, but Momma stayed a good while longer talking and loving on me until I fell back to sleep.

*   *✳❋✳*   *

"Hey, Millie Rose."

"Ray Parker, don't nobody call me that but you."

"Well, that's your name, ain't it?"

"I don't know who told you that, Ray Parker. My name

Schaumburg's Sweet Reminisce

is Millicent Rose Fouraukis and I don't know that it's proper you calling me by my middle name, nohow; and I only let folks I like call me Millie."

"Well, what can I call you?"

"You sittin' right here beside me, Ray Parker, so you really ain't got to call my name at all."

"You ain't like most girls."

"Well, I guess you know who my momma and my daddy be?"

"I know who they be."

"Well, then why you go and say such a fool thing, Ray Parker?"

"I don't know."

"Boy, you wanna go get some watermelon? I'll race you."

"Alright."

Ray Parker was the first boy Momma and Daddy let me sit with on a blanket by myself at the church picnic; but only because it was Pastor Tisdale's great-nephew and neither one of us quite knew what misbehaving was in the manner of relations. Ray Parker's daddy had done run off before he was even born and his momma would send him south during the summer so Pastor Tisdale could teach him how to be a Godly man.

"My uncle said he see a little preacher-man in me. I think I'm gonna be a preacher like my uncle when I grow up. You can be my first lady, like my auntie."

"You hush that fresh talk with me, Ray Parker, before I tell my daddy."

"Okay, okay, don't tell your daddy."

"I ain't gonna tell him this time, but you better mind your mouth and your manners."

"Girl, you got a bug on you!"

"No, I don't."

"Girl, yes you do! You want me to get it off?"

"No, I don't, Ray Parker!"

"Alright."

By the time we made it home that evening, I had a whelp on my arm the size of a nickel and it stung real bad.

"Babygirl, what done happened to your arm?

"I don't know, Daddy."

"Marjorie, come look at this-here whelp on babygirl's arm."

"Millie, what done happened with your arm? Look like something done bit you."

"I don't know, Momma. Ray Parker told me I had a bug on me and I told him, 'No I didn't' two times. He asked me if I wanted him to get it off and I told him 'No!'"

"Well, child of mine, look like you ought to done told him yes, because I don't know the likes of what done got a hold of you. Ben Charles, what it look like to you?"

Schaumburg's Sweet Reminisce

"Marjorie, I declare I don't know."

The more Momma and Daddy talked about it, the more scared I got. Momma started checking me for fever and other things.

"Well, babygirl, did you feel it when it took a bite out of you?"

"Yes, sir. I just thought it was a mosquito or a chigger or whatnot."

"Ben Charles, will you please call over there and see if Ray Parker know what done bit this girl?"

Daddy was headed to the phone before Momma could even finish saying what she had to say.

By the time Daddy got done talking to First Lady, Pastor Tisdale, and Ray Parker, Momma had done fixed me up with a little kerosene and black pine tar – took the sting right out.

"Well, Ray Parker didn't know what kind of bug it was. He said he asked you if he could get it off and you told him no, babygirl."

"I did tell Ray Parker no, Daddy."

"Well, don't you think he was just trying to be kind to you? I believe he was just showing hisself friendly."

"I didn't ask him if he was trying to be kind or not, Daddy, on account I didn't think I had no bug on me. And Ray Parker ain't no saint. Ray Parker called me out my name."

"How's that, babygirl? That don't sound like Ray

Parker."

"Ray Parker called me Millie Rose, Daddy, and I told him my name wasn't no Millie Rose. I told Ray Parker my name was Millicent Rose Fouraukis."

"Well, babygirl, I don't think Ray Parker called you out your name. I think it's alright for him to call you Millie Rose."

"But Daddy, don't nobody call me Millie Rose. And Momma, Ray Parker come talking about I was gonna be his first lady when he start preaching."

Daddy looked at Momma and started laughing. I knew then for sure that Ray Parker wasn't gon' be no preacher.

Momma told me to go get my bath and get ready for bed and that's what I did. She said that her and Daddy would be in later to talk to me about the way I treated Ray Parker; said that I was gonna have to make things right. Momma and Daddy both kept sniggling but I didn't know what was so funny.

Everything in and around Schaumburg was changing – even me – and the likes of Bosch Jacobs had almost everybody fooled. Claimed he was just passing through the deep south on to wherever his thoughts and the few coins in his pocket took him next. But we all knew better. Bosch Jacobs turned out to be a big-time movie producer from California. Put our little town on the map when he brought all them Hollywood actors and actresses to Schaumburg.

Wasn't too long after that the well-to-do started coming out the woodwork. Bought up every farm and acre of land they could in Ned County just on account they could, I reckon. Folks around Schaumburg had done seen more money from the sale of just a few acres of land than all the generations before 'em had done made they entire lifetime.

A politician all the way from Maine made Brother and Sister Godfrey an offer they couldn't pass on. Fella never even set foot in Schaumburg, went off the word of a few people that had seen it and told him about it.

Momma cried when she heard the news. Said she was losing her best friend-girl. Sister Godfrey couldn't even now bear to tell Momma in her own words. Everybody hated to see 'em go, but Brother and Sister Godfrey had been looking forward to taking it easy and now they could sho' nuff.

Folks was after our land too. Too many to count. Before Daddy could even get a word out about what them folks was offering at his meeting, Momma had done already put a big "NOT FOR SALE" sign at the end of the road. It was hard to tell if it was meant for them rich folks over there in that meeting place or if it was meant for my Daddy – I reckon it was meant for all of 'em.

"Woman, I saw your big sign up at the end of the road there. Don't you even wanna hear how much they's offering?"

"Ben Charles, I already know they's offering a whole lot of money for this-here house and all of this-here land, but quite frankly, I don't care how much they's offering. You built me this-here house with your bare hands from the ground up. This-here is our home and home to all them that God see fit to allow to come after us. Ben Charles, you hear me good now – the only other home I aim to live in is the one that my Lord and Savior Jesus Christ promised that He done gone away to prepare for me."

Sheriell Scott

"I hear your heart, woman."

I reckon the thought of Momma living anywhere other than the home that she'd made for me and Daddy all those years didn't set too well with her. Daddy said he was grateful that Momma was content with the life he had made for us in Schaumburg. Said every man needed to know that his family was happy.

Not another word was spoke on the matter for several years, that is, until Daddy got a letter in the mail letting him know that the value of our land had more than tripled and offers to buy were still coming in. Daddy picked up Momma and swung her around the front yard like a little rag doll until they both run out of breath, Momma from laughing and screaming and Daddy because Momma had picked up a little weight.

＊　＊※＊　＊

I was becoming a young woman and Momma couldn't have been more beside herself. Every now and then she would share cause to mention how beautiful I was and how certain parts of me was filling out right nicely, much more than she had at my age. Always found herself of the mind to tell me how she had done run into so-and-so, so-and-so, and how their cousin's son's nephew had grow'd up to be a handsome and respectable young man who was in the church; or how the Reverend Dr. Bishop's son was following in his footsteps.

I often heard her talking to Daddy about grandbabies. Those talks always seemed to be one-sided at the beginning because Daddy didn't want to hear talk of it, but by the time Momma finished daydreaming, she had Daddy more excited than at first and by the time Daddy finished daydreaming, the

Schaumburg's Sweet Reminisce

whole house was crawling with babies; and since Momma's womb had since been long closed, I reckoned they all belonged to me.

Chapter Thirteen

Nearly half the town of Schaumburg came out to help me lay Momma and Daddy's earthly forms to rest. God gave us such a beautiful fall afternoon. A great showing of love from hearts and hands, old and new, near and far. My heart couldn't help but be uplifted.

It served me well to have both the funeral and burial service out beneath Old Moses. There was something about that old tree that just gave me comfort. Daddy used to always joke that that old oak would outlive every soul born to Schaumburg. He may have been onto something. Old Moses was once said to be well over 700 years old and still standing strong, just like my Daddy used to.

After we returned dust-to-dust, we all headed back up toward the main house for the repass. As I rode in the back of that freshly painted, flower-filled wagon drawn by two of the finest white mares you ever did wanna see, I watched in the distance as some still stood graveside saying their last goodbyes while others walked arm-in-arm reminiscing, probably about the good old days judging by the laughter and also by the tears. Hearts were sho' nuff heavy at times, but all-in-all, I reckon we did our best to celebrate life in death for two of the finest folks we ever know'd to live. Hard days lay ahead, but we'd all return to our joy in due time – there ain't a sorrow known to man that heaven can't heal.

Everybody was asked to wear white and did so in kind, one of Momma's many requests. It looked like a field of white gardenia, Momma's favorite flower. Blankets and picnic baskets lined the ground and some even brought along a little nip for the home-going celebration.

The air was stirring a wee bit – smelled just like it used to when I was a little girl and Momma and me would shortcut through the meadow down into the bottoms to pick muscadines and huckleberries. And nobody made muscadine wine like my daddy. Though she would never admit it, Momma resented the fact that muscadines was so plentiful year after year. She couldn't understand why people couldn't pick they own muscadines and make they own wine.

*   *❋*   *

"All I'm saying, Ben Charles, is that if they can make they own preserves and whatnot, why not they own wine? Not that much difference, all's I'm saying."

Momma never liked the idea that so many people looked to Daddy year after year for their Christmas nip. People we hadn't seen nor heard from all year would start coming around in late August, talking right loud and overly friendly; a lot of the women who wouldn't give Momma the time of day after Sunday service were all smiles and compliments come Sunday meeting muscadine fermenting time. By the close of October, the phone would start ringing at all hours of the morning and night – people placing orders and Momma taking 'em; drove her plum-out of her mind most days.

Most anything church folks did in and around Schaumburg that might cause a brother or sister to stumble was to be brought before the elders of the church to be weighed and voted on; and whatever was agreed to was what would stand.

The men around town would buy their wine from Daddy by the quart, but the women could only buy their wine from Momma by the pint; and Daddy wasn't backing up off on that. Momma wasn't too set on none of that wine-selling business but she wasn't all the way against it neither. She just wanted whatever part she had in it all to be nice and done proper. She would take and write a verse of scripture on every jar sold; figured she had a duty to remind those that partook of the fruit of the vine to not be given to drunkenness.

Things seemed to be coming along just fine until a few of the church elders decided that enough was enough. Said that all that wine-selling business was giving place to Satan and wouldn't no good come of it and called a church meeting.

Now, certain men of the church had a strong word for those elders. Said that as long as my daddy's muscadine wine kept they wives from raisin' Cain and more than willing to perform their wifely duties, they aimed to keep right on buying it. Some got a little hot under the collar while others tried to keep the peace.

Momma and Daddy wasn't allowed to come to the meeting – they wanted everybody free to speak they mind whether they was in agreement or not.

After a good while into the meeting, they still wasn't no closer to making up they minds than when they first started. Voted nearly five times on account people kept coming and leaving at different times. The elders agreed to bring that meeting to a close and have another meeting after church on Sunday – wasn't doing nothing but fussing and fighting nohow. They figured folks ought to be pretty tame on the Lord's day. The Elders was hoping that the Lord would give Pastor Tisdale a rhema word to set things right on the matter.

Just as they was about to give the benediction, some of the wives had done got together and decided to show up and be heard on the matter; and all those that couldn't come, signed they name on a piece of paper for it to be made known that they was in agreement to keep their Brother Ben in business. They'd already been praying for increase in next year's harvest. Those women of God had come to be heard and Sister Mae Esther made it known that they wasn't leaving until every woman had had her say. Sister Mae Esther told them elders that she and her ladies didn't much care if they left or stayed, but they were there for the meeting and would stay there all night talking to one another if they had to.

"Sister Mae Esther, what is all this here? I declare, a woman ought to know her place and stay in it," rebuked Elder Brother Deacon.

"Go on and hush him up now, Sister Mae Esther, but don't shame him too bad." Sister Mae Esther had full backing from nearly every woman that knew herself to be one.

"And just where is a woman's place, Elder Brother Deacon? In the home? Well, I've been there all day, until now. My house is kept and put in order. My children done been fed, done had they baths, and done said their prayers. And not to shame you in something you already know, Elder Brother Deacon, but there sits my husband on that-there church pew you sittin' on. Now, he told me that it'd be alright for me to be here if I felt the need to be here. So, I'm here and I'm reminded that I'm standing in the house of the Lord, but I'll remind you, Elder Brother Deacon, that the doors of the church is always open – not just on Sunday."

"That's right, Sister Mae Esther. I reckon he heard you."

"Amen."

"I know he shame."

"I say my wife know her place pretty well, Elder Brother Deacon. You and the rest of the ladies go head on and have your say, baby."

By the time the very last woman had done had her say on things, they took another vote and decided to allow Daddy to keep selling his wine. Daddy promised to be his brother's keeper and he was. If you bought wine, your name went in a ledger, and anybody that wanted to see how much wine you bought and when you bought it was to have no problem doing so.

* ❋❋❋ *

Momma and Daddy saved every dime they made from the wine sales, but couldn't no more figure out what to do with the money after they tithed off it. Momma had one thing in mind and Daddy had something or another, but they couldn't have been more different. They had always said if they couldn't agree on a matter, they'd pray and let it be until somehow things met on one accord.

Daddy had dreams of me attending Harvard and becoming a Supreme Court Justice, something he remembered reading all about in high school when he wasn't chasing my Momma. Momma just wanted to keep saving so I would have a good start in life or a little something put away after she and Daddy went on home to be with the Lord. She had hopes of me being married with a whole heap of babies – maybe start my own little schoolhouse for girls.

"Millie, you been thinking any about settling yourself down with a nice young Godly man, give me and your daddy a mess of grandbabies? Sho' would be nice to live long enough to see my great, great grandchildren. I probably won't have eyes well enough to see 'em, but if I could just hear whichever one call on the name of the Lord, I'll be sho' nuff satisfied. What you think about what I said, Millie?

"I don't know, Momma."

"What you mean you don't know, child?"

"I mean, I don't wanna get married none, Momma. And if I don't get married, I ain't got to be worrying about having no children."

"Why, Millie!? Lord Jesus! Child, you's got to tell me something. Ain't you got all those silly feelings for any of them young men that attend Sunday morning service, or Sunday evening service, or Wednesday night Bible meeting? All them young men that visit from them other churches? Child of mine, is you blind?"

"I seen 'em."

"Well, what you think about 'em?"

"Nothing, Momma. I just don't think about 'em."

"Don't none of them young suitors make your

stomach nervous? Make you laugh and feel silly when you see 'em?"

"No, ma'am."

"Don't none of 'em make you feel shame-faced?"

"No, ma'am."

"Well, don't you think you might wanna give me and ya daddy some grandbabies."

"I don't think about that neither, Momma."

"Child, go on outta here. I just don't know what else to say. Benjamin Charles!"

"What is it, woman?"

"Your Millie gonna have to tell you, 'cause I don't understand nothing she saying and neither do she."

I believe Momma's heart died a little that day. Truth was, I hadn't yet decided what I would do with myself – because I didn't know. Not much about the world excited me. Schaumburg was my world. Nothing in me desired marriage, not in the least bit. But even if it did, I knew that any man I married would always be second to my daddy. The way I figured, if it was God's will for me to get married, He would will my heart to desire marriage.

*　*✻❈✻*　*

Schaumburg's muscadine fermenting time wine-selling days came to an end about three years in. Looked like more than a few had found cause to stumble.

Schaumburg's Sweet Reminisce

On they way home one Saturday evening after setting up for Sunday morning communion, Deacon and Deaconess Puryear caught a bunch of the church's young people red-handed down by Old Man Tarver's creek swimming in their bloomers.

To hear Deacon Puryear tell it, them young people was so full of that wine and carrying on so 'til they didn't know if they was coming or going; one right after another, sipping, cussing and carrying on like they had done forgot they'd been saved.

Deaconess Puryear could barely set her eyes on it all on account she helped raise 'em up – most of they mammies and pappies, too. Anybody who knew Deaconess Puryear knew she held a special place in her heart for every child that was born of a woman, so it nearly drained her heart dry to see them kids down there on that creek bed half-naked, gyrating, and getting fresh with one another still wet behind the ears, or at least she still hoped they all was. Told Deacon Puryear that she had a mind to go straight in to see the Pastor first thing Sunday morning and have each one of those youngin's turn in their purity cards and take the month-long class all over again on account of what her eyes had seen.

"Puryear, you put the fear of the Lord in 'em, now – down there carrying on like wild animals."

Deacon Puryear grabbed his shotgun from the gun rack in his truck to let off a few rounds just to clear 'em all out of there – had to. Scared if he didn't get 'em outta that water, one of 'em would surely drown, if not all of 'em.

"Aim towards the sky, Puryear. You don't see too good."

Sheriell Scott

"Alright, woman. If you gon' tell me to shoot... don't tell me *how* to shoot. You just sit there and put your head down and I'll tell you when to cover your ears."

"I'll just go on and cover 'em now, Puryear. You just don't mess around and shoot one of them children."

"I won't. Cover your ears now, woman. I'm about to let off a few."

"How's that, Puryear?"

"I say cover your ears, woman!"

"My ears was covered, Puryear. That's why come I couldn't hear you the first time."

It took a month of Sundays, but the kids finally fessed up and admitted to stealing the wine from they own mommas and daddies. They'd been tip-toeing and sneaking around for weeks until they each had their share to add to an old milk bottle.

Pastor made every last one of 'em confess and ask for forgiveness before the church. Put 'em all in a circle and the whole church prayed for 'em, one-by-one.

Not too long after that, Pastor Tisdale said that some of the deacons was complaining privately that they had nearly lost control of their wives.

First Lady Tisdale had more than her fair share of wives confide that now that they were more than willing to fulfill their wifely duties, that their husbands wasn't able to satisfy. A few of the ladies were even so bold as to ask First Lady if she would talk to the Pastor and see if he wouldn't deliver a sermon on 1 Corinthians 7: 3-5, and maybe cut

Schaumburg's Sweet Reminisce

those Monday and Friday night deacons' meetings a little short – just until muscadine season was over.

Church house was known to be a little scarce come some Sunday mornings during muscadine fermenting time, but it wasn't no secret as to why. Folks who had a little too much the night before would rather folk assume what they would than see with they own eyes what was.

For weeks Daddy wouldn't seem much like himself, carrying around a nagging feeling that he hadn't been setting such a good example for the church with his wine-selling business. Thought that it might ought to come to an end. He'd have to put about five young men out of work, but he felt in his heart that God would provide and He did. Thought he'd talk it out with Pastor Tisdale and see what he had to say on the matter.

"Man is free to make his own choices, Brother Ben, but if you feel in your heart that you give cause for your brother to stumble, be obedient to the Word of God."

"Yes sir, Pastor, I believe that's me and Marjorie's feelings on things. We believe it be for the best to shut everything down. Everything lawful don't need to be lived out."

With all the money they saved, Momma and Daddy figured on paying off the last year owed on the church's debt – felt like it was only right. They kept that matter between 'em so not to have any of the church members tempted to hold back they tithes and offerings.

I reckon a handful of folks who hadn't been coming to church before muscadine wine fermenting time found a little more of something they'd been needing on account they kept right on coming; and just as He would have it, God kept right on adding to the Church.

Pastor Tisdale used to always say that God has a blessing in every storm, but you got to have your eyes open and on Him whilst you ridin' it out.

*   ✳✳✳   *

Call 'em crazy, but some folks 'round Schaumburg used to say that there was a certain kind of smell that stirred about the air when a family laid a loved one to rest. Daddy always said that he never smelled nothing except fresh dirt, but said it was probably what educated folks referred to as nostalgia – heavy hearts thinking on days past is how he described it.

Every now and then, Daddy would get a good whiff of his granddaddy's tobacco barn and the musty salves he used to work into his muscles in the evenings to soothe his aches and pains. Said his granddaddy taught his daddy how to make a stout batch of that salves and his daddy taught him.

PopPop started using that salve to heal the scars from the first and last toe-to-toe he had with his daddy for stealing tobacco out the barn one night to trade for a pistol, one of them old guns from the war. He traded it with some old up-to-no-good fella passing through town looking for trouble. The pistol didn't even now shoot, but Granddaddy Myles didn't care to know all that on account he didn't ask. To hear my daddy tell it, Granddaddy Myles beat PopPop like he stole something – on account he had. PopPop said at the time he really thought that my Granddaddy Myles might have killed him with his bare hands; told him that he would rather have seen any man kin to him dead than to know him to be a thief or an unbeliever.

Schaumburg's Sweet Reminisce

"A man only need to take another man's pride… not his life, if he can help it. Only need to kill what he plan to eat and a shotgun'll suit any man just fine."

PopPop said that was the only thing Granddaddy Myles said to him after nearly beating him into the ground.

While my daddy was alive, you'd never catch him with a pipe in his hand let alone his mouth or drinking hard whiskey unless he was fighting some kind of nasty fever – had no desire for such vices.

*   *❉❧❉*   *

Just before those beautiful white mares pulled up to the house, I had a bit of my own nostalgia – Stankin Ben. Of all the things in my mind to think on.

Stankin Ben was the biggest hog I had ever seen in my life and he ate everyday… all day. After he started growing tusks, Daddy pinned him up all to himself to stank on his own.

Somehow it became my job to slop the hogs and by that time Stankin Ben had done got so big and lazy he could barely move. After Daddy made that special trough, Stankin Ben ate the majority of his meals laying down with his eyes closed. Wasn't much to say about Stankin Ben other than he lived, he ate, he stank, and he somehow died.

Momma was the last one to see Stankin Ben alive on account she had to slop him because I was helping Brother and Sister Godfrey out at the store. Nobody ever really knew what happened that day out there in that hog pen; nobody but Momma, Stankin Ben, and the Lord Jesus Christ Himself. But what we did know was that Stankin Ben was dead, Momma was covered in slop and mud from head to toe, and from that day forward she got real fussy whenever anybody brought up Stankin Ben.

From time to time, me and Daddy would share a good laugh and try and guess what happened, but that wasn't a conversation we would ever dare let Momma hear. The only thing we could think of was that old Stankin Ben may have made a sudden move toward Momma and scared her. Daddy said Momma probably just beat old Stankin Ben to death after that. Old Stankin Ben was stankin' and just big for no good reason – never bothered nobody, except Momma.

That evening Stankin Ben came up dead, I stood outside the hog pen and watched while Daddy dressed him. We talked about all the bacon and sausage we was gon' get to eat. Daddy was happy because now he had more than enough meat to try out some of his new rubs in his best smoker. Figured he'd dress about a quarter of old Stankin Ben and sell him over town. Wasn't no way the three of us could've ate all that meat before it went bad. Daddy planned to make lard, hog head cheese, and cracklings.

We'd put our plan together and we couldn't wait. Daddy was of the mind to smoke half a shoulder that night but decided against it. Had been curing a whole heap of wood chips since early spring and they wasn't yet ready – but they would soon be. He reckoned they'd be ready just before the winter hit.

Daddy had old Stankin Ben dressed and put up in no time. Had to on account he didn't know how old Stankin Ben died. And even though Momma was tight-lipped on things, Daddy said it wasn't no way that meat could have spoiled that quick; and if me and Daddy had our way, old Stankin Ben was gonna make for some good eatin'.

Schaumburg's Sweet Reminisce

Momma beckoned for us to come up to the house. Daddy started to grin and I knew why he was grinning because I was grinning too. We could smell how pretty Momma had made herself after killing Stankin Ben and we was both well-pleased without having laid eyes on her. We met her coming up the walkway from the back of the house.

We was pretty happy about things and Daddy couldn't wait to tell Momma what all we had talked about. "Well, woman, look like we done seen the last of Stankin Ben. Me and Millie, we got all that meat dressed and put up."

"Well, I'm glad to hear that, Benjamin Charles, but I don't wants to have nothing else to do with that stankin hog of yours. Should've let the buzzards have at 'em."

"Is that right?"

"Every word I said, Ben Charles."

"Well, I sho' hate you feel that way, woman. That's a whole lotta meat to let go to waste."

"All them rubs and smokers you got, you can get a pretty penny for that meat selling it over town – stand to make more selling it that way than you would selling it at the market. I done already called Brother and Sister Godfrey; said they'd be more than happy to sell all the bacon, sausage, and chops you got."

"Alright, woman."

"Millie, you come on with me so I can put you in the tub. Gotta little cobbler waiting for you up at the house. You coming on now, Ben Charles?"

"I'll be on in a minute, woman. Headin' to the shed to

wash some of this-here blood off me. Don't wanna track it in the house."

"Alright, but don't be long, I got a big bowl of cobbler waiting for you, too."

"Alright, I'll be on in a minute."

"Momma, can I eat my cobbler first?"

"No, ma'am. You get your bath, you eat that cobbler, and you go to bed."

"Yes, ma'am."

Chapter Fourteen

Like any other repass, the menfolk huddled together to talk their talk about crops and fishing while the womenfolk shared recipes and beauty remedies and fixed plates for the children and their menfolk.

Everything seemed to be going along, as it would. The day wasn't too happy and it wasn't too sad neither; but I still had my joy. If you ask me, it was just how Momma and Daddy would have wanted it; but there was something mighty special about the repass, something particular that stood out to me in the midst of such a great show of love – much unlike how the world had started to turn, even Schaumburg.

Every blanket with young children had a husband and a wife; every blanket with a silver-haired widow had a son or a daughter sitting at her side, gently holding the hand that still proudly wore its wedding band. Every blanket with a silver-haired man had a silver-haired woman. Some blankets sat three, four, even five generations; some even more if you cared to count the generations still in the womb and even now in some of the quilts they was sittin' on.

The love of family was the one thing on Earth that was supposed to bear you up until you got your ticket to heaven. Nowadays, ain't too many folks thinking about going to heaven and if the thought do cross they mind, they don't give much thought to sending nothing ahead of 'em; ain't making sure nobody coming behind 'em neither.

I didn't have a family or a blanket of my own to sit on that day, but I could have rested myself and my life's sorrows on any one of them-there blankets I so chose.

Looking out across that pasture had me thinking what it would've been like had I given Momma and Daddy a blanket of their own – a son and a mess of grandbabies. That would have made both her and Daddy real proud, but the good Lord knows best. Momma and Daddy hadn't been gone long, but the memories shared that day with friends and loved ones have held me tightly through the years.

What Momma and Daddy had was nearly next to perfect, but I wondered if folks who got married ever gave thought to the one promise that life offers – death, if the Lord tarries. You try to make the most of life doing right by one another only to somehow overshadow the natural course of things to come, all the while hoping not to end up graveside draped in sorrow begging for just a little bit more time, telling that old empty shell that it should have been you. But, if truth be told, don't nobody really want to be the first to go; they just don't want to be left behind to witness life departing death – because as sure as we living, we dying.

Daddy had never been one to hide his feelings and the way he mourned Momma even in her sickness made a lot of people wonder if they would respond in kind if they were in my daddy's shoes. Momma and Daddy had the kind of marriage they had because they always prayed for God's perfect will to be done no matter what it cost 'em. I remember how pitiful Daddy was. Never know'd him to feel that way about nothin' or nobody, except the Lord. I never wanted to feel what Daddy felt, ever.

About a year or so after I left home, couldn't have been no more than 17, Momma and Daddy decided to turn that big empty house into a bed and breakfast. Momma wasn't truly herself unless she had somebody else to look after, whether it be family or a complete stranger. With all that she did taking care of us, her wifely duties never seemed like work even after all those years.

Folks came few and far between but always managed to stay a good while longer than they had planned too. I always looked forward to our talks, especially when they had a boarder. Momma would be sure to fill me in real good. We'd sometimes talk for hours.

Daddy was the type of man that didn't think it was proper for a husband and wife to go to bed one before the other, so with Momma perched on his lap, Daddy went to sleep and Momma talked with me all evening. And like always, a few seconds into that old hide of his and he was out. Not sure how Daddy slept through it all because Momma's voice carried and we laughed often, but Daddy still managed to call on a few hogs. One thing's for sure, as a child I dared not pretend as if I didn't hear something she said. One time I tried it and lived to regret it.

"Millie, how you doing, baby?"

"I'm doing just fine, Momma. How you and Daddy doing?"

"Me and your daddy, we doing alright, doing just fine. Elder Sinclair is doing mighty fine, too. We was just talking about you the other day. Real nice conversation. You put on any weight yet, Millie? Is you getting enough to eat?" Momma wasn't looking for an answer to either one of her questions, but that was her way of telling me that she wasn't going to let up. She was holding out hope for some grandbabies.

"Maybe a pound or so, Momma."

"Oh poor child, a pound ain't hardly worth mentioning, but just make sure you don't lose that one pound you gained, you hear?" We both laughed. "Would love to have you come visit for a while so I can fatten you up."

I sho' nuff missed my momma's cooking. She could make a meal out of oil and water if she knew of a hungry child that needed feeding. One day I got to craving her smoked turkey jowl, collard greens, and hot-water corn bread and all I had was a dry peanut butter sandwich. I had slimmed down a bit but I wouldn't dare tell Momma. She was already calling me every single day, bless her heart. I could tell something was on her mind, but she wouldn't let on. Had she had her way, I would have never left home.

"Me and your daddy been talking about taking a short trip up to Memphis for a few days. We was hoping you could get away and look after things whilst we gone. Elder Sinclair will be 'round to help out. You know our anniversary is coming up soon. You didn't forget, did you, Millie?"

"No, ma'am. It's been on my mind."

"Well good, child – now make sure you keep reminding your daddy closer to the time. His mind ain't what it used to be and that's the God's honest truth. Me and your daddy done got some old, Millie. Done been 'round a lot of years."

Daddy was already ahead of Momma; we talked on the whole matter several days ago. He only made it seem like he had done forgot so he wouldn't have to tell her everything.

"Daddy talked to me on his plans a few days ago or better. Said he aimed to make it a special time."

"My Ben said that?"

"Yes, ma'am. Y'all gon' have a real nice time, Momma. Daddy made some really nice plans and I ain't saying nothing more on it so not to spoil it."

"Child, I can't wait. Millie, you know your daddy sho' is a good man."

"I know, Momma. Daddy say the same about you."

Momma seemed so happy. "Me and your daddy really hope you can get away to help out while we gone. Up to five guests now, counting Elder Sinclair. I reckon Schaumburg is growing on him. Did I mention that he'd be staying on with us for six months, maybe even longer?"

"Yes ma'am, you did."

"Oh, I did? Well child, I couldn't remember if I'd said anything today or not. I guess I'm gettin' like your daddy."

Momma's mind was slowly fading, but it was kind of funny the way she carried on all the time about Elder Sinclair. Never could have a talk without his name falling from her lips, no matter how short the talk was.

"I declare Elder Sinclair's been some kind of blessing 'round here to me and your daddy, but he can't boil water, I don't believe. No ma'am, I reckon he need to find a good woman of the marrying kind."

Knowing Momma, she hadn't let Elder Sinclair nowhere near her kitchen except to eat. That was her favorite place to be – in the kitchen over that hot stove.

"Yes Lord, been a long time since I seen Ben so excited; been teaching Elder Sinclair a whole heap of things. Running that city boy right on up out of 'em. Got your daddy running 'round here like a young boy hisself. Tuned up the trolling motor on that old boat this afternoon. Gonna take Elder Sinclair to a few of his special fishing holes on tomorrow morning, Lord willing, and I pray that He is. Me and your daddy both done had a taste for some perch the past few days."

"Lord willing, Momma."

"Elder Sinclair been wondering when he'd get a chance to meet you, Millie. We talks about you all the time, me and your daddy. Thought you'd be home by now at least for a visit."

"I'm sure we'll meet soon enough, Momma."

"Now, Deaconess Puryear agreed to come and stay over with you and help out as much as she could. Said she didn't want any of the church members to get the wrong idea and start gossiping 'bout you and Elder Sinclair. I told her she was right. It just wouldn't be proper."

"That'll be more than fine, Momma. It'll be good to spend a little time with Deaconess Puryear. Been a good long while since I laid eyes on her."

"And you shouldn't have no troubles. No troubles at all. But it'll be nice to have Elder Sinclair here to help you look after things."

Schaumburg's Sweet Reminisce

"Alright, Momma."

"Alright, baby. Now, the other house guests is all married, husbands and wives – all the way from Philadelphia. Real nice people but they all eat like birds. Been the best of friends as far back as they can remember and they do everything together. The wives even dress alike. And Lord help 'em, they drink that coffee morning, noon, and night. Say it keeps 'em going. I really hope you can make it, Millie. I sho' would like to lay eyes on you, me and your daddy both."

"I can make it, Momma. Just let me know when."

"Well, Millie, I don't wanna put you out."

"I can make it, Momma."

"Oh, well that's good news, Millie. I'll be sure and let Elder Sinclair know you coming. Ben and Deaconess Puryear, too. You can always come a little early and get acquainted with everybody, got more than enough room for you."

"Momma?"

"Yes, Millie?"

"How long those guests plan on staying?"

"Well, right now they only aiming to stay for a couple of Sundays. But you watch what I tell you; once I get a few of my hot sweet-potato biscuits, fried catfish, and fresh collards into them little frail bodies, they'll be changing they minds."

"Well, you can cook, Momma."

"Thank you, baby. Been working on a few new

recipes. I 'bout got 'em ready. Your daddy say they already ready. But I reckon I'm gon' have to have the last say on that."

"How is Pastor Tisdale getting along these days?"

"Well, he's yet holding on; Pastor Tisdale done got mighty feeble. Was having a whole heap of trouble making it through his sermons on Sunday mornings. First Lady Tisdale expect him to take to the bed any day now. Hadn't preached in month of Sundays – just ain't been able to make it. Deacon Wilkes announced this past Sunday that Pastor Tisdale gon' be steppin' aside. Don't know who they gon' get to stand in for him. But now, Pastor Tisdale is still the Pastor of Mount Hope Church. I don't much care to lend my ears or my time to the whispers."

"I sho' hate to hear that Pastor Tisdale done gone down like he have. I got to get by there to see him and First Lady. Just as soon as I get there and get settled. I want her and Pastor Tisdale to know that I've been remembering them in my prayers."

"Well, keep 'em lifted in prayer, baby."

"I will, Momma."

"Met anybody special?"

"No, ma'am. I'm not much looking and not much expecting to be found."

"Child of mine, I wish I knew what was going on in your heart. It wouldn't hurt to entertain a nice Christian man. Let him take you to church on Sunday and for a nice picnic afterwards. Don't you just wanna talk and hold hands or be held sometimes? Have somebody this side of life to bare your soul to? Ain't you got no womanly urges or desires that need taming? What you aiming to do with them child-bearing hips and that nursing bosom the good Lord done gave you, child?"

I could hear the disappointment in Momma's voice. It had deepened over the years, but she'd still talk often about her hopes for me and for her some grandbabies. I listened to her heart and knew that I was loved.

* **** *

"Got something on your mind, Momma?"

"Just blessing the Master for His bounty. Come on over here and let your momma scratch your dandruff up and oil your scalp. You ain't too old for your momma to play in your hair, is you?"

"No ma'am, I'm not."

"Well, come on and don't fall to sleep on me. Talk with me for a while."

We both laughed. I'd oftentimes fall to sleep when Momma combed my hair and she'd wake me straight on up with a swift swat of her comb.

"You know what, Millie?"

"Ma'am?"

"If I had had my way, you'd have stayed my little Millie, forever…"

I could hear the tears filling up every word she spoke. I stayed tight-lipped so not to cry myself, but my heart was full.

"I been praying for you. Always have and always will."

"Thank you, Momma. I appreciate you." I reached for her hand. I know she smiled without even turning to see it for myself, but she also knew that I needed her to ease up on my scalp.

"I guess you ain't quite made your mind up about what you want to do next?

"No ma'am."

"Well, you ain't got to be in no hurry. Always best that you be led by the Spirit in anything you do. Me and your daddy tell you that all the time."

"Yes ma'am, y'all do, all the time."

"Millie?"

"Yes, ma'am?"

"I ain't giving up on my grandbabies."

"I know, Momma."

"You know why?"

"No ma'am, but I wonder sometimes."

"When you was born, I didn't know of another thing I would ever have need to ask the Lord for, but them days is as long-gone as you are old. I ask the Lord for grandbabies all the time now. Look like sometimes I just can't help myself. I know settling down and having babies ain't a longing in your heart. I reckon all's I can do is hope and pray that the

Schaumburg's Sweet Reminisce

Lord'll make it so."

"Lord's will be done, Momma."

"You know, being a helpmate to my Ben done brought me a life of great joy over the years – and the best part of me wants the same for you."

I knew Momma's heart was in the right place. Family was everything to her, but I didn't know how to get her to understand that nothing in me desired to marry nor bear children. I didn't know if it would ever be so.

Momma let up for a while after our talk that day and we just loved on one another as often as we could like family should. I thought about her sadness and wondered if I couldn't just forsake myself and honor them with a family of my own, knowing that it would mean the world to the both of 'em.

Daddy settled it in his mind years ago that he might not ever get to give me away in marriage, but Momma just couldn't seem to let it go. She didn't much care if I got married on top of a chicken coop just so long as I did and the marriage was centered in Christ.

And now, she would have six months or better to get good and acquainted with Elder Sinclair. I could tell that she already had us at the altar.

I was often reminded that marriage, like Salvation, wasn't to be taken lightly. Momma made sure to tell me not to marry a man that I didn't feel like I could respect and love at the same time on account I'd have to part with both everyday all day if I wanted a real good marriage.

"It's hard for one to stand without the other, Millie.

Once you're married and the storms finally come, because they's sho' nuff coming, respect will take you a lot further along together through life's ups and downs.

"A woman can be mad as fire at her husband, can't stand the sight of him, let alone his touch; but, if she respects him, she can put her anger aside and tend to her wifely duties. Now, love will keep you by his side when you have cause to leave him; and in spite of everything that's happened down through the years, it'll keep you at his bedside if he was to ever get down and feeble in his body.

"Can't nobody but the good Lord put that kind of love and respect in your heart and He the only one that can keep it there. Keep Him first and He'll give you the grace to overcome until death departs you. Let the husband take his rightful place and the wife stay in hers – that's how marriage supposed to work."

Daddy said a husband is supposed to be three things for his family – a high-priest, a provider, and a protector. Momma agreed. He said any husband truly given to those three areas in the eyes of the Lord blesses the way of his whole family for generations to come. Said that every man ain't deserving of my conversation no matter what he say or what's said about him. Told me not to even lend too much of my time to a young man I couldn't see myself married to.

"And if he ain't half the man that I am, don't even bother telling him to come 'round here to see me about nothin' unless he reckon he ready to stand toe-to-toe with a real one."

Momma used to always laugh when she heard Daddy say that. It was the same thing her daddy told her when she became a young woman, mature enough for courting. Daddy didn't too much laugh or talk hardly after I left home. Felt like he'd been put out to pasture. Momma understood and just let him be.

* **** *

"Call me in a few days, Millie, why don't you? Me and your Daddy should be done settled on them dates for our trip to Memphis by then."

"Yes ma'am, I will."

"Well, you know me and your daddy love you. Take care yourself, you hear?"

"Yes ma'am, I will. I love you and Daddy, too."

"I try not to call you every day, but you know, me and your daddy worry about you when we don't hear from you."

"Momma, you and Daddy ain't got to worry none."

"Well, you's the only child we got. I reckon that gives us cause to worry some, don't it?"

"I reckon you right, Momma."

"Well alright, you know I love you."

"I love you, too."

"Bye-bye for now."

"Bye now, Momma."

* **** *

Schaumburg seemed to welcome Elder Sinclair like a sweet summer's rain. And it wasn't long before he took to

Daddy like the son I'm sure he'd often prayed for over the years. I could only imagine how lonely that made Momma.

Made Daddy feel proud to have a strong man around the house. Said he'd been able to teach Elder Sinclair a few things about farming and that he wasn't bad for a city boy. He was able to manage the farm while Daddy took a much-needed rest. Elder Sinclair may have been from the city, but he looked every bit of country-fed and bred to me.

Daddy made it a point to keep me up on things concerning Elder Sinclair, too – it made him happy. He'd tell me all the time how smart and hardworking he was; but I believe he found joy in telling me how Elder Sinclair wasn't stuttin' 'bout none of them gals running 'round Schaumburg, dropping by unannounced with they bloody fried chicken and runny cobblers. I didn't quite understand why that made me feel some kind of way about Elder' Sinclair, but I sure did look forward to my daddy's phone calls – almost as much as he did.

"Hey, daddy!"

"Heeeyyyyyy, babygirl!"

"Think I might be able to visit real soon, Daddy."

"Ah well now, babygirl, that'd make me and your momma real happy. All your momma seem to be able to talk about nowadays is you meeting Elder Sinclair. She done talked you up so got old Elder Sinclair anxious to meet you."

"Is that so?"

I still felt as awkward and comely as the day I was born when it came to menfolk and not in the least bit as fine a young woman that others told me I was. And to hear

Schaumburg's Sweet Reminisce

Daddy talk of a man of Elder Sinclair's character in every way pleased to make my acquaintance made me a little more than nervous.

"'Come on over and set down beside me Elder Sinclair and let me show you our, Millie.' That's what your Momma said to him the other evening after supper. Nearly run me over gettin' to your momma. You remember that old hat box your momma had chucked full of your pictures, don't you, Millie?"

"I remember, could hardly keep the top on it."

"Well, it ain't chucked full of pictures no more."

"All the pictures gone, Daddy?"

"Naw, your momma and Elder Sinclair sat there and put every last one of 'em in that big old picture book of hers."

"Momma told me she wanted *me* to help her do that."

"I reckon it may have slipped her mind, babygirl. I'm just glad to see Marjorie and Elder Sinclair coming along."

"How's that, Daddy?"

"Well, all the while me and Elder Sinclair was getting along, I had been noticing that your momma wasn't much like herself. Started distancing herself and wasn't partial to too much conversation with me or Elder Sinclair. Every now and again I'd catch her eyeing him, you know. Elder Sinclair was none the wiser."

"That's not like Momma."

"That's what I know. I told her it wasn't ladylike, was unbecoming of a Christian woman, let alone my wife. After I

214

said my peace, she just said she had her reasons. I asked her if I needed to handle anything… if anything had happened, you know, and she just said that she was trusting the Lord to make it all plain in His time. After that, things turned all the way around. She started asking Elder Sinclair all kinds of questions, took to him like a son. *'Elder Sinclair, what you think you might be wanting for supper? I aim to try out that rhubarb pie you was telling me you liked so much. It ain't much, if anything, I can't whip up in this-here kitchen of mine. What you think you might be wanting to go with your pie this evening?'*

"Elder Sinclair looked at me and I looked at him. I said, well Elder, she didn't ask me, she asked you. Tell her what you want so we can go work this farm before the sun run us up out them bottoms.

"*'Well, Mrs. Marjorie, I imagine I'll be satisfied with whatever you set in front of me.'* The smile that come across your momma's face that morning took me back to those Sunday dinners she used to make for me when her old man allowed me to start courting her. I'd come down to the house after church and her old man would talk at me until he allowed me to put my feet under his table and eat the fruits of his labor.

"It'd take your momma nearly all evening to put dinner on the table, but it wasn't much talking going on once she did. *'Can I put some more food on your plate, Daddy?'* *'Naw, babygirl, I done had my fill.'* And then she'd turn to me. *'Benjamin Charles, can I get you something more to eat?'*

"Before, I could even now answer, Marjorie had done already had my plate in her hand and back on the table with a second helping. She'd heap my plate up so to where I wouldn't eat all day just to be able to eat all that she put in front of me.

215

Schaumburg's Sweet Reminisce

"Her Momma told her to watch me because I might be a little shame-faced to ask for seconds in front of her old man. Said if I was still sitting up close to the table that meant I could still eat, but if I had done reared back like her old man, that was a sign that I had just enough room left for dessert. Yessir, sometimes she'd send me home with extra dessert for the next day; but if she baked sweet potato pie, it didn't even now hardly last me the walk home. Every now and then she'd try her hand at something new and bring me a little taste and, I declare, after all these years, ain't never tasted nothing she done prepared that I ain't like. I believe that woman of mine could make a meal out of dry grass if she had to.

"The other evening here, Elder Sinclair offered to do the dishes after supper. Marjorie took him up on his offer. Told him she'd help on account she don't too much like nobody messing around in her kitchen. I can count on one hand the number of times I done helped your momma with the dishes and she had to ask me to help her then; so, I let 'em both have at it and I went on in there and sat down in my chair and tried to take me a quick nap. Them two kept up more noise than them pots and pans they was supposed to be gettin' after – so I went on back in the kitchen to supervise the noise.

"After we finished up the kitchen chores, Marjorie put on a big old pot of coffee and we sat around in the parlor well into the night. Babygirl, you done took a whole lot of pictures over the years. And I declare, your momma was just beside herself – seemed like she had a story to go along with every one of 'em. Elder Sinclair didn't seem to mind. He hung on your momma's every word, asked a lot of questions about you, talking just as much as your momma was. Had a real good time that evening, laughing and talking – sho' nuff did; felt real good to think on old times – the Lord been mighty good to us. I declare He have."

"Yes, He have, Daddy!"

"But now, it wasn't but a few nights later, I just all a sudden woke up out my sleep – hadn't been down long neither; but you know me, once I'm up, I'm up. I grabbed my Bible, figured I'd walk through the house and check on things and stumbled up on Elder Sinclair in there in the parlor looking through that picture book again. I didn't think nothing of it until I was on my way back through and found Elder Sinclair on his knees, praying with that photo album clutched in his chest. I felt a bit shame standing there watching him that way, you know, him not knowing and all, but it was just a beautiful thing to see. I slid on back out the way and went back to minding my own business so not to disturb Elder's prayer. But that old boy sho' know how to petition the Lord.

"I had to think long and hard about what I was gon' tell Marjorie. Didn't tell her right away on account I know she'd been praying too, and well, I didn't want your momma getting too excited and make Elder Sinclair start to feel some kind of way. But when I finally did tell Marjorie, she near 'bout shouted. I mean that woman near 'bout come undone at the seams. Made me tell her three times and again what I'd seen.

"Marjorie, I'll ask that you don't go putting pressure on Elder Sinclair. Now, I feel sure about what I seen the other night, but Elder hadn't spoke one word to me 'bout no special feelings towards our Millie. Besides, Elder Sinclair much older than our Millie. We need to just let the Lord move if He aim to.

"'Alright, Ben.'" "Is that all you got to say, woman?'" "'I seen the look on Elder Sinclair's face for myself, Ben. After we sat there and put all of Millie's pictures in that photo book, *he sat there holding it like a newborn baby. I'd say the Lord was moving right then.'*

"Ummm hmm. Well now, I didn't take notice none, but all I'm asking is that you don't go troubling the man none.' *"'I heard you the first time, Ben Charles, and my answer hadn't changed. Come now, get your breakfast.'* "Your momma was right, cause you sho' nuff on his mind. Elder Sinclair done started asking a whole heap of questions about you. We supposed to be working and he steady asking questions. So far that old boy seem to be a pretty good man. Working out just fine. He ain't always lived upright, but he under the Blood, if you's wondering. Near 'bout eat you out of house and home but he works real hard – smart, even-tempered, too; but now he got his flaws. What man don't? Well, that's all I'm gone say on that.

"But now, I tell you, that Marjorie of mine put a scare in me a few days ago. Nearly all them gals over town got eyes for Elder Sinclair, ya know. Ain't seen nothing like it – I reckon they know a good catch when they see one.

"One in particular just showed up here to the house, ya know. Figured she bring all the fixings for a Sunday supper, thinking she was gon' call herself strutting around your momma's kitchen in there to show off for Elder Sinclair. Marjorie must have felt her coming down the road. Before I could stand to my feet to see who it was, your momma had done come out that house across that threshold and stopped that woman cold in her tracks before her foot even hit the first step. Swept by me like a runaway freight train.

"Your momma kindly took them fixings out her arms, handed her a few choice words, and sent her running and stumbling right on back down that dusty road to relay the message to any of the others who'd be so bold. To this day, I don't half-know what Marjorie told that woman or what that

woman told them other women over and around town, but
there ain't been naan' 'nother woman to show up to the
house since that day.

*"'Not in my house and, sho' nuff, not in my kitchen.
Never seen women act so bold before in all my life,
downright loose is what it is. Elder Sinclair belongs to my
Millie and it shall soon be, if I got anything to do with it.'* Had
your momma pretty stirred. Well Lord, if it be Your will,
Father, make it so. That was all I knew to say about that-
there."

Chapter Fifteen

M s. Millie?"

"This is."

"Elder Sinclair, Ms. Millie."

"Elder Sinclair?"

"Yes ma'am, Ms. Millie."

"Elder Sinclair, is everything alright? You scaring me." I sensed a bit fear in that baritone voice of his.

"I don't aim to do that-there, Ms. Millie, but I think you may ought to get on home. Your daddy been trying to reach you the last couple of days but the phone line been down because of the storms."

"Oh Lord. What's done happened? Is Momma and Daddy alright?"

"Your daddy is fine, Ms. Millie. He with your momma at the hospital in Belmont."

"All the way in Belmont? Wh… What on earth done happened, Elder Sinclair?"

"Your momma took ill a few days ago. Doctors here in Schaumburg say they couldn't do nothin' for her. Sent her on over to Belmont Memorial; been there for the last two days. The doctors there sending her home tomorrow. They say it ain't nothing more they can do."

"Please, Lord Jesus – keep my momma. Keep her, Lord."

"That's been our prayer for the last few days, Ms. Millie. Your momma ain't in no pain or nothin'. Your daddy said she just resting, but she been askin' for you."

The tears started coming and just wouldn't stop. Couldn't even now half-talk.

"I don't wants to make you cry, Ms. Millie."

"Elder, what did them doctors say is wrong with my momma?"

"Ms. Millie, I wish I knew. Your momma had all of 'em standing around scratching they head before I left. Your daddy told me to get you home as soon as you could get here. I done already took care of everything to where you'd be here when they get back. Told the man over there at the train station everything that happened. Said he knew your momma and your daddy – visited the church down this way with his wife and family a time or two past. I hope that was alright. He said you could change the time if you needed to. I'd come for you myself, but your momma and daddy gon' need my help gettin' back here."

"No, that's quite alright. You've already done more than enough and I'm ever so grateful. Elder Sinclair, would you hold the line, please – just hold the line for me if you would for just a second?"

"Sho', I'll hold the line, Ms. Millie – I sho' will."

"Elder?"

"Yes, ma'am?"

"Forgive me, Elder Sinclair – needed to pull myself together and get me something to write on."

"You alright, Ms. Millie. You ain't harming me none."

"Well, I appreciate you. How soon can I get to my momma and daddy?"

"Oh, yes ma'am, Ms. Millie. First train set to leave out tomorrow morning at 7 a.m. Now, I'm sorry 'bout the short notice, but your daddy said to get you here as soon as I could."

"That's quite alright, Elder."

"Yes ma'am, Ms. Mille. Now you got one stop, so that should put you arriving at the station over there in town around midday. I'll be there waiting to pick you up and bring you on to the house. They holding your ticket at the station and it done already been paid for. It'll be under Elder Toby James Sinclair."

"Elder, I can't thank you enough."

"It's the least I could do. Your folks been mighty good to me, Ms. Millie."

"Elder?"

"Yes ma'am, Ms. Millie?"

"Elder, how bad is it, really?"

"Well Ms. Millie, your daddy tells me that your momma is in a really bad way; but nearly all of Schaumburg is believing God for divine healing. We serve a merciful God and we know that every sickness is not unto death, so we praise God for what is and that which is to come."

"Amen. Amen. Elder, I thank you in kind for those comforting words."

"Lord willing, and I pray that He is. I'll see you tomorrow 'round midday, Ms. Millie."

"Lord willing. Goodbye Elder and thank you kindly, you hear?"

"Good day, Ms. Millie."

I was able to rest my eyes that night, but just for a spell. I mostly cried and talked to the Lord – reasoned with Him like a little child to restore Momma's health or at least keep her until after I could be at her side for a time.

By morning, I was fresh out of tears with nothing to give but thanks to the good Lord for another day and for the mere fact that I hadn't yet lost my mind. I had hoped that I had told the Lord all that filled my heart on last evening. I could feel His presence. His peace was upon me and I was hemmed in 'round about. For such a time as this, I was glad that I knew Him – that I was His.

From where I was sittin', Elder Sinclair possessed all the markings of tall, dark, and handsome, and from what I had been hearing, he was truly a man of God. I don't reckon them women 'round Schaumburg had much choice in losing they mind over Elder Sinclair. Any woman would have cause to make a little fuss, even if she was good and saved.

Schaumburg's Sweet Reminisce

I had already settled it in my mind on the ride into Schaumburg to be the last one off the train; partly because I didn't know what would befall my eyes when they rested on my momma. I told myself I was ready, but saying you ready for something don't always make it so.

And then there was the matter of making the acquaintance of Elder Sinclair. I'd never been properly introduced to a man before and because I was my momma's child, I had a lot to live up to. I didn't know what all Momma had done told Elder Sinclair and that made me nervous.

I breathed deep and clutched the strand of my pearls Momma gave me before I left home to be caretaker to the two little old Johnson widows in Casper Downs, Georgia. Best friend-girls and blood kin. Twin sisters as God would have it.

*   *❄️*   *

Vera and Queenie lived in a mansion so big you could look out one window and see water for miles and out another and see mountains that touched the sky. Married their menfolk the same day, in a double wedding in that very house – made that pact when they was little girls. Always said that was the only way they'd get married – together and to good-looking men; and the men had to be as good-looking as they were. Took 'em nearly all they life, but they finally jumped the broom.

Lived in that great old mansion with they husbands for almost 50 years until they menfolk made 'em widows. Whole lot of folks was of the mind that they menfolk only married 'em for they money; but Vera and Queenie didn't mind the gossip. Their menfolk made 'em happy and they both had more money than they could spend anyhow.

Sheriell Scott

When Queenie was in her right mind, they talked all
the time about their menfolk, things they'd learned, important
people they'd met, and every place they'd ever seen.
Sometimes they'd forget I'd be sittin' there and get a little
loose at the mouth and have my ears tingling for days – but
it may have been them sweet whiskey sugar cubes they
used to taint they evening coffee. I'd have to fill that sugar jar
almost every other day.

Nice little old ladies though – didn't mean much harm
just trying to live out they last days together. Used to fuss
and fight every now and then about which one of 'em was
supposed to die first. The fussing and fighting never did last
long. Soon as it would come to mind that neither one of 'em
really wanted to die, they decided they'd just die at the same
time and start talking about something else. They figured
they had done everything else together so when they
prayed, they would always just ask the Lord not to take one
before the other.

Vera and Queenie was mighty good to one another;
looked after one another as best they could all they life. But
Vera's eyes had started to dim and wasn't able to look after
Queenie like she had; needed somebody there with 'em
when Ms. Pearlie, their caretaker, took time off for herself.
Vera and Queenie would run you plum-out your mind if you'd
let 'em.

Ms. Pearlie would go to all different kinds of places
and stay a good little while when she did; and she'd always
send Queenie and Vera a little something from every place
she got a chance to visit. If she didn't, she'd never hear the
end of it.

Ms. Pearlie had only planned on being gone for a
month this last time, but ended up staying near 'bout the

whole summer, longest time she had ever been away at one time.

They'd often read Ms. Pearlie's secret desires from her diaries without her knowing. It wasn't until they'd done read each one cover-to-cover that I'd come to know what they'd been up to all that time.

To keep their minds busy, Vera and Queenie would spend their evenings making up stories about why Ms. Pearlie hadn't yet come back. They'd somehow convinced themselves that Ms. Pearlie had done run off and up and died on 'em – even cried real tears. Never could agree as to just how Ms. Pearlie died, so they changed their story; figured she found a man to run off into the sunset with.

When three months turned into four and then five, Ms. Pearlie sent a letter and said that she was getting married. They seemed right happy for Ms. Pearlie at first, but then not so much. Next thing I knew, Vera and Queenie had done up and told them folks that was over their estate that they wanted me to stay on with 'em at least until they could find somebody. Never did even think about askin' me about it first.

A good many was expecting me to go to college somewhere up north, but school didn't interest me none, not much did; but the truth is what everybody knew – I didn't wanna leave my momma and my daddy and they didn't trouble me none about it neither. Said I could go on off up north when I got good and ready, but if I never got ready that'd be fine too. Nothing stirred my thoughts like Schaumburg.

Vera and Queenie had all kinds of books, but Vera and Queenie's books was just for show. Some you couldn't even now touch with your bare hands – had to wear special gloves and whatnot. They had this one big old room with nothing but books from the floor to the top of the ceiling with a ladder on each wall that moved sideways all the way around that room. If you could climb that ladder, you could reach any book you wanted anywhere in that room. I'd never seen anything like it. All them books and not one Bible in the midst. Made me wonder when they prayed who they was praying to.

I reckon I could have learned everything I needed to know for myself right there in that big old room, probably more than what they was gonna try to teach me in one of them colleges.

Momma said most folks wouldn't use much of that fancy learning if they was able to learn anything at all.

Daddy said a man was likely to forget everything he learned if he never put what he learned to use.

Knowing anything is only necessary if there's a reason for you to need to know it; most people could make a good life for themselves with just the basics. The world will have you believing that it got so much to offer until you find out that it don't. King Solomon thought it so until he come to know better.

Vera and Queenie both thought I'd meet a nice southern gentleman in Casper Downs and settle down, but I was just a small-town country girl barely of age and Casper Downs was a bit too showy for me.

Vera and Queenie had been so many places and seen so many things to where just being in that house on all that land near all that water listening at the both of 'em made it seem like I was further away from home than I really was.

Schaumburg's Sweet Reminisce

Now, that Queenie and Vera, I tell you, were some kind of fancy. Never wore regular folks' clothes and hardly ever the same thing twice. Didn't think too much of bloomers neither.

They called me Ms. Millie; said I carried myself like a proper lady, so in their mind, it was fitting to do so. Maybe Elder Sinclair would think so too.

I hadn't yet let go of my pearls, still had every last one; but, if I'd held on to 'em any tighter, they'd all be rolling around on the floor of that train.

Momma said I needed a strand of pearls of my own to clutch every now and again as a reminder – every young girl did:

To every young girl her very own strand of pearls.
Received and worn in chaste.
You say you got one missing pearl, young girl?
Fasten that latch then, child!
And make sure that one don't soon turn into two.
'Cause one day you'll reach for your pearls and they'll be of no use to you. Once they gone... they gone forever. Then what you gon' do?

"Pleased to finally make your acquaintance, Ms. Millie, though I'd have it for happier times. How was your train ride in?"

"My pleasure, Elder Sinclair. I've heard more than a good bit about you. And as for the train ride, I was favored with safe passage; I hadn't need for much else."

To keep from staring, I searched every inch of that town square, foolishly carrying on like I had been gone longer than I had.

"Not much has changed that I can see."

"Well, I reckon not. I was only in Belmont for half the morning."

Elder smiled. I did too, but didn't show my teeth.

"You traveling mighty light, Ms. Millie. You ain't of the mind to hurry back, is you?"

"No plans to rush on back, Elder Sinclair. I'm here to see after my momma and my daddy, however long it takes. Momma made sure I didn't take too many of my favorite things, anyhow. Said I'd always have a reason to come back to visit if I didn't."

My suitcase fit like a matchbox in Elder Sinclair's hand. He reached for my pocketbook but I declined. I clutched my pearls again and pressed them flat against my neck to make sure the latch was still fastened. I felt a little ashamed carrying on while Momma lay in pain, but it was plain that I fancied Elder Sinclair more than I should have or at least more than I thought I would.

I couldn't get the words to come to ask Elder about Momma outright, scared I guess – but I sensed the Holy Spirit working.

"Elder?"

"Mrs. Marjorie, she doing a little bit better this morning; still asking for you. Few of the mothers from the church dropped by to prepare the house. I told your daddy we wouldn't be long. I reckon I ought to get you on home; everybody waiting to see you."

"Elder, I… I don't…"

"You gonna be alright, Ms. Millie. Everything gonna work out just like it supposed to. God is in control of this-here thing we dealin' with."

"Thank you, Elder. I'm just a bit nervous, is all. I've ever only know'd my Momma to be one way."

"Ms. Millie, I sure could go for a ice-cold Coca-Cola. You care for one?"

"Elder Sinclair that's mighty fine of you, but you help yourself. I don't think I'd much care for one."

"Now Ms. Millie, your momma told me that in all her years, she'd never known you to turn down a Coca-Cola."

"Well, she told you right, Elder; but don't you trouble yourself none. I'm fine, really I am."

"Yes ma'am, Ms. Millie."

While Elder went into the station for his Coca-Cola, I stayed outside to calm my nerves, nerves that wasn't yet old enough for the present worry. God promised He'd be a present help in my time of need. I just needed to trust Him.

"Well, Ms. Millie, I don't mean you no harm, but I figured you might change your mind after you get settled." Elder wasn't long with his shopping. I didn't expect him to be – most men shopped like men and he seemed a bit anxious.

"No harm, Elder." I'd been so caught up in my thoughts, I didn't even now notice Elder come out the station with both hands full of Coca-Colas. I was sure to be partial to at least one later that evening. Funny thing is, I had never had a boy buy me nothing nor take me nowhere – 'course I never had a boy come around none. Elder Sinclair wasn't no boy none though.

"Well, I reckon we may ought to get you on home now, Ms. Millie. I aim to keep my word to your daddy."

The ride in from town up to the main house was quiet, not much talk between Elder and me. I'd like to think he understood the reason for my ill-manners. I was wrestling so with all kind of thoughts and feelings – the kind I needed my momma to help me understand – but now she needed me.

In that quiet stretch of ride, I tried to remember all the things Momma'd ever told me about faith, about life, about love. From the first time she had to tap my hand real good 'til the day she allowed me to leave her side for a world that she nor my daddy thought much of.

I wanted to think on my momma in the only way I've ever known her – God-fearing, beautiful, and strong. The way she loved on me and Daddy and what she'd come to mean to us over the years couldn't be explained with just words.

Though my heart was heavy, I took to mind a lot about Elder Sinclair in our short time together. Elder Sinclair was tall, solid, and plain, but easy on the eyes. His hands looked strong and had started to callous in places. I was sure that that was Daddy's doing – made sure Elder earned his keep.

Elder hummed a tune while I braced myself against all the bumps and turns in the road that seemed to bother him none. Whatever was on his heart sho' brought peace to mine. I wondered what was in Elder's heart behind the song.

Schaumburg's Sweet Reminisce

* **❊❊❊❊** *

I fell on my daddy's neck and wept like a child. He was weak, I could tell – but I remembered asking the Lord to give each of us just enough grace to bear the other one up.

"Sho' is good to see you, babygirl."

"I missed you, Daddy."

I felt like a little girl again wrapped in my daddy's arms. He'd made a lot of things alright with just a hug over the years, but what we were facing was something bigger than us and we both knew it.

Me and Daddy sat and talked in the parlor until I could get my bearings. I was home but it didn't feel the same – Momma's presence wasn't there. I couldn't smell Momma's favorite perfume or her good cooking. It was like she was already gone. I needed to feel her touch and I needed her to feel mine.

Mother Leola brought me a cup of hot tea, one cup after another while Daddy looked on. I could have sat there and drank tea all afternoon and Daddy knew it.

"Another cup of tea, Millie?"

"Yes ma'am, Mother Leola."

"That's enough. Sister Leola, I believe Millie done had her fill of that-there tea. No need to trouble yourself no further."

"Alright, Brother Ben. I'll leave the kettle on the stove for later. Got a meal in the oven and some stock on now for Sister Marjorie. Y'all need anything else, you just give me a holler. If you need anything, just holler, now."

"Sho' do appreciate you, Sister Leola, for everything. I believe me and Millie gonna be alright."

"We can't thank you enough, Sister Leola."

"Now, now, Millie. The whole church been fasting and praying for the Lord to move in a mighty way on your momma's behalf, so you keep leaning into the Lord, ya hear?"

"Yes, ma'am. I will and I'm so grateful for the prayers of the saints."

"Oh, now child, you just give Sister Leola a great big ole hug and as soon as you able, you get on by the church and let us love on you. You done grown into such a fine young woman. Every bit of your momma's child. Just beautiful. We got to hurry up and get you married off child. Get some grandbabies runnin' 'round here just as soon as the good Lord see us through this storm."

Sounded to me like Momma had Sister Leola on board with her plans for my womb. I gave Sister Leola another hug, hoping that she wouldn't get started in on me with that baby talk.

Sister Leola sensed Daddy growing weary, knowing what lay ahead. "Well, I'm gonna leave y'all to it. Millie, you ain't yet laid eyes on your momma and Brother Ben you look like you need your rest. I'll stand here talking all day if you let me."

"The Lord will bear you up, Brother Ben."

"I sho' aim to let Him, Sister Leola. Sho' do appreciate

everything."

"Millie, you be sure to give me a holler now if y'all need anything. Don't forget to turn that stock off after while. And hug your momma's neck for me, hear? Bye, bye for now."

"Yes ma'am, I will. Thank you, hear?"

"Alright, baby."

I watched Sister Leola until the tears flooded my eyes.

"Come now, babygirl. It's time you lay eyes on your momma."

"Daddy… Daddy…"

"Come now, Millie, come now… Everything's gonna be alright."

"Elder, you come now, too."

"Yes sir, Brother Ben."

"Just you, Daddy," I whispered. I didn't realize Elder Sinclair had come into the parlor.

Daddy gave Elder Sinclair a nod to hold off, but he knew to stay close by on account Daddy needed more strength than he had just to hold me up.

Before Momma took sick, just one glance at my daddy, even in his old age, told you that he wasn't one to be reckoned with – that is, until he smiled back at you with them big ole hazel eyes of his. Watching the life seep out of his Marjorie had done near 'bout broke him, left him feeling helpless and less of a man on account he couldn't help

Momma help herself.

When my eyes finally rested on my momma, her eyes were closed, and from where I stood, she didn't look like she was breathing. Stopped me cold in my tracks.

Ever since Momma was a little girl, she had always been known to be as strong as an ox and didn't care who said so neither. She had been sick for months, but you'd have never know'd it. Had I known she was as sick as she was, I'd have never left home for Casper Downs; she knew that.

"She alright, babygirl. Your momma, she just resting."

Seeing Momma on her bed of affliction hurt my soul. She wasn't yet gone, but she didn't have long and anybody that knew anything knew that. I never allowed myself to think on Momma and Daddy not being around here; they was all I had.

I didn't know nothing other than what they'd taught me, and I was good with that.

I only knew the people that knew me because they knew my Momma and Daddy – and I was alright with that.

I was my daddy's babygirl and every bit of my momma's sweet child – and that was enough for me.

That was all I could tell anybody about Millicent Rose Fouraukis on account I didn't know nothing else about her.

I needed my momma to be alright because I needed her to know that Elder Sinclair made me some kind of nervous. The kind of nervous she always talked to me about. She'd be so beside herself if she knew. I needed my Momma to live on account I told myself on the ride in from the train station that that would be the first thing we'd talk about – but I could barely hold myself together. I could still see her, touch her, but I couldn't feel her presence. I didn't think it'd be this hard.

"Momma." Hot tears poured down my face, and if ever there was a time that I needed the Holy Spirit to groan for me, it was right then. "Lord, please don't take my momma. Don't take my momma, Lord."

As strong as my daddy was, he was just as weak when it came to me or my momma being in pain. "Come now, Millie. I got you now."

Daddy was starting to struggle under the weight of my grief and his. I felt his hands trembling. I wanted to be strong for my daddy but I couldn't; I didn't know how. The harder I cried, the tighter he held on to me. I looked all around that room for strength, for God to show up and set things right, hoping that by the time I laid eyes on my Momma again, she'd be there, full of life. That she'd be upright reaching for me, ready to love on her sweet child, like she always did.

"Daddy, I can't." I was crying so hard, I could hardly catch my breath.

"I'm right here, babygirl. It's alright. Come now. Your momma's been asking for you."

"Ben."

Momma's frail hand fought the air. Her voice was weak and fading. She never opened her eyes.

"Right here, baby." Daddy started towards her, but I needed him to not let me go.

"Elder, take care my babygirl. You take care of our Millie, now."

"Yes, sir. Yessir, Brother Ben."

"Daddy, don't let me go."

"I got you now, Ms. Millie."

"Ben…"

"I'm right here, Marjorie." Daddy went to Momma, fell on his knees beside the bed and grabbed her hand to steady it so. "Come now, Marjorie. Settle down here, now." Daddy kissed Momma's hand like he would any other time and then came the tears.

"Ben."

"I'm right here, Marjorie. I ain't going nowhere."

"Ben, did our Millie make it?"

"Our Millie is right here – she can't wait to see you."

I stood there in Elder's hands shaking like a cold wet puppy, too afraid to move and too choked up to say anything. Elder Sinclair held me close and beared me up the rest of the way.

"Come and see your momma now, babygirl. Let her hear your voice."

"Momma… Momma… It's me, Millie."

"That's right, she in there. Search for her."

"Is that my Millie?"

Schaumburg's Sweet Reminisce

"I'm right here, Momma."

She was so tired. I reached for her frail hand and held it in mine. I squeezed just a little and she squeezed back as best she could.

"I missed you, sweet child."

I should have been here, is what I silently told myself. I rested Momma's hand on my face and watched her. I could only hope for my faith to one day be as strong as hers. She allowed my tears to fall as they would, all the while knowing that she was the cause of them.

I never could hide anything from my momma and still couldn't.

"The Lord shall be your peace, Millie. You hear me? I say the Lord shall be your peace."

"Yes ma'am, Momma."

"Then make it so, child."

"The Lord is my peace."

"That's right."

"I love you, Momma."

"Momma loves her Millie, too."

Hearing those words part my momma's lips wasn't nothing I hadn't heard a hundred times or more before. I'd always felt safe in my momma's love, but there was something in the way she said what she said this time, a boldness, like the words had come straight from the mouth of the Lord my God Himself.

It was all too clear that Momma would soon be forsaking me in death, but her love gave me peace in knowing that there was a greater love in God and that He would pick up where she left off; and in that very moment, God showed up just like He promised He would.

I didn't leave my momma's side after that. I bathed her and kept her hair done up so she'd feel pretty for Daddy. Daddy fed Momma her breakfast and lunch and I fed her dinner when she had the stomach to eat.

Momma held on for a good while after them doctors gave her up. So much so, we was all able to make one last trip to her childhood home. By then, everything had run on down to pieces. She didn't say much, but every now and then she would smile just a little. I guess she was remembering the good times. Daddy wasn't of the mind to take her all that way, figured it be too much for her, but Momma had been getting on about it for days.

With Momma being on the bed, Daddy had done got used to not getting up 'til well after sunrise. That morning, Momma rose up and managed off that bed with no help at all and called to my daddy.

"Ben, I'm ready to go."

Daddy's soul drew heavy because he knew in his heart that Momma meant more than she'd said. Her voice was soft but sure in every word that fell from her lips.

"Marjorie, I think we may ought to talk about this, now."

"We can talk on the way, Benjamin Charles. You get ready, now. I'm ready to go."

Schaumburg's Sweet Reminisce

Daddy couldn't bring hisself to tell Momma "No" and break her heart, so he loaded up his old truck and we struck out for her childhood roots one last time. Daddy drove steady to get there and back before nightfall. Cat seemed to have our tongue for most of the ride. Me and Daddy didn't want to wear Momma out even though she slept a good part of the way. She seemed so peaceful so we made the most of the day.

Momma seemed to be getting along real good after our little trip – look like to me that she might get better, but then the Lord saw fit to come for what was rightly His. She never seemed to fret none. Took each breath as it came until it didn't. Always said that she was content with whatever the Lord's will was. I took care of my momma like my very own child.

"How you feeling, Momma?"

"I'm tired, Millie, but I'm yet holding on."

"I reckon so, Momma. We all are."

"I'm in a lotta pain and I's anxious to meet the Lord. I don't wants to leave you and my Ben, but there's a greater joy waiting for me on the other side."

"Momma."

"Thy will be done, has always been my prayer – the Lord knows best."

I had done cried so much since I'd been back home to where I'd learned to cry and smile at the same time. Momma could barely keep her eyes open; but each time they opened, I wanted her to see me smile even though I was dying on the inside.

Sheriell Scott

"Elder Sinclair is a good man, Mille."

"Yes, ma'am. I believe he is."

"Done been real good to me and your daddy. We's both grateful."

"Yes ma'am, I know."

"Do he make you nervous?"

"Yes, ma'am."

"Sho' nuff?" Momma smiled just a little bit more than she had. It hurt some for her to breathe.

"Yes, ma'am. Momma, Elder Sinclair make me real nervous, like I might lose my breath."

"Now Millie, you set your mind clear on what I told you now 'bout menfolk. You take your time and you wait on the Lord. If He don't move, don't you move neither."

"Yes, ma'am."

"Alright then."

I rubbed Momma's hands and feet and oiled 'em down with a little coca butter. We didn't talk at all for a good little spell on account she fell asleep and again my mind wondered on all the things she'd taught me over the years. Funny how I remembered so many.

"I wasn't snoring, was I, Millie?"

"Just a little bit, Momma."

"Child, was I snoring loud?"

Schaumburg's Sweet Reminisce

"Just a little, Momma."

"Lord have mercy, child don't you tell your daddy that."

We both laughed because we both knew how bad Daddy rode Momma about her snoring. I never knew Momma to fall asleep in mixed company and for good reason, but truth be told, she was snoring louder than I let on.

"I sho' would love to be here with you on your wedding day. Would love to see you tighten some britches, too. Look like I'm gonna have to let the good Lord tell me all about it. You just make sure you don't get ahead of God now, Millie."

I was sad knowing that Momma wouldn't be with us much longer, but I was glad for the time we had; and more than grateful for the life she gave me and the world she prepared me for.

"Momma, I wish you wouldn't talk like that, like you just waiting to die. I ain't seen you cry one tear for your trouble. You don't even sound sad when you talk about leaving me and Daddy."

"Child of mine, you hush that kind of talk now, you hear? I's still your momma."

"Yes, ma'am."

"Now I've lived a good life, better than most, and the Lord ain't gonna take me no sooner than time for me to go. When I'm gone, you just make sure you live for the Lord and take care of my Ben."

"I will, Momma, but it sho' breaks my heart."

"You just scared and hurt, that's all, Millie – and that's alright. It's gonna hurt for a while… a good while. I know how much you love me, but God's grace is sufficient. The Lord is thy strength. He promised it so and I believe every word of every promise. Millie, all a man really got is the Lord and He's been proving to me all my life that He's all I ever really needed."

I curled up beside my momma and read aloud some of her favorite Psalms and sung a few of the hymns she liked to hear, more so for me than for her. It was just like her to let me know when I sung out of key or wasn't giving it my all. Reading those Scriptures made me understand how she could be so at peace knowing that her bodily form would soon be going the way of the earth, but that her soul would live on forever in the presence of the Lord.

Momma had served the Lord well and it brought me comfort knowing that once she was absent from her body, that she would be present with the Lord.

To most people, Momma came off as judgmental, a "goody two-shoes…" But God alone would decide her heart. I'm just glad the good Lord saw fit to borrow her to me for a short while.

"Millie, have I been a good momma to you?"

"Wouldn't even now wanna be born into this world to any other. I love you, Momma."

"Momma loves you too, Millie. Benjamin Charles, have I been a good wife and helpmate?"

"Marjorie, the Lord gave me the best he had and only a foolish man would ask for better. Woman, you done served me well, better than I deserve. All our years, woman, you added and never took from me. In all my toils, I've never had a day of regret. You've proved me a man, Marjorie. Proud to be the husband of one wife. You've honored me in marriage and done give me a many good memories to bide my time here on earth. There ain't nothing that I could part my lips to ask for that you ain't already done gave to me. I knows you tired, woman – a special part of you is gonna live on through our Millie. But when we all get there, oh what a day it will be. I loves me some you, Marjorie Rose, more than life itself."

Momma and Daddy made a promise to one another early in their marriage. The promise was to love the Lord thy God with all of their heart, mind, soul, and strength so that when it got hard to love one another, they could rely on the grace of the Lord to keep 'em together.

*　 ✳✺✾✺✳　 *

We held off on the funeral on account Daddy took to the bed just days after Momma passed. I reckon it was just too much for his poor heart to bear.

Said he remembered how his spirit was drawn to hers the first time he laid eyes on her and how he always made sure that my momma knew she was the prettiest little, dark-skinned, bow-legged girl he'd ever seen and the only woman that he'd ever love. Been cherishing his Marjorie Rose since the day they met.

He loved her well over the years and lay right there by her side every night holding her until the very end. Benjamin Charles loved his Marjorie Rose – said that she was his earthly reward. That's just how he looked at things.

At night, after I shut up the house and everything was still, I'd hear Daddy dampening his pillow with tears; that was up 'til his very last night on Earth. I hadn't never seen that kind of brokenness before. I wondered if he ever asked the Lord to take him, too. Daddy had always said that he never wanted to be anywhere without his sweet Marjorie Rose.

When it came close to Momma's time, Daddy wouldn't even now hardly get out of bed. It pained him to leave her side, so he'd lay there beside her, holding her as tight as she could stand it.

And so, it wasn't long after Momma passed that that old spirit of despair calloused Daddy's heart. I never would have took and thought that Daddy would go down as fast as he did, so it wasn't long after Momma passed, my daddy was gone – too heartbroken to go on without his Marjorie Rose.

Chapter Sixteen

The repast table looked like it stretched a mile long and a mile or better wide. Made me feel real proud of the life that Momma and Daddy lived. Wasn't hardly none perfect, but as much as they was able, they walked in peace and tried to bless others with the good measure God had blessed them with.

Don't think there was a soul there that Momma and Daddy hadn't stood in the gap for in one way or another. Gave out of what they had and always from the heart. Never expected in return from man – only from the Lord. Prayed that the few deeds they'd done while passing through on this tedious journey of life would live on through those they'd helped if they was so led to pay it forward.

Momma was always praying and patching up folks when they couldn't afford to go to the doctor none. Folks used to always say that she should have gone to school to be a nurse or a doctor, but she would always tell people that she was called to be a good wife, mother, and a servant to whoever the good Lord sent her way to keep after.

Daddy sometimes wondered if he may have kept

Momma back from a better life.

"Ben... Baby, you alright, ain't you? Ben.... Baby, I said you alright, ain't you?"

"Woman, do any part of you ever want for better?"

Just like Daddy, Momma had her own way of settin' things right; she knew Daddy liked it when she talked soft and sweet.

"Husband of mine, now you listen-here to me. If all of the writers in the world came together to write a book about the perfect life, they wouldn't be able to write about a better life than the one that I have with you and our Mille – only God can do that."

"Marjorie, I just wonder sometimes if I make you happy, if after all these years you'd been better off if you'd left Schaumburg. Don't you ever think on such things?"

"Ben Charles, you go on with that foolishness, now. Come here to me. If God had of wanted me to run off up North to some college or another, He would have put it in my heart. Now, if I done gave you any reason to think that the life you done made for me ain't enough, husband of mine, I'm sorry. It ain't never entered in my heart or mind to sin against you in that way. I am a truly favored woman, Ben Charles – above all that I could ever even think to ask for. Benjamin Charles Fouraukis, that world out there will never come close to doing better by me than you've done by me and our Millie all these years. I don't know how much more plain I can make myself, but I don't mind trying."

Daddy's eyes filled with tears but Momma caught each one before it could fall. Most men would be shame to let they woman see 'em cry, but not my daddy. Momma and

Schaumburg's Sweet Reminisce

Daddy knew each other like they know'd they own self, if not better.

Momma had a real kind way about her and that's what people loved most, maybe even more than her cooking. She liked to build people up in the Lord whether they appreciated her Bible talk or not; and she always loved on purpose – was always planting seeds.

Daddy wasn't without his seed planting. Figured he'd help a few folks that couldn't half-make ends meet, which was most people on account most of the town was made up of folks nearly too old to work. At the start of every planting season, he would ask God to provide his strength and the increase and he would make sure His will never failed. Started out small, but each passing harvest seemed to yield more than the last… and year after year, Daddy worked until he was knuckle-boned tired – but he never seemed to tire of it.

People would come from a little bit of everywhere looking for food. Whatever they could pick, they could have. The women elders of the church, mainly the few widows and the deacons' wives, rolled up their sleeves and canned a lot of what was left over for the church's pantry, wasting nothing.

Even the sheriff had done made a deal with Daddy. Said that he would supply all the labor he had for one square meal a day; said if a man didn't work, he shouldn't expect to eat. Sheriff said he'd heard that somewhere before but couldn't remember where from. Daddy told him it was Scripture, 2nd Thessalonians 3:10-13.

Daddy invited that old sheriff to Sunday morning church service. Two Sundays had done passed before he showed up, but when he did, he brought everybody that he had locked up at the time on account he didn't have nobody else to watch the jail.

*　*✳❈✳*　*

Deaconess Puryear took and sent everybody home just before evening set in, figured I'd had a long enough day and needed my rest. I reckon it was time I set with my own thoughts for a spell.

My mind was as tired as the day was long, but I didn't feel no ways tired. My soul was made glad and my spirit was made full today even through the tears. Oh, how I hoped and prayed I never emptied.

Mother Fentress, Sister Stella Jean, First Lady Tisdale, and a few other ladies finished up the kitchen chores, tidied up the house, and parted ways too; but I made 'em all promise to get everybody together and get back by there to help me eat up all that food that they'd left in the freezer box. I was sure I'd be needing to lean on each and every last one of 'em in the days and months to come. Told 'em to send over anybody in need of a meal or a place to rest they feet for a while.

The phone had been ringing off the hook the week prior with folks wanting to make arrangements to stay at the bed 'n breakfast. Deaconess Puryear asked to be heard and said that she didn't think it was proper for me to be in that big old house all by myself on account everybody and they momma knew that Momma and Daddy had done passed. Said any old fool could come 'round knocking with the wrong intentions.

I told Deaconess Puryear that I'd be alright. Told her that Daddy had taught me to shoot all his rifles and every last one was locked and loaded. Deaconess Puryear got so tickled to where her teeth almost fell out her mouth; but after

Schaumburg's Sweet Reminisce

a little back and forth, she let things be – but not before she told every Deacon under the sound of her voice that she'd be calling for somebody to get by here and check on me every day for as long as needed. Deaconess Puryear still saw me as that little, sweet, quiet child who used to come by and sit on her lap and help her shell purple-hull peas until both our fingers turned black – and in most ways I still was.

I milled around for a good while that evening trying to keep my mind settled; Satan is always at his best when you find yourself at your lowest point.

In all my years growing up in that house with all the love and joy any child could stand, I never thought I'd see the day to where I'd look around and find myself in need of either one.

I couldn't see the flicker from the porch light through all them thickets. I reckoned Elder Sinclair had done already bunked down in the east farm quarters for the evening. He gave such a beautiful talk today – made me so proud. Said that it was the first time he'd ever eulogized anyone let alone two people at the same time. Momma and Daddy was so much alike; if you knew the one, you knew the other. I never did get a chance to thank Elder Sinclair; Lord willing, there'd be breath in my body come morning.

I thought I might make myself a cup of hot tea and set out on the porch and listen to the sounds of the night, but I set my thoughts against it. I wasn't sleepy, I wasn't hungry, and didn't much feel like talking or thinking, quite frankly. I didn't know what to do with myself; I just wanted to be. I didn't much know what that meant or even looked like, but somehow I just felt like that was what I needed.

I made my way back into the kitchen and sat down at the supper table, first in Momma's chair, then Daddy's.

Thought about all them evenings we sat down to supper, how Daddy would give thanks and we'd eat and share with one another even if all we had to share was our own selves. I was gonna sho' nuff miss that.

But I guess I be grown now, all on my own. Only had myself and the good Lord to answer to, but I wouldn't dare let Momma and Daddy's rearing be in vain.

Didn't have a wild hair in me. Wasn't moved by much; I was what old folks referred to as an old soul. Didn't bother me none. I liked the company of older folk, just liked being around 'em, and they didn't seem to mind having me come 'round neither.

I looked around that big old kitchen and finally knew why Momma loved being in it so much – and it wasn't because most folks preferred her cooking over their own. It was because Momma could control the entire house from this-here kitchen. It was center mass of everything and it echoed loud.

When she called out, her voice would fill every room, so no matter where I was in that house, because I had ears to hear and I was the daughter of Majorie Rose Foraukis, it was best that I get in there to that kitchen the first time she called.

Momma always sounded louder than she was, but if I was in trouble, it didn't matter how soft she spoke – I was still gonna get it, always did; but somehow her singing would always make me feel a whole lot better after my whooping. I don't know why Momma always sung a hymn after she tore my bottom to pieces, but I used to wonder if it woulda hurt a whole lot less if she'd sung her hymn while she was whooping me.

Schaumburg's Sweet Reminisce

No telling how many songs and hymns had been sung in that kitchen, how many biscuits, cakes, and pies had done baked in that oven, hams and turkeys roasted, and stoves Momma burned out over the years. Them old cast-iron skillets of hers was like looking in a mirror. Was hoping to be able to put 'em to use in the coming months along with that old iron caldron of hers. Fill it to the rim with some gumbo or some fresh chitterlings and hog maws and invite the whole church out to the farm. We'd had our fair share of fellowships over the years.

Daddy showed me how to take coats and hats and how to help little old ladies up from they seats. Said I needed to be gentle on account old folks break easy. Daddy would get so tickled at me sometimes. If Momma had her hands full in the kitchen, she'd send me with my daddy to receive our guests. I'd be right there stepping on his heels until he grabbed me by the hand to help me along. I practiced my welcome all the time so I would always be ready. Those times made me feel like the woman of the house in a way – and now I was.

Whenever Momma was trying to get supper on the table, I had to be in eyesight but not under-foot. Started washing dishes when I was old enough to balance myself on an empty coffee can. Taught me the right way to make dish water and the easiest way to soak a pot if I needed to, but told me that if I didn't burn nothing, I wouldn't have to worry about that at all. Told me it was always best to cook with gas, if I could. Taught me how to pull together a little something real quick if somebody just showed up without calling first. Taught me how to stretch a meal and how to serve up leftovers so it'd taste like you just made it – even though everybody know leftovers is the best kind of eatin'.

Momma'd always tell me that one day I'd put supper

on my own table all by myself, but not until it was time. Said three women could cook a pot of greens with the same fixings and each pot of greens would come out tasting different on account every woman had her own special touch in everything she did. Told me to leave my touch only where it counted. Didn't ever wanna hear tell of me playing house.

        *   *❄❆❄*   *

"Now Millie, don't worry yourself none if you burn a meal every now and then starting out; just don't burn your house down. We done all burned more meals than we wanna lend truth to."

I don't reckon nobody nowhere can say they rattled pots in this-here kitchen but Marjorie Rose Fourakis. She just felt some kind of way 'bout folks prancing 'round her kitchen, always had.

"Ben, that child of mine, picked 20 pounds of chitterlings today. Didn't take her no time. Ain't a soul alive that could pick chitterlings cleaner than our Millie. I was telling Sister Gertrude and Sister Irene about it and they both now asked if I would let our Millie pick a bucket a piece. I almost told 'em 'No.' Who you know standing in line to clean chitterlings? I think they may need to clean they own chitterlings. I told 'em I'd have to talk to you about it and see."

"Well, I don't want to know nothin' 'bout no chitterlings 'til they ready for my fork."

"Well, we both know that, Ben, but what you think? Might we oughta?"

"Woman, I reckon you going on about how good a job babygirl did put 'em up to asking."

Schaumburg's Sweet Reminisce

"I guess it serve me right on account I was going on and on about it. They said they'd pay her, but they gonna have to pay her what she want. I'm not gonna make her. She gonna have to agree to it."

"Oh, I think she will, Marjorie. I think Millie will make 'em a fair offer, if she charge 'em anything at all."

"Ben, you know, I asked our Millie why she like cleaning chitterlings. Guess what she told me?'

"How's that, woman?"

"She said it ain't that she like cleaning chitterlings, but while she cleaning 'em she get to thinking on how the Lord just keep on cleaning her up on the inside. But now, she say she eat 'em because they's the fruit of her labor. I got happy and tickled at the same time, Ben Charles."

"Ain't that something? I wish I could have been standing there to hear my babygirl minister that Word."

"Yes, Lord. That child of mine sho' is something special. Her cornbread came out so nice and pretty the other evening."

"Babygirl made that cornbread?"

"Couldn't you tell?"

"Well, come to think of it, cornbread was a lot sweeter than it usually be."

"Umm hmm. That child's hand just as heavy as it wanna be with that sugar."

"Now that I think about it, that's why babygirl kept smiling. She didn't say not one word."

"She ain't all the way there on that fried chicken, but I'm gonna keep working with her on it. It take a little time to get good at frying chicken, but my Millie is getting mighty close. I keep telling her she got to get that grease just right, drop that chicken in that oil, and let it alone. That child be turning that chicken like she turning rope, you hear me? I said, 'Now Millie, you can't be poking and prodding that chicken, put'd in there, and let it be. It got to cook down to the bone."

"Scared she gonna burn it, I reckon. Babygirl get a little anxious at times – always in a hurry to get things done. Only thing worse than eatin' burnt chicken is eating chicken that's half done."

"Say it again. Know what she told me, Ben?"

"How's that, woman?"

"Told me she wanted me to teach her everything I know."

"Yeah?"

"I ain't told her yet, but I done gathered up all my recipes. I'm gonna have to rewrite 'em all, but I done got 'em all together none the same. Gon' find me a nice fancy hat box to put 'em all in there for her."

"Woman, I think that'll make a mighty fine gift for our babygirl."

"It'd make an even better wedding gift, but I'm just gonna let that alone."

"Everything in God's time, woman. Don't go letting your thoughts go to getting you in your feelings about things.

Schaumburg's Sweet Reminisce

If the Lord see fit for us to see grandchildren before we take our last breath, we will; and if He don't, it is well with our souls."

"Ben, I hear you, baby."

"Babygirl told me she had done fixed up her own little special rub for that old hen I plan to put on the grill for you for Mother's Day."

"Sho' nuff?"

"I got a good whiff of that old rub and it 'bout took me off my feet. Had a good bit of kick to it. She had done put something in there that I couldn't quite put my finger on."

"Well, what it remind you of?"

"Woman, I don't even know. Look like I ought to been know'd what it was. She'd been out there in my salt shed mixing up some of my old spices. Ain't no telling what Babygirl done mixed up out there. I got some old herbs out there I done had for years."

"That rub ain't gonna make us sick now, is it, Ben?"

"I doubt it. Might cure some things we never now know'd we had."

"Well then, I reckon that'd be a blessing."

"That'd be a blessing indeed, woman. I bet you that rub gonna be pretty good on the old bird."

Daddy always did all the cooking on Mother's Day. Most times he'd just fry up some perch for breakfast and put some meat on the grill for later. Momma didn't mind taking the day off because she loved her some perch and Mother's

Day was the only day she chose to allow Daddy to do everything. But I'd gotten old enough to share in preparing the meals too.

Momma took me over town to buy everything I'd be needing and, because I was spending my own money, I could fix what I wanted even if it was Mother's Day. Me and Momma liked most of the same things anyhow.

Momma was telling any and everybody who would listen that day how proud she was to have me cook her Mother's Day meal. Made me shame-faced and nervous all at the same time. They'd be asking later how good of a meal I put on the table.

After being over town half the day, I told Momma that we needed to get home so I could get started on my supper. Made me feel real good on the inside to say that. Momma smiled and held her head up high.

We was near 'bout to the house and I still was going over my list in my head making sure I hadn't forgot nothing – had done forgot I had the list in my hand. Momma laughed. She know'd I was nervous. This was my very first supper all by myself.

"Millie, you got everything?"

"Yes, ma'am."

"I'm glad. You look like you planned a mighty fine meal."

"Yes ma'am, I believe I have."

"Now Millie, I'm gonna turn you loose in my kitchen. I done taught you nearly everything I know, so I know you ready. You and your daddy make sure you clean up real proper now. Y'all know how I feel about my kitchen being left a mess."

"Me and Daddy decided we gonna cook outside on the grill, Momma."

"You gon' fix your sides on the grill too, child?"

"Yes ma'am – on the pit. We got things already laid out. Daddy said cooking over that pit was kinda like cooking on a gas stove, but I had to watch them hot spots."

Daddy stayed out the way and let me do what I needed to do to get my sides together, but he stayed close enough to keep a eye on them flames and on me. I gave Daddy some of my special rub the night before so his hen would be nice and right. I didn't really know how it was gonna turn out, but I had a good feeling about it.

Daddy took his time and roasted that hen nice and slow. Him and Momma seemed to be real good at everything they did.

"Babygirl, you ready?"

"Yes, sir."

"Alright then, what you got?"

"I got some ox tails, collards, red beans and rice, candied yams, and hoe cakes."

"Babygirl, I can't wait. You got everything you need out the house?"

"Yes, sir."

"Alright, we may as well get started. Them coals is probably right where they need to be. You remember where I told you them hot spots was in that pit, don't you?"

"Yes sir, I remember."

I let Daddy taste everything before we called on Momma for supper. I followed Momma's recipes to the letter except for maybe a dash, a pinch, or a sprinkle here and there.

"You think it taste alright, Daddy?"

"Babygirl, it's better than alright. You cook almost as good as your momma. You got your own special touch. Let me go on in here right now and get your momma. We been at it nearly all day and your daddy ready to eat."

While Momma pulled herself together from her nap, Daddy came on back out and helped hisself to another taste of everything.

"Come on out here, Marjorie. I'm ready to get to these ox tails and candied yams Babygirl done made."

"Ben, I'm on my way. Don't y'all start without me."

"Babygirl done outdone herself, Marjorie, do you hear me?"

"You ain't got to tell me none. I smelled that good eatin' all the way in the house. As soon as I smelled them yams, I drifted on off to sleep so I'd be good and ready to lift my fork a few more times than I probably should."

We'd fixed up the picnic table out in the yard. Daddy had run off while the hen was roasting and cut Momma some wildflowers. Made everything look real nice. Used Momma's fine plates and silverware too.

"Everything looks so nice. Y'all didn't have to go out your way, but I'm glad you did. All this food? All this-here for me?"

"It sho' is, woman, and I'm mighty glad you can't eat all this-here by yourself."

Daddy grabbed Momma up in his arms and gave her a kiss on the cheek. "I reckon I might ought to eat dessert first. What you think, Millie?"

"Ben, you go on somewhere now. You come get some of this-here good food in you first."

"Happy Mother's Day, woman!"

"Thank you, Ben. I'm a blessed and happy woman, indeed."

"Millie, I declare that was one of the best meals that done ever graced my tongue. I'm so proud. You cooked everything out here on that-there pit?

"Yes ma'am, while Daddy kept watch."

"She sho' did, Marjorie, and I didn't have to hardly tell her what to do or how to do it."

"Well, I'll be. Millie, fix your momma another plate of food, would you? A small helping, but heavy on the ox tails. They seasoned just right and falling off the bone."

"Woman, when you start eating two plates of food?"

"Benjamin Charles, now I know you not counting plates when you got two sitting on your belt already and eyeballing your third. And I saw you off in them pots before I even now made my way out here."

Daddy got real tickled at Momma's fussing and leaned over and gave her another kiss.

"And Millie, from now on you gonna be in that kitchen cooking all by yourself. One Sunday out the month ought to be enough to get you started and me your daddy'll get after them dishes for you."

"Yes, ma'am. Thank you, Momma."

"I declare, child, food tasting this good need to be on the table every day of the week."

"Happy Mother's Day, Momma!"

"Well, I thank you, baby. You and your daddy done made this-here Mother's Day mighty special for me. Ben, won't you bring that ice cream out the freezer while me and Millie sit here and talk a spell. My stomach can't hold not another thing, but I at least wants to taste it."

Momma threw such a fuss about my cooking, folks started inviting they own selves over for dinner on Sundays. I didn't much mind none. Momma always said if you can cook for one you can cook for one too many – all that matters is that you able to cook to start with.

I never had no special company come visit me directly, so I just settled it in my mind that all of Momma and Daddy's company was my company too. So, if you really think about it, I had company all the time.

Schaumburg's Sweet Reminisce

We liked gettin' company. It was always somebody wanting to make a fuss over me. They liked asking me a whole bunch of questions, too – most times the same ones each time they saw me.

Mr. Pratt would always ask me how a little girl like me come to be so pretty. I told him it was favor from the Lord.

Mrs. Florence would always ask me what I was gonna do with all that hair I had on top my head. I told her that she would have to ask the Lord because He had every hair on my head numbered.

Mrs. Patricia would always tell me how straight and pretty my teeth was on account she didn't have none of hers. I told her that she could have all my baby teeth because the tooth fairy was of the devil.

Another somebody would ask me if I was getting my lesson like I was supposed to, and then one somebody or another asked me if I was reading my Bible everyday and minding my momma and daddy.

Momma would let me visit with our company in my own way for a good little while before giving me her special look to let me know I had overstayed my welcome. I just always felt like I could be myself around old folks. They made me feel like what I had to say was so important.

One time I felt I had cause to correct Mother Pratt in front of everybody. I had been standing on the other side of the wall and listening the whole time. Mother Pratt didn't seem to mind; she excused herself, corrected her grammar, gave me a kiss on the cheek, and complimented Momma on how smart I was. Told me that before long, I'd be the smartest girl in all of Schaumburg, if I wasn't already. But the look on Momma's face spoke a word to me that it didn't speak to all of her lady friends. I was sent back out to the kitchen to wash up the dishes and sweep off the back porch.

Me and Momma always did the dishes together when she had a lot of friend-girls over at one time. It was a lot of dishes in that sink and they was still being dirtied. Didn't look like Momma and her lady friends would ever stop eating and drinking. Most times she would buy me a little something or give me a few dollars for helping out during one of her get-togethers. I could tell that Momma was mad, so I didn't figure on her getting me nothing this time.

Momma drew the double doors to the parlor to where I couldn't half hear no more. They was all talking at the same time anyhow, but the parlor was so far from the kitchen, all I could do was hear them laugh every five seconds. If I stood real still, I could make out some of what they was saying, but I needed to get all them dishes done before Momma came back in to check on me. I knew all of Momma's friend-girls and I could always tell who it was laughing or talking without being in the room if I could hear 'em.

Momma always laughed the loudest, but not so much that day and she was sure to let me know why a little later after her company left. Ms. Sadie chuckled, Mrs. Rosa Mae cackled, and a good bunch of 'em hollered. After a few hours, the ladies thanked Momma for having them over and planned they next get-together.

I can remember each one of 'em hugging me real tight, just long enough to pray God's mercy over me. They knew my momma all too well.

I'd find out that while Mother Pratt was full of forgiveness that Momma wouldn't be so merciful toward my ill-manners. Later that night, Momma snatched me from my sleep, slob and all, and tanned my backside something good.

Chapter Seventeen

Momma had used the same lavender and sweet pea, talcum powder she did as a little girl to freshen her and Daddy's bed sheets. It was Daddy's favorite, so she never gave thought to changing it, plus Daddy made sure she never ran out of it. Had two whole tubs tucked away in the back of her vanity that hadn't even yet been opened. When I was a little biddy thing, if I was near when Momma was setting the bed, she'd dust both my wrists and behind each ear and that would send me running straight to my daddy's arms to love on me.

Just like Momma used to, I dusted both my wrists and behind each ear and wore that special lavender and sweet pea talc powder for the funeral to have 'em both near to me, but it hurt my heart that my daddy wasn't there for me to run to.

Like anybody else, I'd have my good days and my bad days. Most days I'd wear just a little bit of that special, smell-good powder, just a little; but on those hard days when I got to missing Momma and Daddy something terrible and that loneliness got to riding my back like the dark of night, I'd get to sprinkling a little bit here and there until I had done filled every little nook and cranny so wherever I stood, I'd be reminded of my momma and daddy. I didn't like thinking about Momma and Daddy so much because it hurt, but I sho' nuff didn't wanna forget.

Daddy always said that fear had a way of talking loud and long – most times to steer you away from the will of God. I loved what Momma and Daddy had together, but settling down and having babies had me downright shook. I hadn't yet figured out what about it all had me the most scared. I grew up telling myself that what Momma and Daddy had was enough for me on account I could never be the woman that my momma was and any man I allowed to love me could never be my daddy.

I climbed the first set of oak-stained stairs in that old house. Daddy had fixed all the squeaks except one, the seventh step – said the seventh step was the step where Momma's water broke on the day she had me.

Momma would be beside herself telling off on Daddy. Would carry on about how he ran back and forth on them steps like a chicken with its head cut off when she told him it was time, hollering louder than she was. Momma said she was in pain, but she got to laughing so hard at him that her water broke right there on that step.

When I turned a year old, Momma had Daddy carve my name and the day I was born into this world on that very step; it's where Momma taught me to spell my name too. Most days I'd be waiting right there on that same step to jump into my daddy's arms when he came in from the field or if I was on punishment.

I stopped short of the top step and looked back. Funny thought came to mind. The whole time I was growing up, I ain't never took and fell down them steps, not once; but now I sho' nuff got up 'em something quick like when

Sheriell Scott

Momma got after me with my daddy's black strap or a fresh switch.

    The door was shut to Momma and Daddy's room. Wasn't a soul in that house but me, but just like I always did, I knocked because I knew better than to let myself in without being invited first. I pretended to hear my daddy on the other side of that door.

    "Who is it?"

    "Me."

    "Who is me?"

    "Me, Daddy."

    "Me?"

    "Yes, sir."

    "What you want, me?"

    "Daddy, I wanna come in."

    "You got any money?"

    "No, sir."

    "You got any food?"

    "No, sir."

    "What you got?"

    "Just me."

    "Who is me?"

Schaumburg's Sweet Reminisce

"*Me*, daddy. Millicent Rose Foraukis!"

"Well, who is that?"

"Daaaaddddy?"

"Come on in, babygirl."

"Okay, I'm coming in."

"Hey babygirl. Oh, that *was* you?"

"Daddy."

A separate set of stairs off to the right took me up to the door of the attic, Momma and Daddy's special place when they needed to fast and pray together on something. Momma said her and Daddy stayed on they face before the Lord in that attic a whole year before I was even a spec in her belly.

Momma's faith was tested time and time again. Wavered more than it probably should have, but it never failed. God didn't allow her to suffer no longer than He knew best for her; gave her my daddy to stick right on in there with her until she got to the end of herself, and when she did, He opened her womb.

The attic was warm, swept clean but dusty – near 'bout empty except for a tattered Bible, two old sitting chairs, a few boxes, and whatnot.

After Momma got sick, her and Daddy would come up here to pray when she was well enough to leave the bed. And just like always, God answered in the way He knew best for her and for Daddy too.

As bare as it was, that old attic had a peace about it

that the rest of the house no longer had. Felt like all the peace I would ever need was right there in that room with me, the kind of peace that almost took your breath.

The sun had been resting for a while, so I lit the wick to a small oil lamp; didn't really need to on account the moon showed almost bright as day.

I felt the tears wrestling in my stomach – they'd be coming for me soon. I wasn't gonna fight 'em. Soon as I sat down, the last bit of strength left my body. Figured I'd just let myself be and trust that the strength of the good Lord would be made perfect in my weakness. I needed to pray, but I couldn't, so I asked the Lord to whisper my name to the Father and to make intercession for me all night if He had too. Then I just held myself tight and thought on the goodness of the Lord and let the tears fall until I fell asleep.

The sun met me first thing bright and early the next morning. I felt rested but like there was something on the inside fighting to get out of me and I thought on the night before when I asked the Lord to pray for me. I'd wondered what the Lord had prayed for on my behalf.

I never came up here much as a child, but I didn't even now wanna leave. I felt in my spirit that I would soon have my own special work to do and reckoned I'd find it within the walls of this special space.

I melted back down into that chair and hummed a verse of my momma's favorite song:

Jesus prayed for me.
Took all of my sins to the cross.
He bore my burdens and all of my shame.
I am empowered when I call His name.
He's rich in grace and mercy unmeasurable.

Schaumburg's Sweet Reminisce

What a Love, Oh, what Love He has for me.

I was soon ushered to my knees to spend some time before the Lord in prayer.

It was day by day after I laid Momma and Daddy to rest, but the food, the phone calls, and visits went on for months. That's what love does – it takes on the burden of another.

Elder Sinclair left out just a few days after the funeral. Got an offer on the railroad paying pretty good money over in East Georgia. The head man over the railroad there had been calling long before Momma took ill. He'd turned 'em down at first. Wanted to serve Momma and Daddy on the farm for a spell and learn a few things; felt it was most important. Took a liking to Schaumburg and figured he'd buy a piece of land at some point, settle down, and maybe start a family of his own.

Elder Sinclair said he'd be back – told me so himself. I wanted to tell him that he didn't have to rush off, but he just made me so nervous. He'd been so good to Momma and Daddy; I really hated to see him go.

"You be hearing from me real soon, Ms. Millie, and I'll be back to visit before you know it. I'll be praying for you."

Elder went his way – looked back twice at me, smiled and waved. I didn't oblige him the first or the second time and I had no idea why.

From time to time, some of the mothers from the church would get together and come for a visit. Sometimes they'd stay through the night and breakfast the next morning. We'd carry on way on into the night, sharing in good times and be 'round there dragging the next morning.

Elder Sinclair started calling every morning to check on me and then again just before sundown to make sure I locked up the house alright. Every now and then he'd ask about how things were coming along on the farm. I'd get tickled at myself when he did. I didn't need Elder Sinclair telling me nothing about farming, truth be told. I knew more about that farm than he did; I was the daughter of Benjamin Charles and Marjorie Rose Foraukis and they'd taught me everything I needed to know about running a farm and keeping house; besides, them mothers at the church wasn't gonna allow me to suffer no harm or no heavy lifting.

"Morning, Ms. Millie."

"Elder."

"How'd things go over the other evening there?"

"Everything went just fine, Elder. It come a hard and heavy rain. Rained all night and near 'bout half the morning. I expect it to be pretty hot today."

"You can count on that, Ms. Millie, and I bet that creek way on up there this morning and running fast."

"I reckon that to be true, Elder. Be time to cut them pastures again before you know."

"Yes ma'am, Ms. Millie. Gonna be a whole lotta hay."

"How's things coming along for you there in East Georgia?"

"Well, everything's coming along just fine, just fine. The head man here want me to stay on a while longer than he talked about right at first. I agreed to it, but I sho' misses the farm."

Schaumburg's Sweet Reminisce

"Lord willing, this-here farm'll be here waiting on you."

"Yes ma'am, Ms. Mille, I pray it so."

"Elder, sometimes I feel like this-here farm is all I got left of my momma and daddy even though I got scores of memories. Some days it fills me up with everything I need and then on them other days, it look like it might swallow me whole. But by His grace."

"Ms. Millie, you keep holding on now."

"Oh, I aim to do just that, Elder. I aim to indeed."

"The church seeing after you alright, ain't they?"

"Everybody's been mighty kind, Elder.

"That's good, that's good, Ms. Millie."

"Elder?"

"Ms. Millie?"

"It means a lot to me to have you call and check on me the way that you do. I sho' do appreciate you."

"Ms. Millie?"

"Yes, Elder?"

"I thinks about you all the time. I hated leaving so soon after the funeral, but I makes sure to cover you in prayer every time you cross my mind."

"Well... Elder Sinclair... I hope to cross your mind more often than not and I appreciate your prayers. Believe you me, I can use every one you can muster up."

Me and Elder Sinclair would carry on for months; he'd write to me often and send me all kinds of fine chocolates and fancy teas, but it'd be years before I'd lay eyes on him again.

But life would soon bring about things that even an early morning phone call from East Georgia couldn't make right.

I'd up and leave Schaumburg for a short spell to study business up north. Momma had done taught me so well to where them folks up north came searching for me to attend their school. They wanted the likes of me and I needed to be equipped to run that bed n' breakfast Momma started before she died. I wanted to do her and Daddy both proud, even in death. They'd be proud knowing that their babygirl was able to teach a few of them city-slickers a thing or two about running a big farm in the backwood bottoms of Schaumburg, Tennessee. Had they been living, they'd been able to witness me give my very own speech and walk across that platform first in my class. It wasn't no more than a handful of us; but for a lazy-talking, home-schooled, southern church-girl, it was good just being numbered among 'em.

I wasn't gone too long. The world outside of Schaumburg didn't interest me much and that fancy schooling didn't teach me much more than what I'd learned watching my daddy run this-here farm all his life. His way of doing anything, even business, come straight from the Bible. But long-gone were the days of folks doing business with just they word and a handshake.

*   ✲❄✲   *

I hastened on back to Schaumburg, but not before I got a chance to visit a few of those well-travelled bed n' breakfasts along my route. I managed seven in all, stayed two nights at each one and made nice with all kinds. After I'd had my fill of sleeping in all those many different beds, I headed straight on back to Schaumburg. I couldn't have been more glad about anything in my life.

Last time I was on a train back into Schaumburg was the year I come back to see after my momma and daddy.

Wasn't many folks taking the rails that day – counted just five in our cart alone. Man sitting across the way from me told the train attendant to offer me the meals meant for his traveling companion on account they was all already paid for.

I'd prepared my own lunch before leaving the last bed and breakfast on my route. Mrs. Sarah Neeley didn't mind me stirring 'round her kitchen none neither; thought in my stirring, I might leave a pinch of my momma's special touch on her pots and pans and whatnot. I didn't know about all that, but she told me she thought I'd make a mighty fine bed n' breakfast madam. Said I could cook like nothing she'd ever dreamt of and she'd been to school a right smart of years for it.

"If you can feed 'em good, don't mind cleaning up after 'em, leave 'em alone until they have a question for you to answer, and then answer they question – you'll keep 'em coming back for years. Most folks just wanna be left alone but still be made to feel like they matter. I've fed and cleaned up after many a'generation in this-here very house, including my own. Sooner or later, you just get a knack for it and your home becomes their home away from home." Mrs. Sarah was sure in every bit of what she told me.

I felt it un-proper at first to oblige the old man; besides, he was a stranger to me and even if he wasn't, a woman ought not to always say yes on account she can. I was but a few years older and still learning myself, but the railway attendant, a good bit older than myself, told me that she thought it'd be alright. Said that the man and his wife traveled by train once a month to see their grandchildren – wife wanted to see their faces as much as she could before she died. This-here trip would have been her last had she not died first.

The attendant told me that she was needing my answer. We waited for the man to look our way. I at least wanted to see what was in his eyes. He was near 'bout a tear away from dry bones his own self. The pain that showed on his face, I'd sho' nuff seen before. Reminded me of my daddy's pain when his sweet Marjorie died.

I obliged the old man from where I sat and since I was brought up to respond in kind to kindness received, I told the attendant that I'd be changing my seat. She nodded and went head on – guess I had took up enough of her time trying to make my mind up.

The closer I got to him, the harder he cried; never lifted his head. I took my seat right beside him and the harder he cried, the harder I prayed for his strength and mine:

"Meet him at his need, Lord, as only you can. Declare a new thing in the midst of his pain right now, Father. In Jesus' name, I pray. Amen."

I laid into one of Momma's favorite hymns… and then another. It wasn't too long after that the man stopped crying. Dried his last tear with one hand just in time to pick up his fork to feed hisself with the other.

We both had a lot to say and share on a whole lot of

things. Never would've guessed we hadn't met before that day. Hadn't ever given too much thought to know how white folks' children was raised, but I guess if you raised to fear the Lord, the upbringing ought not be too much different.

"Ms. Mille, it's good to know them that belong to the Lord."

"Yes. Yes, it is, Mr. Montgomery, and even better to know Him for thyself. I thank you kindly for the meal, Mr. Montgomery. That was mighty kind of you."

"Well, the joy of your spirit made for a fine time, Ms. Millie. Remember me in your prayers, if you'd be so kind?

"I sho' will, Mr. Montgomery, I sho' will."

"We'll be seeing you." Mr. Montgomery smiled, tipped his hat, and stepped down off the train.

I wondered what would become of old Sterling Joe Montgomery. I believed to see him again and prayed his strength in the Lord.

*　*❋❂❋*　*

I still had a'ways to ride, but I could feel the pull of Schaumburg from every direction. Couldn't now hardly wait to get home and rest a while, but it was clear to me, I had much work to do – Kingdom work that would stretch far and wide.

The need would come to me and be met in the way of the Lord. I told the Lord that it was just me and Him now, knowing good and full-well that it was all Him on account I couldn't do nothin' without Him. I told the Lord whatever He wanted me to do, I'd do – but the Lord already knew what was in my heart for Him. He put it there.

Deaconess Puryear was the first face I seen when I stepped off the train, but Mother Fentress got the first hug and she sho' nuff knew how to give a good hug – put all her back and full bosom into it.

"Bless God... Schaumburg's Rose is finally home. You come on over here and give Mother Fentress a big hug. It sho' is good to see you, baby."

"Yes ma'am, Mother Fentress, I've been needing one of your hugs for some time now."

"Well, baby, my arms is always open to you."

Mother Fentress was the oldest mother in the church. Nobody really knew how old she was; she just always said she was the oldest and Mother Fentress didn't argue with you.

"Don't you leave away from 'round here and stay gone this long again now, child. We been missing you all this time, but I still gots all your letters, every last one."

"Yes, ma'am. I'm home and I aim to stay put, Mother Fentress."

"I love you, baby. So glad you home."

"I love you too, Mother Fentress."

"It sho' is good to finally lay eyes on you, Sister Mille, and you just as pretty as you ever did wanna be. You even now look smart, don't she, Mother Fentress? Your momma and daddy would be so proud."

"Well, I thank you kindly, Deaconess Puryear. It's

good to be home. I've had my fill of the big city, and if not for all my days, for a good long while I imagine."

"Well, you welcome, Sister Millie, and it's sho' nuff good to have you back with us. Ain't that right, Mother Fentress?"

"Yes Lord, Deaconess Puryear. It's a mighty fine day, a fine day it is. Bless God, bless His holy name!"

"I hope I learned more than I'll ever need to know about business to do right by Momma's bed n' breakfast and Daddy's farm."

"Sister Millie, you gonna do just fine, just fine I say."

"Thank you, Deaconess Puryear."

"Baby?"

"Yes ma'am, Mother Fentress?"

"If I didn't know no better, I'd say you done put on a little weight, child."

"Yes ma'am, I did."

"Is that right?"

"And she carrying it all in her hips, Mother Fentress – just like Marjorie."

"Sho' nuff is, just like our Marjorie Rose."

I had filled out quite nicely. Momma'd be so tickled to see me with a little weight on these old bones of mine.

Sheriell Scott

"Well, you care to sit a while, Sister Millie, or you ready for me and Mother Fentress to take you on out to the farm? You been on that train for several days now. I imagine you ready to get on home and look things over. They kept it up so nice whilst you was gone, just like your daddy, but not nearly as good."

"Shouldn't have much to tend to nohow now, Sister Millie. Me and Mother Fentress let ourselves in and found work for our hands to do whilst the house aired out. Ain't good for a house to be shut up that long. Took me and Mother Fentress two whole days, but we managed with no problem at all, Sister Millie."

"Baby, that's a mighty big house. I reckon you could fit a whole army up in there if you tried."

"Well, I'm mighty grateful to the both of you. I know it was a lot of work on account I done had to clean it more than a few times by myself. Never did seem to bother Momma none – but not much did."

"Well, me and Mother Fentress was more than glad to do it."

"I wasn't doing nothing no way and ain't no way in the world Deaconess Puryear could have swept and pulled together that big old house all by herself."

"Well, since I ain't got to do all I was thinking I had to do, I reckon we ought to sit for a spell. Care for a Coca-Cola? A slice of pie?"

"Baby, Mother Fentress will have a Coca-Cola *and* a slice of pie."

"Yes ma'am, Mother Fentress. Deaconess Puryear,

you have anything?"

"I'm fine, Sister Millie, I'm still holding my breakfast."

"Well, Mother Fentress, I reckon I'll have a Coca-Cola, too. Y'all excuse me; I'll be right back."

"Okay baby, be sure to pull them Coca-Colas from the back; they keep the coldest ones back in the back. Pull 'em way from the back now, ya hear? And I'll have a slice of chess pie –"

"Yes ma'am, Mother Fentress."

"Mother Fentress, that sho' is a lot of sugar."

I was thinking the same as Deaconess Puryear but dare not say.

"Now, Deaconness Puryear, don't you think I know that? She asked me what I wanted, not what I needed."

"I'm just saying, Mother Fentress, that's a heap of sugar."

"You saying a bit more than you should, Deaconess. The child had done asked me what I wanted. What? I'm supposed to tell a tale when I know the truth? I know it's a whole heap of sugar; reckon I'm just gonna add it to the rest of my sugar."

"Add to the rest of it? Mother Fentress, what you talkin' 'bout?"

"That's right, Deaconess Puryear. That old doctor say I gots the sugar anyhow – so, I reckon I'll just add this-here sugar to the rest of it."

"Mother Fentress, you's a mess."

"Deaconess Puryear, I know that and I know one other thing, too. I know that pie I'm 'bout to eat ain't gon' taste nowhere near 'bout as good as mine."

"Is that so, Mother Fentress?"

"You'll know it to be so, Deaconess Puryear, just as soon as our Millicent Rose bring it on out here to me."

"Mother Fentress, you was right about them Coca-Colas – they both now even got a little ice in 'em. Here's your pie. I got you a nice piece, I believe."

"Thank you, baby. You have some?"

"No ma'am. I thank you kindly though."

"Well, I'm not gon' ask you twice, child."

"You go head on and enjoy yourself, Mother Fentress. They still got quite a few pies in there. Woman said they been trying to sell 'em for three days now. I hope it's to your liking – can't nobody make 'em as good as you."

"That's what I been sitting here trying to tell Deaconess Puryear. Is you a believer now, Deaconess Puryear? You heard what she said. Everybody seems to know 'bout Mamie Fentress' chess pies except you."

"You sure you don't want nothing, Deaconess Puryear?"

"Sister Mille, you and Mother Fentress go head on, I'm alright. I be just fine."

Schaumburg's Sweet Reminisce

"Sister Millie, just before your train pulled in, I was telling Mother Fentress that you got pretty close to 500 bales of hay between them two barns and down yonder there in that bottom."

"Millicent Rose?"

"Yes ma'am, Mother Fentress?"

"Baby, what in the world you plan to do with all that hay? Reckon you be able to sell it all?"

"That's a whole lot a hay. By the time I try to sell it all, I'll been done cut and baled that much more or better, but I sho' would hate for all that hay to go to rot on me. I reckon whoever need it, can have it; and then, once I get them herds back up, I'll be alright."

"You sho' 'bout that, Sister Millie? That's a right smart of money you stand to make if you sell it."

"Deaconess Puryear, folks would have to come from near and far and I'd have to get that price way on down there to get folks to buy up that hay on account most folks got fields of they own they can cut."

"Well, Sister Millie, you right about that. Best way to get rid of anything is to give it away. Folks liable take you up on anything that's free whether they need it or not. Mother Fentress, what you got to say on things?"

"Well, I believe in my heart Brother Ben would agree to the same. He just had a way about him, didn't he? Alwayst' to give, expecting nothin in return. If he had it, you could rest sure that if you needed it, he'd sho' nuff put it in your hand."

"Ben and Marjorie both, Mother Fentress. But I reckon when you speak of one, you speak of the other. And speaking of hands, Sister Mille, them they hired to work the farm whilst you was gone done already been paid and done left, so you got the farm all to yourself now."

"Did a real good job from what me and Deaconess Puryear could make out."

"Well that's mighty fine to hear, Mother Fentress. I aim to look everything over once I get settled."

"Sister Millie, I don't know what you plan to do out there on that big old farm all by yourself whilst you running that bed n' breakfast, but I'm sure all that fancy schooling will help you think of something."

"I got a few things I been thinking on, Deaconess Puryear."

"Well, whatever you decide to do, you just let Deaconess Puryear know when you ready and she'll let me know, so we both'll be ready... 'cause I ain't gonna be doing nothing nohow. And another thing, baby, don't be too shame to ask for help, hear?"

"Yes ma'am, Mother Fentress. I'll be sure to let you know when the time comes."

"Mother Fentress, how's your pie?"

"Well, like I told you before she brought it out here, Deaconess Puryear, it don't near 'bout taste better than mine but, because our Millicent Rose done spent her money on it, I reckon I'll eat it. I don't believes in wasting nothing and I'm of the mind to let 'em know that putting this-here pie on this-here fancy plate ain't do it a bit of good."

"Mother Fentress, now how you know it don't taste better than yours? You's just one person."

"Deaconess Puryear, didn't you hear Millicent Rose tell you that the woman said they been trying to sell this-here pie for three days now? That ought to tell you something. If they'd been my pies, they wouldn't still be in there."

* ****** *

Mother Fentress and Deaconess Puryear couldn't be left to sit and stir together for too long. Funny thing was, most times when you seen one, you seen the other; but too much had been said and done over the years for one or the other to let bygones be all the way gone.

One year, Mother Fentress and Deaconess Puryear fell out over who was supposed to MC the program at church for First Lady Tisdale's appreciation. Now, Mother Fentress had been MC'ing First lady Tisdale's appreciation day for as long as anybody could remember, but at the time, she thought she might still be wrestling with her gout and told them to let somebody else do it and that she would send her love offering and a letter of love to be read before the church. Said she wanted to give First Lady Tisdale her flowers while she was yet living.

Mother Fentress thought that since she had been knowing First Lady Tisdale the longest, that she ought to been able to say who could MC her program. Thought it was only right because she was the one who come up with the idea from the git-go.

But now, whilst Mother Fentress was at home nursing her gout, the church board voted in favor of Deaconess Puryear to MC the program. No sooner than Mother Fentress got wind of things, she called for all the Elders of the church to pray and lay hands on her. You'd a thought Mother Fentress was on her death bed, but she was a firm believer that "the effectual fervent prayers of the righteous availeth much." The Board moved to let their vote stand anyhow. Mother Fentress threw such a fuss, near 'bout had the whole church divided.

Reverend Tisdale wasn't bit more pleased than a sow eatin' slop and sat her down for a whole year. When Mother Fentress finally humbled herself before the church, Reverend Tisdale told her that she could continue on as Head Mother. Mother Fentress wouldn't open her mouth to speak a word to Deaconess Puryear for the longest time unless Reverend Tisdale was nearby, but she did see fit to wave her hand on first Sunday.

* **** *

"Deaconess Puryear wants to know if you heard from Elder Sinclair, baby?"

"Mother Fentress?"

"Well, ain't that's what you was wondering out loud about before we got here, Deaconess Puryear?"

"I don't know what I'm gonna do with you, Mother Fentress."

"Well?"

"Sister Millie, I don't means you no harm. I don't means to pry."

"Can't say that I have as of late, Deaconess Puryear. Can't say that I've heard from Elder Sinclair in quite some time."

Schaumburg's Sweet Reminisce

"You mean since them Deacons run him off?"

"Mother Fentress, why come you say the deacons run him off?"

"I say them deacons run him off, Deaconess Puryear, on account them deacons run him off. They did, now. They sho' nuff did."

"Well now, Mother Fentress, I don't think it happened quite like you letting on. Besides, our Sister Millie's been gone for a good long while now. That what you speak of was so long ago."

"Deaconess Puryear, them deacons ran Elder Sinclair out from 'round here. Now that's the truth. Ain't much different than when I was a young girl coming along. If a young buck even smelled like he might be trouble, a bunch of them elders would get together and reason with him and when the young man finally come to his senses, he'd pack up and strike out on down that road; and whenever somebody was to ask about him, they'd say the elder's run him off – and it ain't no different with this-here child and Elder Sinclair. A blind man could see he felt some kinda way about the child. Her own momma and daddy even now know'd it."

Listening at Mother Fentress and Deaconess Puryear carry on, more than a few things was starting to make sense. But I believe they was more set on getting after one another than getting after the truth about why Elder Sinclair left Schaumberg so soon after the funeral.

"Baby, that Elder Sinclair's a mighty fine man of God. And if I dare say, a strong handsome buck."

"Mother Fentress, you ought to be shame."

"Shame of what, Deaconess Puryear? This-here child know what I say to be true. Anybody with eyes could see how handsome Elder Sinclair was – even you."

"Yes ma'am, Mother Fentress. I don't believe I've laid eyes on a man of God more handsome than Elder Sinclair. Made me nervous to be in the same room with him. Sometimes I thought I'd just lose myself."

I don't know what made me speak of Elder Sinclair in such a way to Mother Fentress and Deaconess Puryear, but "from the abundance of the heart the mouth speaks." I did miss him. Thought about him all the time while I was away, even after the phone calls stopped.

"Well, you still got all your pearls, ain't you, baby?"

"Oh, yes ma'am, Mother Fentress. I still got my full strand. I aim to keep 'em."

"That's good, baby. Real good."

"Well, last I heard, he had taken up with a woman with a whole heap of children somewhere's down there near South Carolina. Folks say that sheriff down there made her a widow a few years back. Heard they was to be married or something or another, but I don't know how much truth it is to it."

"Well, then maybe you ought not speak on it, Deaconess Puryear. That's why come them deacons run him off on account folks let the first thing enter they mind slide off they tongue. If I had any doubt that Elder Sinclair had the mind to mess over our Millie Rose, I'd have run him up outta Schaumburg myself with a beatin' he'd never forget. He did a lotta good in the church and for Brother Ben and Sister Marjorie too. It just wasn't right to run him off like that."

Schaumburg's Sweet Reminisce

It hurt my heart to hear that folks thought less of Elder Sinclair. Momma and Daddy thought the world of him and so did I. He'd been real kind to us for a time and, apart from my daddy, Elder Sinclair was the first man I guess I ever loved. I reckon it was love. Didn't know how I was supposed to feel about him being yoked to some other woman and her children. It'd been a good long while since I'd heard from Elder Sinclair, yet still, it felt like my heart would nearly give out on me when Deaconess Puryear said what she did.

"You hear Mother Fentress on this here now, Millicent Rose. Whether I feel like them deacons was right in doing what they did or not – what's been done is done. Now, we all made a promise to Brother Ben and Sister Marjorie to look after you like you was our own as long as we drew breath on this earth. Them deacons didn't mean you or Elder Sinclair no harm. Reckon we all thought that your heart was too heavy to resist temptation. So, the deacons asked Elder to give you some time. Next thing we know he was gone and then so was you. There's gonna come many a'Elder Sinclair's. You watch what I tell you, baby. You just keep letting the Lord heal your heart so that you good and ready to be found."

"Yes ma'am, Mother Fentress."

"Deaconess Puryear, you think it's time we get our Millie Rose on home? I reckon we done kept everybody waitin' long enough."

"I reckon you right, Mother Fentress. Millie Rose, First Lady Tisdale put together a homecoming celebration for you out on the farm. They's all there waiting to see you."

"Well now, I hope First Lady Tisdale didn't put herself out."

"Well child, wasn't a soul in or around Schaumburg that was against it. Schaumburg's got only one Millie Rose."

"Amen, Mother Fentress."

"Well, Mother Fentress... Deaconess Puryear, I reckon we ought not keep 'em waitin'."

I couldn't have asked for a better homecoming. Even took my mind off of Elder Sinclair, for a while.

The house and the farm was all pulled together. I couldn't think of a thing that needed to be done; so, I spent a many a'morning before sunrise up there in that attic before the Lord, waiting for Him to answer just like Momma and Daddy always said He would. Took a little while, it did, but I always knew that as long as my heart was open to Him, that the Lord would hear and that He'd answer. I figured the Lord just wanted to love on me a little while longer before He put me to work. I reckon He had to be sure that I was good and filled up with Him before He did. In time I would learn to trust the providence of God for myself.

God wrote His vision on my heart and after He wrote it, He made it plain to me.

"You have taken delight in Me, my child. The desires of your heart are mine – they belong to me. I have placed them there, forever. I have sanctified you unto myself and have given you to be yoked to no man.

"I AM will be your husband. I AM will sustain you in every season. I will send to you in great number those that are empty to be watered and filled from My fountain. Your going out and your coming in will be like that of the Jordan River and I will be your spoil. That which is to be... already

is. It is inside of you to fulfill My will. Do my will and you will know fullness of joy in your devotion to Me."

No sooner than seven days and seven nights later, I received my first guest. A woman with seven children in tow bearing the name of Eloise Sinclair.